BEST FRIEND TROUBLE

By
Alex McAnders

McAnders Books

*****

The characters and events in this book are fictitious. Any similarity to real persons, living or dead, is coincidental and not intended by the author. The person or people depicted on the cover are models and are in no way associated with the creation, content, or subject matter of this book.

All rights reserved. No part of this book may be reproduced in any form or by any electronic or mechanical means, including information storage and retrieval systems, without permission in writing from the publisher, except by a reviewer who may quote brief passages in a review. For information contact the publisher at: McAndersPublishing@gmail.com.

Copyright © 2022

Official Website: www.AlexAndersBooks.com
Podcast: www.SoundsEroticPodcast.com
Visit Alex Anders
at: Facebook.com/AlexAndersBooks & Instagram
Get 6 FREE ebooks and an audiobook by signing up for Alex Anders' mailing list at: AlexAndersBooks.com

Published by McAnders Publishing

Titles by Alex McAnders

M/M Romance

Serious Trouble & Audiobook; Book 2 & Audiobook; Book 3; Book 4
Serious Trouble - Graduation Day; Book 2; Book 3

*****

MMF Bisexual Romance

Searing Heet: The Copier Room; Hurricane Laine; Book 2; Book 3; Book 4; Book 5; Book 6

*****

Titles by A. Anders

MMF Bisexual Erotica

While My Family Sleeps; Book 2; Book 3; Book 4;
Book 1-4
Book 2
My Boyfriend's Twin; Book 2
My Boyfriend's Dominating Dad; Book 2

*****

MMF Bisexual Romance

Until Your Toes Curl: Prequels; Book 2; Book 3; Until Your Toes Curl
The Muse: Prequel; The Muse
Rules For Spanking
Island Candy: Prequel & Audiobook; Island Candy & Audiobook; Book 2; Book 2
In The Moonlight: Prequel; In The Moonlight & Audiobook

Aladdin's First Time; Her Two Wishes & Audiobook; Book 2 & Audiobook
Her Two Beasts
Her Red Hood
Her Best Bad Decision
Bittersweet: Prequel; Bittersweet
Before He Was Famous: Prequel; Before He Was Famous
Beauty and Two Beasts
Bane: Prequel & Audiobook; Bane & Audiobook
Bad Boys Finish Last
Aladdin's Jasmine
20 Sizzling MMF Bisexual Romances

*****

M/M Erotic Romance

Their First Time
Aladdin's First Time; Her Two Wishes & Audiobook; Book 2 & Audiobook

*****

Suspense

The Last Choice; Dying for the Rose
It Runs

*****

Titles by Alex Anders

MMF Bisexual Erotica

While My Family Sleeps; Book 2; Book 3; Book 4; Book 1-4
Dangerous Daddy's Double Team & Audiobook; Book 2 & Audiobook; Book 3 & Audiobook; Book 4 &

Audiobook; Book 1-4
Black Magic Double Team & Audiobook

M/M Erotic Romance

Baby Boys
Baby Boy 1: Sacrificed; Book 2; Book 3; Book 4; Book 1-4

MMF Bisexual Romance

As My Rock Star Desires; Book 2; Book 3; Book 4; Book 5

BEST FRIEND TROUBLE

Chapter 1

Lou

What type of idiot invites a guy to meet their parents for their third date? It's like when someone hops the fence around the gorilla cage at the zoo… and then takes the gorilla to meet their parents for their third date. It's crazy talk that only a psycho would do.

But here's the thing. We've been texting so much. And he told me that he was falling in love with me after the second date. That's right, I went on a second date with someone. I bet no one had that on their bingo card.

But I did and he took me into the mountains to watch a meteor shower. And he had a blanket and a picnic basket. I'm practically crying just thinking about it. No one has ever treated me like this. So when my parents said they were coming to visit me, how could I not take the opportunity to prove them wrong?

'We don't have a problem with you being gay,' they said. 'We just don't think that anyone will love you if you are.'

What? Did my parents just say that? They don't think their son will ever find love?

Well, let me tell you something Mom, there's a guy who's hot and rich that any girl would die to have. And he's falling in love with me, your gay son who you don't think anyone will ever love.

I've always said, if life gives you lemons, you make sure you use them to prove your parents were wrong about you. Seymour is my lemons. Does Sey look like the guy who tosses his keys to the nearest Mexican to park his yacht? A little bit. But according to my parents, I look like a guy who would never find love. So, looks can be deceiving.

The only issue now is that I texted Sey the time and place we would be meeting my parents and he hasn't texted back to confirm. The guy texts me 'Good morning, beautiful,' every day. And on the morning he's supposed to meet my parents, crickets?

Did I make a mistake? Was I moving too fast? He was the one who said that he was falling in love with me. I didn't go there. So, how far off is that from inviting him to meet my parents?

I ruined things, didn't I? Oh god, I did! I took a guy who offered me an olive branch and I spanked him with it. Didn't he see me pulling off the leaves? He could have stopped me. Did we even have a safe word? We didn't have a safe word. Crap, I scared him off!

Approaching a full-on panic attack, I pulled out my phone and called the only one who knew how to handle me when I got into a state like this.

"Titus?"

"Lou, what's up?"

I could hear him smiling through the phone. Didn't he know my life was falling apart? How could he be smiling at a time like this? Who's the crazy person now?

"What's up? I'll tell you what's up. I'm headed to meet my parents and the boyfriend, who I invited for the sole purpose of making my parents eat their words, hasn't told me he's coming."

"Wait, he's your boyfriend? When did that happen?"

"I don't know. Sometime after our second date. He told me he loved me and…"

"He told you he loved you after your second date?" he asked cutting me off.

"Yeah. Or maybe it was a text. And he might have said that he's falling in love with me. But that's just one block away from love-town, right?"

"I… guess."

"So, he told me he loved me. Then I told him my parents would be in town and that he should meet them. He said he wanted to and we agreed. But this morning when I gave him the details, nothing. Not even a meme. And I love the funny memes he sends me. It's one of the best things about our relationship."

"Wow! That's a lot."

"What's a lot?"

"You just said so many things that…"

"Oh my god, I'm here," I said cutting Titus off. "What am I gonna do? What am I gonna do?"

"First, calm down."

"I tell you that my life hangs in the balance and you tell me to calm down? This is the perfect time to panic."

"Lou, listen to me. Take a breath. Breathe."

Staring at the pastry shop I told my parents to meet me at, I did what Titus said. I took a breath. It was hard considering the giant hands squeezing my chest, but I did. It helped. I barely felt like I was going to pass out anymore.

"Are you doing it?"

"Quiet, I'm trying to breathe," I told him struggling to take another breath.

After my heart slowed to a deer on caffeine from a chipmunk on speed, I gathered myself.

"You still there?" Titus asked me.

"I'm here."

"Okay. Where are you?"

"Standing in front of my doom."

"I meant physically. What's your address?"

"I'm in front of Nutmeg."

"Alright. Do you need me to come there?"

"Aren't you jetting around the world or something?"

"I wasn't jetting around the world. I was helping Nero get set up at his new place. You know that. You also know that it was his team's jet. I couldn't even afford the peanuts on that thing. Nero had to pay for my ticket back."

"So you're coming back?"

"We're about to land. I could catch a taxi and be there in 15 minutes."

"Oh wait! Wasn't I supposed to pick you up at the airport? I'm so sorry. My parents told me that they were going to be in town for the day and my mind just stopped."

"I understand. I get it. Don't worry. I'll catch a cab. And if you want me there, I could be there in minutes."

I thought about it. I had told my parents that there was someone I wanted them to meet. How humiliating would it be to show up by myself? It would prove that everything they ever thought about me was true. I couldn't take that. Just thinking about it made me want to fall to my knees in tears.

"Could you?" I asked loving Titus more than I thought possible.

"Of course, I can. The stewardess is telling me that I need to shut off my phone. But don't worry. I'll be there as soon. I got you, Lou. You know that."

"I do. Thank you," I said finally calming down.

It was going to be alright. I didn't know what was going on with Sey, but I didn't have to worry about that now. And sure, I had implied that they would be meeting someone I was dating, but they haven't met Titus. I could have meant that I wanted them to meet my best friend. I was going to be alright.

Staring at the pastry shop again, I thought about who would be waiting for me inside. Frank and Martha hadn't come to visit me since the day they dropped me off at University. They weren't one of those caring parents who called their children to see how they were doing. I was their accessory.

Despite them having a lot of money, I grew up like we struggled to get by. I can't think of a single gift they gave me that cost over $20. Meanwhile, they bought themselves new cars every year. Whatever made them look good in the eyes of the horrible people around them, they did. Making me feel loved or provided for didn't qualify.

The only reason I could afford to attend East Tennessee University was because of my grandmother. She paid for everything I had. Even when I was a kid, if I wanted a video game or new clothes, I would go to her. She was everything to me.

I definitely wouldn't have survived my childhood without her. She was the one who told me that it was okay for me to be who I was and that she would love me no matter what. That was before I came out to anyone. Grandma Aggie probably knew I was gay before I did. She seemed to know a lot of things before others did. It was like she had a connection to the beyond.

Yet, she didn't use that knowledge the way my parents would have. With knowledge like that, Martha would turn everyone into her slave while Frank would become a super villain. Frank was quiet but when he stared at you, you could see the horrible things he was thinking.

Grandma Aggie was my only refuge from all of that. I wouldn't have survived without her. Life was too hard and lonely. I could cry thinking about the number of times she held me in her arms telling me I could get through something. In the times I didn't believe her, she kept holding me until I did.

Grandma Aggie's arms were my only safe space in all of Tennessee. I think about her every day and call her a lot. Drawing on the strength she gave me is the only reason I'm able to continue towards the pastry shop now.

I didn't have a boyfriend to show them, but I had Titus. He was going to be here soon and the friendship we have will prove to them that I am worth something.

Even if they don't think so, someone does. Just like Grandma Aggie always did.

Taking a final deep breath, I stepped in front of the glass door and peered through it. The two of them were sitting there dressed impeccably like they always were. Martha was wearing the navy power suit that made her look like a sailor and her signature pearls.

Frank wore a green polo and khaki pants. He was the most invisible person in the room. I might have been their accessory, but Frank was Martha's. And his job was to not outshine her in any way. He made the money and opened all of the doors. But he wasn't allowed to have a personality of his own. That was always fine for him.

Stepping inside, I stiffened my back and walked over. Approaching the table, they turned around.

"Mother, Father."

My mother winced. "You know I hate it when you call us that."

I did know it. That was why I said it.

"Sorry. Frank, Martha."

I also knew that Martha liked to hear her name first.

"Would it have killed you to be on time for once in your life?" my mother groaned.

"I don't know. Would it?"

Martha turned to Frank.

"I can't deal with him if he is going to be like this. I can't do it. Not today."

"Louis, respect your mother," Frank muttered.

"He speaks," I said genuinely surprised that he did.

"Do you see what I mean," my mother told him.

"Louis!" my father said raising his voice.

"Alright!" I said throwing up my hands in defeat.

He hadn't spoken loudly. But any display of emotion from him was unnerving.

"Must you do this every time?" my mother continued.

"Do what? All I've done is say hello. You're the one who's been criticizing me since the moment I got here."

Frank spoke up again. "Lou, we've been waiting here for thirty minutes."

He was right. I had been late. I was giving Sey as much time as I could to get back to me.

But it wasn't like they hadn't ever kept me waiting. For example, I'm still waiting on my gift from my thirteenth birthday. There had to be a $0.99 Store around here somewhere.

"You didn't touch your croissant," I said looking at the prop in front of them. "Are you going to eat it? I didn't have lunch."

Martha huffed in disgust and pushed it in front of me. I know it was a small thing, but this was the first thing they had given me in years. Maybe they did love me.

Tearing into it, flakes from it fell onto my plate and the table around it. Both of my parents watched me like it was feeding time at the zoo.

"So, how is school?" my father asked.

I almost choked. Neither of them had ever asked me that before. I didn't know what was happening. And as much as I wanted to reply with something snide, I didn't dare. What if the concern they were showing me was real? What if, despite a lifetime of evidence to the contrary, they actually did care about me? I couldn't risk ruining that.

"It's okay," I said sincerely. "Umm, classes are going well. I have a really cool roommate… Quin. Umm, I have a boyfriend," I said suddenly desperately wanting their approval.

"I see," Frank said lowering his eyes.

Had I ruined the moment by reminding him I was gay? I had, hadn't I? If I would have kept my mouth shut and just said things were fine, he wouldn't have looked away. I always do this. I always keep talking when I should be shutting up.

"And here he is right now," I said seeing him open the door.

Sey had come. He was here! I could have cried seeing him. And behind him were five of his football teammates. What was going on?

As soon as he saw me, his eyes lit up. Throwing the door open, he stepped inside.

"Lou!" he bellowed from across the room. His teammates lined up behind him.

"Sey, what's happening?"

Sey looked back at the guys. When he did, they started singing.

"Wise men say, only fools rush in. But I can't help falling in love with you."

As the guys continued what had to be the sorriest rendition of one of my favorite songs, Sey crossed the room to me. Overwhelmed, I looked at my parents. Both were looking down and away. They wanted no part of what was going on and they weren't hiding it.

I didn't care. Whatever was happening was the most romantic thing anyone had ever done for me and I wasn't going to let them ruin it.

"Lou, I know we haven't known each other very long. But when you meet the person you know you want to spend the rest of your life with, you know. And if you do, what's the point in waiting?"

"Wait what?" I said both horrified and delighted.

"Like a river flows, surely to the sea, darling, so it goes, some things are meant to be."

"Lou, what I'm saying is that we might have just met, but I know you. I've known you my entire life because you were the dream I prayed every night would come true. So…" he said getting down onto one knee in front of me and pulling a ring out of his pocket.

"Oh my God!" I gasped.

"Louis Armoury, will you marry me?"

My head spun. Was this real? It had to be. I would never put such horrible singers in one of my fantasies.

Could I do it? Should I do it? We had only just met. But, as he said, when you know, you know. And I have never had anyone treat me like he has. Never.

"Yes," I said. "Yes, I'll marry you," I told him with tears rolling down my cheek.

"You will?" he said as happy as I was.

"I will," I repeated knowing it was the best decision I had ever made.

He took my hand and slid the ring onto my finger. It was a little big but that was okay. We could fix it. We were in love and love could fix anything.

He got off of his knee and kissed me. It was my first kiss as an engaged man. It was wonderful. I had never been happier in my life.

With Sey's arms around me, I turned to my parents. They still hadn't looked at Sey. They hadn't moved their eyes from the floor. Was it that they couldn't stand to be wrong? They had said that no one would ever love me, but this was the proof that they had been wrong.

A man loved me so much that he had asked me to marry him after two dates. Didn't that say every there was to say about me? I was lovable. I was worth someone's time.

"Well? Aren't you going to say anything?" I asked needing to hear their defeat.

It was then that my mother looked up at me. Her eyes locked on mine.

"Your grandmother Agatha died. Her funeral was yesterday. There will be a reading of her will. We expect you there and try not to be late," she said before both of them got up and walked out.

I watched them stunned. I couldn't speak or move. I had to have heard them wrong. Or maybe it was a joke.

"Grandma Aggie is dead," I heard someone say.

I was the one who said it. It was meant to be a question for the two people who were leaving taking my grip on reality with them. But they couldn't hear me. I could barely hear myself. And as they left the shop and crossed in front of the window, they brushed past another familiar face. That person was holding a bouquet.

"Titus," I whispered before his devastated eyes turned towards me, and he ran past the window and out of sight.

Chapter 2

Titus

I couldn't have seen what I had, could I have? Lou, the guy who had been on more first dates than there are trees in Tennessee, had gotten engaged? That can't be right. But I had seen it. I was standing there watching it.

Lou had told me who it was he had been texting with. It was with a transfer student who was on the football team. He had arrived this semester so it was after I had been cut. But I definitely recognized the guys singing behind him. They had been my teammates.

Having to close my eyes as I reached my truck, I steadied myself and took a breath. Tears were fighting to get out but I wouldn't let them. Yeah, I had waited too long. Yeah, I had ignored everything Nero and Quin had told me about telling him how I felt, but I had finally listened. This was going to be the day.

I had made a detour to get the flowers. If I hadn't, could I had been there to stop it? If I had told him how I felt, would he have still said yes to that guy?

My phone rang snapping me out of my building despair. Pulling it out, I saw Lou's name. I couldn't talk to him right now. Knowing I couldn't pretend to be happy for him, I shoved it back into my pocket.

Looking at the dozen red roses that had cost me an arm and a leg, I tossed them onto the ground. I had been such a fool. I couldn't be here. I needed to get away. Glad that I had stopped back at my place to pick up my truck instead of coming here directly from the airport, I got in and pulled away.

Within moments, my phone rang again. Pulling it out as I drove, I again saw Lou's name.

"I don't want to hear that you got engaged! Don't you understand that?" I shouted at the phone before tossing it onto the passenger seat.

Knowing that I needed to get as much distance as I could from what just happened, I didn't head to my dorm. Approaching the freeway home, I turned onto it. Just as I did, the phone rang again. I wasn't sure why Lou wasn't getting the point. There was no way I was going to pick up.

Yeah, I had told him I would meet him at the pastry shop but only because his boy had flaked or whatever. But he showed up. Lou didn't need me there. So, why won't he stop calling me?

After he called for the fourth time, I turned off my ringer and turned on the radio. I didn't care what was playing as long as it took my mind off of what I had just seen.

I couldn't accuse Lou of anything. He had always been upfront about who he was. He wanted to find love and he was going to go out with every guy in the state to find it. I was the one who was too chicken-shit to admit what I was.

The only person I had ever told about liking guys was Quin. I still haven't even told Nero, and not only had we grown up together, but we were roommates when he proclaimed his love for his boyfriend on national TV. Nero risked his chance of being drafted to the NFL for the man he loved and I still couldn't come out to him.

So, if not Nero, then who? Certainly not Lou, the guy I was in love with from the moment I saw his puckish smile and big, adorable brown eyes. And instead of accepting who I was, what did I do? I became his buddy, his best friend.

Well, ya know what? I'm tired of being everybody's friend. I want to be desired. I wanted Lou to want me.

But it was too late now. He had found his guy and had gotten engaged. He had only mentioned having two dates with him. I thought I had more time. But I was the only one to blame.

Unable to stop thinking about it on my hour and a half drive to Snow Tip Falls, I was glad to see Glen's General Store come into view. It was the unofficial start of our little backwoods town. The drive to my mother's place wouldn't take long after passing that.

Pulling up to the split-level log cabin I had grown up in, I took a deep breath. I was home. And, although it wasn't the house Quin bought in Snow Tip Falls to be with his boyfriend, Cage, it was still a nice place. It was on a hill that overlooked a tree-covered valley. You couldn't ask for much more than that in a town like ours.

Whereas Quin was born into ungodly wealth. My mother just had the pension the Air Force gave her after my father was shot down during combat. She raised me by herself. I wasn't the type to consider my mother my best friend. But she was my rock. No matter what bad thing happened to me, I knew I would always have her.

Getting out of my truck, I walked to the front door knowing that I wouldn't have to deal with everything going on around me once I stepped inside. It's not like I'm scared of change. I'm the one campaigning to open up Snow Tip Falls to tourists. I'm a big fan of change. I think change is good.

But with Lou getting engaged, Nero moving to a new state, and me getting a new roommate all in less than a week, I could use a little stability. That was my mother. Etiquette, traditional values, and the status quo were the things she lived by.

Flinging open the unlocked door, I looked around for my mother. When I found her, I froze. I probably should have looked away. But the first time you see your mother and her boyfriend sprint from the couch to the bedroom naked, it takes a moment to process.

"Oh my God!" I yelled as the horrible image burned into my brain.

Was this why people in Greek mythology gauged out their eyes? I think I finally understood.

"What are you two doing?" I shouted horrified.

Although it was too late and I would never be able to close my eyes again, I spun facing the opposite direction. I considered leaving but what good would that do? The damage had been done. Besides, where else could I go?

"What are you doing here? Aren't you supposed to be at school?" my mother said sounding as horrified as I felt.

"I thought I would come and visit you. Maybe I should go."

My mother exited her bedroom.

"You don't have to leave. But this might be a good time to tell you something."

I slowly turned around finding my mother tying the waist of her robe. After what had happened, even this was too revealing.

"Yeah, what's that?" I asked hesitantly.

"Mike, can you come out, please."

Oh no!

Mike came out in jeans, suspenders, and no shirt. The man had a receding hairline, a blond beard, and the biggest beer belly I had ever seen. He was the owner of the local diner and growing up, I had always seen the flirting between the two. I wasn't blind. But this?

"What's going on?" I asked nervously.

"Honey, Mike and I are going to be moving in together," she said firmly.

"Mike's moving in?"

"No. I'll be moving in with him."

"I just bought a house on the lake. It's up near Tanner Cove," Mike explained.

"It's beautiful, Titus. And I will be moving there."

"I know how your Mama likes nice things. Only the best for her."

I turned to my mother.

"So, what are you gonna do with this place?" I asked her wondering how I fit into all of this.

"I haven't decided. Maybe I'll sell it."

"I see," I said feeling my chest clench. I winced and then crossed to the couch to sit down.

"You okay, son?" my mother asked.

"It just seems like everything's changing. Nero's playing professional football. Lou got engaged. You're moving in with Mike. Everyone's getting what they want but me."

"Mike, could you give us a minute," my mother said headed toward me.

"Actually, I need to get back to the diner to prep for the dinner rush."

Mike grabbed his shirt and shoes. "I'll see you later?"

My mother smiled and watched him go. When he was gone, she joined me on the couch. She took my hand in hers.

"Things change, Titus."

"I know that. I'm the one who has been trying to convince you of that, remember? It's just that everyone seems to be changing without me. What am I doing wrong? Why am I the one being left alone?"

"You're not alone, son."

"Aren't I? You're with Mike. Nero has Kendall. Lou has that guy, whatever his name is. And who do I have? Tell me, Mom. Who do I have?"

My mother's eyes dipped. She had that look like she wanted to tell me something but couldn't get herself to say it.

"What is it?"

She gathered herself. "It's nothing."

"No. Stop it, Mom. You always do this. If you have something to tell me, just say it. Is it about this place? Did you already sell it? Are you thinking about moving out of town, too?"

"Titus, you have a brother."

I froze. Of all of the things she could have said, that was the last thing I expected to hear.

"What are you talking about?"

"I can't say any more than that. But, it's been weighing on me for a while, and…"

"What? You think you can tell me I have a brother that I never knew I had and then leave it at that?"

"I can't say any more," she said resigned.

"Why not? Who is he? Is he in town? Did you have a child before me?"

"No, nothing like that." My mother took a deep breath. "You two share the same father."

I stared at my mother as the reality of what she was saying twisted my body. "Mom, you have to tell me who it is. Does he live around here?"

"I made a promise that I wouldn't say anything."

"To who? My dad?"

"No," she said uncomfortably.

"Mom, you can't just drop something like that and expect that I'm gonna let it go. At least tell me something about him. Is he older than me? Younger?"

"He's younger," she admitted.

"So, my Dad had him before he got deployed to Iraq?"

My mother looked down.

"Come on, Mom. At least tell me that? Does he live in town?"

Her eyes flicked up meeting mine.

"He does," I realized. "Do I know him?"

"Titus, stop it. You're trying to get me to say things I can't say."

"You can do whatever you want, Mom. It's what you've always done. I mean, how could you keep this from me my whole life?"

Her resolve returned. "This conversation is over."

She got up and headed to her room.

"Oh because you're done talking about it, you think it's over."

"Just let it go, Titus!"

"Let it go? You dropped a bombshell like that and you expect me to just let it go?"

Entering her room, she slammed the door behind her. I stared at it stunned. What the hell had just happened? I had grown up lonelier than I could stand, wishing I had a brother, and I had one this entire time? I couldn't believe it.

It destroyed me that I couldn't call Lou and tell him about this. But, he was probably celebrating his engagement. Why had I waited so long to tell him how I felt about him? I felt like my whole world was coming apart.

Not wanting to be here anymore, I headed for my truck and drove. Being a small town, I didn't have a lot of places I could go. I could hike out to one of the falls that the town was named after. But I didn't feel like being by myself.

Approaching Mike's diner, I saw his truck parked in back. I thought about him and my mother. How long had things been going on between the two of them?

It wasn't that Mike was that bad of a guy. When Nero was going through his asshole phase, Mike was the only one to give him a job. Considering my mother's dating options, he was a catch. I guess my problem was everything that came with their relationship like potentially losing my childhood home.

Look, I get it. I'm not a kid anymore. I could find my way on my own. But my world was shifting under my feet.

I had lost the guy I love. I was losing the only home I ever had. And somewhere out there was a brother I might never meet. What the hell was I supposed to do now?

Driving further down Main Street, I next approached Dr. Sonya's Bed & Breakfast. Dr. Sonya was my new roommate's mother. Since Nero got drafted and Cali was coming to East Tennessee University as a freshman, us rooming together made sense. The two of us were the only ones there from Snow Tip Falls. We had to stick together.

Remembering what other project Dr. Sonya had going on, I pulled into her driveway and parked next to a truck I didn't recognize. Following the path to the back of the beautiful two-story, craftsman home, I circled onto the large stone back porch finding three small two-tops.

"Titus! What brings you here?" Dr. Sonya said exiting the house's back door to greet me.

"Cali told me you were doing this and since I was in town, I decided to check it out. How's it been going?"

"Surprisingly good. Marcus is beyond thrilled," she said showing a hint of her Jamaican accent. "He's here every morning baking. It's become a real adventure."

"That's great! Now if we can just get the rest of the town on board, we could put Snow Tip Falls on the map."

"Literally," Dr. Sonya said touching my arm with a laugh.

She shared my frustration with the town's apathy. I was sure that Snow Tip Falls could be the most popular destination in Tennessee for Eco tourism. We had more beautiful falls per square mile than any other part of the state. It would benefit everyone.

But there were people like Mike and my mother, who preferred to keep things the way they were. What they didn't realize was that my generation needed a reason to stay. If we can't find our opportunities here, we will look for it somewhere else. And, how long would the town last when its only residents were over 50?

Dr. Sonya got it, though. It helped that she was born on an island that survived on tourism. That was probably why she opened her bed and breakfast. It was the only place in town a stranger could stay the night.

Without her, the town would be a general store, a diner, and a crumbling high school.

"You don't seem to be your usual jovial self. Something wrong?" Dr. Sonya asked.

I hadn't expected her to pick up on it. I thought I had been hiding it pretty well. But could I tell her that the boy I've been secretly in love with got engaged before I had a chance to tell him how I felt? Could I tell her that I walked in on Mom and Mike and now they're moving in together leaving me nowhere to live?

"I was just told that I have a brother."

Dr. Sonya looked at me with as much shock as I felt when I found out.

"Really?"

"Yeah. Turns out I've had one for most of my life and my mother never bothered to mention it until now."

"Did she tell you anything about him?"

I shook my head. "She said he was younger than me and that my father had him before he got deployed to Iraq."

"Your father was deployed to Iraq?" She asked confused.

"You didn't know?"

"I didn't."

"Yeah, my father was in the Air Force. I've honestly been scared to ask if he and my mother were married. She doesn't like to say much when it comes to him. But after telling me I have a brother, I'm starting to understand why. Do you know anything about any of this?"

"This is all new information to me," she admitted.

I shrugged. "So I guess I have that going on."

"I guess you do. By the way, did you want anything or did you just come to check out the place?"

I thought back to the pastry I saw on the table in front of Lou.

"Do you have any croissants?"

"Marcus has made these delightful croissants with chocolate striped over top of them," she said bugging her eyes with excitement.

"I'll take one of those. And maybe of coffee."

"You got it. Sit. Relax. Enjoy the sights," she said pointing at the view.

"Thanks," I said choosing a seat and sitting down.

The view from Dr. Sonya's back porch had to be one of the best in town. Tree-covered hills rippled off into the distance. And on the furthest peek was a cloud of mist from the largest waterfall in a hundred miles.

I was lost in both the view and thought when I heard a voice I hadn't heard in a while.

"Titus?"

I turned to find Claude, the only kid from my graduating class to go to college immediately after high school.

"Claude! Good to see you. What are you doing here?"

"Here in town or here at Dr. Sonya's pastry shop?"

I shrugged. "Both. Please, sit."

Claude made his way to the seat across from me. Memories of Claude washed through my mind. I had always been a little jealous of him. Not only was he one of the best football players on our high school team. But he was always so damn good-looking.

The man had perfect features and the most amazing brown complexion I could imagine. I didn't know how he felt about being the only black kid in our high school. It might have been the reason he kept to himself. But I had always wished we could be friends.

"Well, I graduated early. That's why I'm in town. And I'm here at Dr. Sonya's because Marcus said that he was making his chocolate croissants today," he said with the hint of a smile.

"I heard they're good."

"They are."

I stared at Claude for a moment.

"You know, out of everyone who got out of this town, you were the last one I thought would come back."

"Same," he said looking down in thought. "But, my mother's here. And she's been needing a little help, so here I am."

"And what are you doing? Are you working?"

"Do you have a computer that needs repair?" he asked leaning forward with a smile.

"You repair computers? Here?"

"Yeah, well, there's not a ton of call for it. But when there is, there's no one else. And I've been slowly convincing a few of the businesses to switch to electronic data management, so you never know."

I laughed. "You mean, to get this town to move into the 21st century? Good luck with that."

"Thanks. But what about you? I thought you were at East Tennessee?"

"I am. I'm just visiting for the day."

Claude shook his head in acknowledgment. "You know, I've been meaning to get a hold of you."

"You have? Why?"

"You give tours of the falls to tourists, don't you?"

"I mean, I have. Why?"

"Have you ever considered that with the right support, it might make a great business? Maybe it could be more than just tours. Maybe it could include some camping or river rafting. You could sell packages for it. I've been crunching the numbers. It might take a while, but something like that might be quite profitable."

I looked at him shocked. "Yes, I have. All the time. Why? Are you thinking about setting up something like that?"

"I was thinking about it. But, I'm only one guy. And I would be much better at the business side of things. If I had a partner, though."

"You seem to be forgetting one thing. You're not gonna get anyone in this town to go along with something like that. Believe me, I've tried."

"You've tried to convince people. But have you considered just doing it yourself? You don't need permission to go after what you want in life. You just need to know what you want and then not stop until you have."

"Claude? I thought I heard you out here. Did you come for more of the croissants?" Dr. Sonya said bringing out my order.

"You know I did," Claude told her with a smile.

"Well, there are only two left, but I'll let you have them if you show me how to do that thing on the computer again. It'll just take a second."

Claude looked at me with a smile that told me that it would take longer than a second.

"Of course."

"I'm sorry to keep bothering you about it. My computer technician is off flagging footballs," she said before fake crying.

"No worries. I'll show it to you now." Claude got up. "Think about it, Titus. What is it that you want?"

I watched the two of them enter the house and then gave Claude's proposal some thought. I had considered starting up a tour business many times. I never knew where to begin. That was probably why I was so focused on convincing people to open up the town. I thought that with it would come opportunity.

But, maybe Claude was right. Maybe it was up to me to make my opportunities. Maybe it was time for me to decide what I wanted.

Allowing my mind to jump from one thing to another, it finally settled. There was only one thing that I truly wanted. It was as clear as the sky over the mountains in front of me. What I wanted more than life itself was Lou.

I left Dr. Sonya's driving around as I thought. What was I willing to do to have him? I was willing to do anything. So, what did that mean?

As it got dark, I returned to an empty home and made something to eat. Knowing I would be heading back in the morning for class, I went to bed early. Lying in the darkness I came up with a plan. I was going to tell Lou how I felt. I couldn't do it over text. It had to be in person.

In the middle of my first class the next morning, my phone buzzed. It was Lou. I read it and all of the others he had sent.

'Where r u?'
'Aren't u coming?'
'I need to talk to u.'

'Seriously, where r u?'
'UR freaking me out.'
This morning's text was different.
'I need you. Please talk to me.'

I knew what he needed to talk to me about. He had gotten engaged. He wanted me to be happy for him like I always was. Usually, I liked being his biggest cheerleader. Lou was a fantastic guy. I was sure he didn't see how great he was. I was only too glad to remind him when I could.

But, I couldn't do this for him. I couldn't pretend to be happy that he had gotten engaged to a guy that he had known for two weeks. There was no way.

I loved him. I wanted to be with him. And there was no way Seymour, or whatever his name was, knew how incredible Lou was.

'6:30 at Commons,' I replied breaking my silence.

He sent back a heart emoji. It made me smile.

I wasn't making a mistake. Lou had to have feelings for me, right? I was the guy he returned to after all of his dates. I was the one he came to when he was sad. I was his guy.

And when I told him I loved him, he would know he had made a mistake saying yes to that other guy. He would then break off his engagement and we could finally have the life we were always meant to have.

For the rest of the day, I did my best to pay attention in my classes. But it was hard to take my mind off of what would be the true beginning of my life. I had loved him for so long. Nero had seen through me months ago. I was into guys and the only person who meant anything to me was Lou.

Returning to my dorm to kill the final hour before we were to meet, I ran into my new roommate, Cali. Amazingly, he had had a growth spurt over the summer. So, the once skinny, dark-haired kid who always had a mysterious look in his eyes, had turned into the quiet, built jock.

He knew it too because he spent most of his day with his shirt off. Luckily, he wasn't my type. But I was starting to get the feeling that our types were similar.

"Hey," he grunted when I entered tossing my bag onto the bed and climbing in behind it.

I looked over at him. He had his shirt off because of course he did. He had to have just come back from football practice.

"Hey."

"You went home?"

"Huh? Oh yeah. I needed to clear my head." I sprung up. "Wait, do you know a guy on the team by the name of Seymour?"

"Sey? Yeah, what about him?"

"What do you think of him?"

Cali got squirrely and looked away.

"He's alright, I guess."

"He's into guys, right?"

Cali's eyes snapped to mine. "Maybe. Why do you ask?"

"I think he asked Lou to marry him."

He looked at me surprised. "Your Lou?"

"Yea," I said with a look that said how unhappy I was about it.

"Damn. Alright. Did you want to go mess him up?"

That wasn't a response I was expecting.

"I wasn't thinking that. But it does sound tempting," I said with a laugh. I wasn't sure why, but what he said had made me feel better. "What do you know about him?"

Cali thought. "Rich guy. Transferred from Nashville."

"He transferred from Nashville?" I asked knowing that despite East Tennessee's string of championships thanks to Nero and his brother Cage, Nashville was a much more prestigious football program.

"Yeah. He said he liked what we had going on here."

I thought about that. Last year Nero had proclaimed his love for his boyfriend Kendall on ESPN and then led the team to the national title. The championships before that were thanks to Nero's brother

Cage who hadn't hidden it when he fell in love with his boyfriend Quin.

"How is he on the field?" I asked knowing why he had transferred.

"He's our starting quarterback. He's not as good as Mr. Rucker. But he's okay."

I smiled.

"He's not your coach anymore. You can call him Cage."

Cali didn't respond.

"If you're gonna join us when we hang out, you can't call him Mr. Rucker. You realize that, right?" I teased.

Cali turned red. He might have looked like a new person, but he was the same respectful, small-town boy inside. I was going to have to look out for him. Without someone helping you through the transition, East Tennessee University could mess you up. I had been lucky to have Nero, Quin, and most importantly, Lou.

Cali and I fell into silence as I considered what I would say to Lou. I wasn't gonna beat around the bush. I was just gonna say it.

'Lou, I love you. I always have. And I want us to be together. Lou, I love you. I always have. And I want us to be together.'

I rehearsed the words until the heat from them didn't make my head want to explode. It took a while but by the time I was ready to meet Lou, I was ready.

"Good luck," Cali said even though I hadn't told him what I was about to do.

"Thanks," I replied not asking what he knew.

Looking into the mirror before I left, I stared into the eyes of the shaggy-haired guy peering back. Was there any reason for Lou to choose me over the rich, square-jawed quarterback who had asked to marry him? If there was, I didn't see it.

But Lou had to know that no one would love him like I would. I would do whatever it took to make him happy. Who else could say that? Lou had to know that that was true.

Crossing campus and approaching Common's big metal doors, I entered heading up a half flight of stairs to the study hall. Lou and I met here a lot. When we were in the same class, we came here to study together. When we weren't, we came to pretend to study while Lou told me about his latest date. I hadn't known there were so many guys who dated guys in the world much less in East Tennessee.

Spotting him across the room on the couch, I headed over. It was our usual spot. It allowed us to get close enough to whisper without disturbing others.

My heart clenched looking at him. My god was he beautiful. He wasn't a big guy but he made up for it in personality. His apple cheeks and puckish smile always made him seem like he was having fun, even when he wasn't. And his lightly-tipped dark hair was just long enough to run your fingers through and tug when the moment was right.

Lou didn't have his usually playful smirk today, however. There was sadness in his eyes. Was it because he was breaking his big news to me? Whatever it was, there was something I needed to get out first. This was when it had to happen. If it didn't, I didn't know when I would have the courage again.

Approaching him, our eyes met. I melted.

'Lou, I love you. I always have. And I want us to be together,' I rehearsed.

Sitting next to him, he did something he never had before. He put his hand on my thigh as his gaze fell to the ground. The gesture froze me. What was going on? Pushing through it, I began.

"Lou, I…"

"My grandmother died," he said cutting me off.

"What?"

"That's what my parents came to town to tell me. The funeral was last Saturday."

"They didn't tell you about the funeral?" I asked shocked.

Lou had told me about her. He had said that his grandmother was the only reason he had survived his childhood. Now she was dead and his parents had stolen his opportunity to say goodbye.

"I'm so sorry," I whispered feeling my heart ache for him.

Then Lou did another thing he had never done. He fell into my arms and cried. I held him forgetting about whatever plan I had. Lou needed me and I was going to do whatever I had to to be there for him.

Chapter 3

Lou

Nothing ever felt real until I told Titus. And having said it, I knew that my grandmother was truly gone. I would never see her again. It wouldn't even be in a casket. My parents had robbed me of that. I always knew that my family hated me, but I never knew they could be this cruel.

"She's gone," I said feeling his warm arms wrapped around me. "I can't believe she's gone."

"I'm so sorry," he kept repeating.

It was enough for me to forgive him for not reaching out to me until now. He had said that he was coming to rescue me from being alone with my parents. I had even seen him standing outside the door. He had chosen not to come in.

Seeing him walk away had hurt me. The only thing I wanted was to do what I was doing now, cry in his arms. But he had abandoned me. I had never felt more alone.

But, none of that mattered now that he was here. We didn't need to talk about why he had gone. There were a lot of things we didn't need to talk about.

I didn't know how I was going to break the news of my engagement to him. It was partly because I wasn't sure if we were actually engaged. Yes, he had proposed with a choir of his teammates singing in the background. It was the most romantic thing anyone had ever done for me and I had said yes. But where has he been since?

My parents dropping that bomb on the day of my engagement was a shitty thing for them to do. There was no doubt. It had ruined what was supposed to be the happiest day of our lives. But I wasn't the one who had done it. I was the boy who had had his heart ripped out of him. There were more important things than grand gestures and Sey had asked to be my husband.

Sure, as I sat stunned, he had sent his teammates home and had held my hand as I tried to process it all. But eventually, he walked me home and I haven't heard from him since.

Did he think it was up to me to reach out to him to talk about how I was doing? Was he trying to give me my space to grieve?

Whatever he was doing, I hated every moment of it. And considering it had been over twenty-four hours since I had last heard from him, I was starting to believe that his proposal had been a joke. Maybe "joke" was the wrong word. Maybe he had done it because he knew how insecure my parents made me feel and decided that this would prove to them that someone valued me.

I hadn't told him anything about the struggles I had had with my family over the years. But couldn't that be a sign that he was the one? Him knowing what I needed without me having to say anything?

"What would you like to do?" Titus asked me eventually breaking the silence.

"Nothing," I admitted. "I just want to sit here."

"For as long as you want," he said meaning it.

"Actually, do you know what would be really nice? Having a game night. Nothing big. Just something nice, you know?"

"I'll set it up."

With his assuring words, I sat up pulling myself from his arms. I stared at him. He was the best friend anyone could hope for. This was probably the time to tell him about my engagement. Even if it hadn't been a genuine proposal, this was my chance to bring it up.

Maybe he would tease me about getting engaged as quickly as I did everything else. Maybe I would then make a few quips about it and brush my moment of insanity aside. Whatever would happen, this was my opportunity to make it real.

"I think I want to go to bed," I told him instead.

"Of course," he said collecting my things for me and offering me his hand to help me up.

I took it and then slipped my arm around his waist. I always felt so small in his arms. For most of last year, he had been on the football team. He still had the body to show for it. He was going to make some girl a great boyfriend one day.

Did I think that there was a chance he was also into guys? Obviously. I had asked enough guys out to know they were all just a drink away from telling me how they kissed their best friend at camp or whatever? But there was a big difference between having feelings for someone and being willing to act on them.

The key was being able to tell the difference. And my gay-dar told me that Titus wasn't there and might never be. Such a waste.

That was fine, though, because he was the best friend I had ever had. I didn't even know that friendship like his was possible before I met him. Why would I want to do anything to mess that up?

It would be the dumbest thing I could ever do. And I have done some dumb things. There was even a time when I agreed to marry someone I had only been on two dates with. Could you even imagine that?

Titus walked me back to my dorm and followed me inside. Quin was home.

"Hey Titus," he said cheerfully.

The two of them had met our freshman year when Quin was looking for his boyfriend's birth parents. Quin was also the one who convinced Titus to attend East Tennessee. The two went way back.

"Why didn't you tell me Lou's grandmother had died?" Titus snapped at Quin.

Quin froze. "Lou, your grandmother died?"

"Yeah, it's not a big deal," I said trying to brush off my oversight.

"When?" Quin asked, his cute face crinkling.

"That's what my parents came to town to tell me."

Quin covered his mouth as tears filled his eyes.

"It's not a big deal," I insisted as I crossed the living room to my bedroom and crawled into bed under the weight of it all."

"Stop saying it's not a big deal," Titus said following me. "It's a big deal. Someone important passing away is a big deal. Your parents not telling you about the funeral is a big deal."

"Your parents didn't tell you about the funeral?" Quin asked as the tears streamed down his adorable cheeks.

"I'm sure there was a reason," I told them hoping that there was.

That didn't stop Quin from crawling into my bed and wrapping his arms around me. He had never done anything like this before. He has never been the touchy-feely type. But as he held me tightly, all I could think was that it felt good.

"I think you're in good hands," Titus said from the bedroom door.

I opened my eyes in search of his.

"Thank you. I don't know what I would do without you," I said sincerely.

"I'll call you in the morning to see how you're doing," he said filling a hole I didn't know I needed filled.

"Umm, not too early," I joked.

Titus smiled. "What am I, a monster?"

I laughed. It was the first time I had since getting the news. I felt more pain than I had ever in my life. But I knew that as long as I had Titus, I was going to make it through… and then I got comfortable in another cute guy's arms. My grandmother was clearly looking after me from above.

It was the following day that I received an email from my parent informing me of my grandmother's will reading. It surprised me that they hadn't waited until the last minute to tell me about that too.

If nothing else, my grandmother always made it clear that she would be passing down her entire fortune to me. It wasn't like I cared about stuff like that, but she had insisted. She told me that it had already been taken care of and that I had to prepare myself for it.

I, of course, did no such thing. That was future-Lou's problem. I was present-Lou. And let me tell you, past-Lou was a bit of an a-hole. He dumped everything he ever had to do on me. Did he even know what responsibility was?

Not having to be at my grandmother's estate until Friday, I decided not to think about any of that until then. I was in mourning. I had more important things to worry about like how to get out of bed.

"Do you think you would be up for a game night on Friday?" Titus asked when he Facetimed me.

"I have to head home on Friday."

"What about Thursday?"

"Sure, I guess."

"Then, save the date."

"I don't have anything else going on so it shouldn't be a problem," I said sadly.

There was a pause as we stared at each other.

"How are you feeling?"

"It's hard to believe, ya know? I used to call her every two or three days. But I hadn't spoken to her for weeks before she died. I didn't even know she was sick."

"Do you know what she died of?"

"My parents haven't said."

"Do you think you could get more details from your brother?"

"You mean the anti-Christ? I haven't spoken to him since the last time we were both home. We're not close."

"Wouldn't this be the perfect time to mend whatever broken fences are between you two?"

"Titus, I do not trust him with a hammer."

"I'm serious, Lou."

"So am I! Once, as a kid, he walked up to me with a hammer, looked me in the eyes, and then smashed my foot with it."

"What?"

"It was one of those plastic hammers and he was five, but he had looked me in the eyes before he did it. Message received."

"How old were you?"

"Four. I'm telling you, he's the spawn of the devil… and my father."

"Okay, well, do you have any aunts or uncles you could contact for more information?"

"Not really."

"I'm sorry, Lou."

I shrugged. "The good thing is that after this weekend, I'll never need anything from my parents again."

"That's good?"

"Believe me, when you have parents like mine, it's like having a pride parade on Christmas. Although, Santa's a bear who spends all of his time with twinks, so I guess that's already called a Christmas Parade?"

Titus smiled. "Then I'm happy for you. But I'm sorry it had to happen like this."

"Thank you," I said seeing his sincerity.

"Are you sure you're gonna be up for Thursday's game night?"

"I think so. You're not going through a lot of trouble, are you?"

Titus thought. "I'm going through enough trouble that you shouldn't cancel it for a date, but not enough that you have to feel bad about it if you did."

I laughed. "You know me so well."

"I'm glad you noticed," he said with a smile.

Hanging up from Titus, I suddenly had the energy to get out of bed. I did have classes, after all. Inheritance or not, no one wants to date a dumb guy no matter how pretty he was.

Forcing myself to get dressed, I thought about Sey. I still hadn't heard from him.

I refused to be the one to reach out to him first. I was in mourning. Didn't he understand that? Titus did. Quin did. It wasn't that hard of a concept to get.

Though, maybe the other reason I hadn't reached out to him was that I was hoping the whole thing would go away. Don't get me wrong, there were things about being engaged that I loved. I couldn't wait to bring him to my grandmother's will reading and rub my engagement in my family's faces.

'Mother, you said that I would never find love because I was gay. Well, gaze at his amazing cheekbones and tell me how wrong you were. Don't be shy, your anti-Christ of a son wants to hear too.'

Yeah, that was definitely a moment that needed to happen. But did I want Sey at Titus's game night? I'm not sure if I did. It felt like something that was only for family. Wasn't Sey now my family? It didn't feel like he was. Should I be feeling this way?

After a day in which I heard from Titus a lot, I decided to be the bigger man and reached out to Sey. This wasn't a battle. At least it wasn't supposed to be. So, I texted him telling him I was feeling better, and told him about the will reading. Why hadn't I also mentioned game night? I guess it slipped my mind.

'I'm glad you're feeling better, beautiful! When's the reading?'

'Sunday.'

'I might have a game on Saturday. Where is it?'

I sent him the address to the estate.

'I'll let you know.'

"I'll let you know?" I said reading it aloud.

Nothing filled me with less confidence than relying on him to let me know about something. I mean, he was going to be there for me, right? He had to know this was important. How could he not know this was important?

"You getting ready for tomorrow night?" Titus asked when he Facetimed me again, this time as I left my final class for the evening.

"Should I be?"

"I would be considering how often I crush you when we play against each other. But, don't worry, I know you're going through something. I'll be taking it easy on you."

"Oh, is this how it's gonna go. Because if you want me to bring it, I'll bring it. You can count on that."

"No, no. Everyone agreed to take it easy on you. We know you can't take another blow with everything going on."

I stared at my phone's screen and Titus's smirking face. Had he gone insane? He had to know that I could wipe the floor with them. I mean, as long as it wasn't a word game because, you know, Quin. But other than that, I would mess up all of them.

With my mouth still hanging open, I heard Titus's voice in duplicate. I looked up to see him standing in front of me. He was still smirking at me with his adorable stupid face.

"You're catching flies," he said reminding me that my mouth was hanging open.

"I'm just so in shock that you think you have a chance at beating me... at anything."

"It's funny how grief affects your memory."

I laughed a vengeful laugh. "Oh, do I have plans for you."

"Save it for tomorrow, Maleficent."

"Maleficent?" I asked having forgotten about anything other than the things I was going to do to him.

"I packed a couple of sandwiches. You wanna find a spot in the grass and chow down."

"You packed a couple of sandwiches, huh?"

"Yeah. Roast beef. Ham. I figured it would be less of a hassle than heading to the cafeteria and getting lost in the crowd."

"You figured it would be less of a hassle, huh?"

"Yeah."

I took a moment from my spiral into villainy to process what he said.

"Oh. That's actually really nice of you. Thank you. But you know this isn't going to protect you from what I'm going to do to you tomorrow, right?"

"I never thought it would," Titus said with a smile before finding a beautiful spot under the trees and sitting down.

Titus and I chatted and laughed for the rest of the evening. When it got dark enough to see the stars, I pointed out my homework.

"I have to ask you this, Lou. When you decided on astronomy as a major, you knew that celebrities weren't the stars you would be studying, right?"

"Oh, ha ha."

"I'm just checking because I'm sure you still have time to switch majors to something useful."

"Astronomy is useful! How do you think cell phones work?"

Titus looked at me confused. "By pressing the little button on the side. Obviously."

I smiled. "There's a little more to it than that. The next time we're away from city lights, I'll give you a better explanation."

"I look forward to it," Titus said looking me in the eyes.

I wasn't sure what was different about the way he looked at me tonight, but staring back at him, I felt something. It was harder to breathe. With the light creating a halo around his large curls, my heart thumped. I wondered if I wanted to kiss him.

This would have been the perfect time to tell him about Sey and my engagement. He deserved to know. I had already gone long enough without telling him. But when I opened my mouth, I said,

"You know I'm gonna crush you in tomorrow's game night, right?"

"We'll see," he replied with his usual big smile… his usual beautiful, heart-melting smile.

Holy crap! I wanted to kiss him. What the F…? I popped up shaken.

"I should go!"

"Something the matter?" he asked looking at me concerned.

"No. I just need to go. It's getting late," I told him before he walked me to my dorm and I shook his hand wishing him a fair, sea-worthy night.

I didn't know what I was saying. I was panicking. It felt like he wanted to kiss me goodnight… and I would have let him.

This is Titus I'm talking about. My best friend. The one person I couldn't take Lou'ing things up with. The one person I couldn't stand to lose.

"What?" Quin asked as I stared at him with my back pressed against our living room door.

"How did you know that Cage was the one?"

"I don't know. I just knew… after a little help from someone smarter than me."

"Okay. So, you're way smarter than me. You're way smarter than everyone," I told him sitting next to him at the dinner table and pushing everything in front of him aside.

Quin looked panicked for a second and then gave into the moment. "What's going on?"

"There's something I haven't told you."

"That you're in love with Titus?"

"No! Wait. Why would you say that? You know what? Nevermind. That's not what I'm talking about."

"Then what's going on?" Quin asked crinkling the skin between his eyes adorably.

"Someone might have asked me to marry him and I might have said yes," I said bracing myself for his response.

"Who… Titus?" he asked in almost a whisper.

"This isn't about Titus!" I said frustrated that he kept bringing up the guy I was suddenly having feelings for.

"Okay! I'm just having a hard time figuring out who else you've known long enough to agree to marry."

I felt every blow from his unintentionally hurtful words.

"Do you remember the guy I told you was texting me every morning and being super romantic?"

Quin searched his near-photographic memory not coming up with anyone.

"The most recent guy!"

"Okay. Sure."

"Well, when my parents came to town, I asked him if he wanted to meet them. He agreed and then proposed in front of them. It was actually pretty romantic."

Quin looked at me shocked. "Lou, Cage and I have been dating for two years and not even we're engaged."

"And I have no idea what you're waiting on," I said finally having the opportunity to say it. "Are you two holding off in case you meet someone hotter than each other? Because that's not going to happen."

"We're waiting for me to graduate and maybe live a little… or something. I'm actually not sure why we're waiting. But what I am sure about is that four dates would have been too soon."

"First of all, it was three dates… and technically he asked me after date two."

"Lou!"

"I know! I know!" I said letting my true panic show. "And he did it in front of my parents. Now I have to go home for the will reading, and they'll expect him to be there, and he doesn't know if he can come, and I don't know if I'm in love with him."

I paused finally getting out what I truly wanted to tell Quin. I was engaged to a guy who I didn't know if I loved. I stared into his soft, forgiving eyes waiting for his response. He simply tightened his lips into a smile, got up, circled the table, and wrapped his arms around me.

"You're getting really good at this," I said awash in his warmth.

"I'm getting a lot of practice," he joked.

"You're welcome?"

We both laughed and he let me go. Allowing Quin to get back to work, I headed to my room. I didn't expect Quin to have any answers for me. He was a literal genius. But, he wasn't what you would refer to as people smart.

He was a good friend, though. So was Titus… which would make it that much sadder when I mopped the floor with him at tomorrow's game night. I say that, but it wasn't like I actually wanted to beat him so bad that his Mama came after me. That was just our way. We enjoyed teasing each other.

I mean, did I have a competitive side that made me need to win at everything I did? Sure. And, did beating him at game nights give me a rush that would keep me up until 4 AM afterward? Of course. But wasn't that everybody?

He and I had a fun rivalry when it came to these things. And in no way would I spend the rest of the night imaging tying his loser ass in a rim and beating it like a drum. It was going to be a few hours at best.

The next morning when I woke up, I was excited about the day. It was the first time since getting the news about my Grandmother that I was. I knew the grief would come rushing back if I let it. But, I didn't want it to. At least not today.

It didn't even bother me that this was the fifth morning in a row that Sey hadn't sent me a 'Good Morning' text. I mean, what had happened? All I had done was ask him if he wanted to meet my parents. He was the one who took it past that. I hadn't asked him to do what he did next.

In any case, today I was in a great mood. Heading to my first class, I Facetimed Titus.

"So, you never mentioned what we'll be playing tonight. I might need to brush up on the rules."

"Trust me, you'll be fine," he said with another of his broad, beautiful smiles.

"Are you just saying that so you'll have the advantage? Because I'm on to you, Mister."

Titus laughed. "Although I wouldn't put it past me, I promise you, you'll be fine."

"Okay. By the way, who's coming?"

"It will be the whole group. I invited everyone. They can all make it."

"Oh!" I said moved.

"Isn't that what you wanted?"

"It is. I just… nothing. It should be a fun night."

"It will be. Promise," he said sincerely.

"Okay. Well, I'm about to head into class."

"Call me anytime," he said sending a warm wave through my body and making my dick flinch.

I hung up.

"Well, that's new," I said wondering how hard my dick would be as I entered class.

The answer was, completely hard. So sticking my hands in my pockets, I found a seat trying not to think about what getting hard meant. Was I catching feelings for my best friend? I couldn't be. Not Titus.

I mean, he was cute and sweet and fun to be around. I think anyone who has met him would agree with that. And he did have quite the body. At least, he seemed to. I had never actually seen him with his shirt off.

'Hmm, I wonder what Titus would look like with his shirt off,' I thought instead of paying attention to anything my professor was saying.

When game time rolled around, I was ready for it. Usually, Quin and I hosted and Quin took care of all of the details. But when Quin didn't arrive home with chips and I was there by myself, I was confused. I was about to call Titus when there was a knock on the door.

"Titus?" I said feeling a rush.

"Hey," he said entering with barely a hint of his usual smile.

"So, who did you say was coming?"

Titus stared at me. "I have a confession to make."

"Okay…" I said unsure if I should feel disappointed or worried.

"The game I set up for tonight is going to be a little different."

"You mean like a strategy game? Is that why no one showed up?"

Titus smiled. "No. It's a scavenger hunt."

Relief washed through me. "Oh! Cool! I love scavenger hunts."

"I know you do. And this one has a theme."

"Okay," I said wondering what was going on.

Titus pulled a scrap of paper out of his pocket and handed it to me. I took it unsure if I should open it.

"It's your first clue."

I hesitated seeing the sincerity in his eyes and then slowly read it.

"Go to the place where your Grandmother first told you that you were beautiful the way you were."

I couldn't breathe. My stomach shook. And before I could get a word out, I exploded into tears. The theme of Titus's scavenger hunt was the love my Grandmother had for me. I fell into Titus's arms sobbing uncontrollably.

"I can't. I can't," I said overcome with grief.

"I'll be here with you. I'm not going anywhere," he said holding me tighter.

I stayed in his arms as long as it took for me to pull myself together. Wiping my eyes I said, "I guess I should attempt to play your game… you sicko."

Titus chuckled. I was glad he did because I didn't want him to think this was anything other than the most thoughtful thing anyone had ever done for me.

"So, let me see," I said reading the instructions again. "Go to the place where your Grandmother first told you that you were beautiful the way you were." I thought about it. "Well, that had to be after I told her I was gay." I narrowed my eyes on Titus. "Did I even tell you about that?"

With his usual smile, he shrugged.

"Clearly, you're not going to be any help. But if I went to where my Grandmother told me that, I would go to her library. Are we supposed to drive to her estate?" I asked Titus.

He didn't respond.

Staring at him further, I said, "No. But, you do want me to go to the library. I'm right, aren't I? That's where I'm supposed to go?"

"You're supposed to be so good at games," Titus quipped. "You tell me."

"Oh, I see what you're doing. Okay. We're going to the campus library."

"Lead the way," Titus agreed.

Feeling more alive than I had in a long time, I rushed out of my place almost sprinting across campus. Approaching the glowing four-story building, I saw a familiar face outside.

"Quin, what are you doing here?"

Instead of saying anything, he smiled and handed me my next clue. I read it.

"Find the book your grandmother would always read to you after your mother said cruel things to you."

I lowered my head and fought back the tears as I remembered the vile things my mother would say.

"She was always my defender. She was the only one who didn't make me feel like I was the worst person in the world." Falling into tears again I admitted, "I miss her so much."

Both Titus and Quin put their arms around me. It felt good. It felt good to talk about her and it felt good that I had people who would be there for me. But pulling myself together, I took a deep breath and answered the question.

"The story my Grandmother read to me when my mother would say the most horrible things to me is, 'The Velveteen Rabbit.' I'm still not sure why. But, I'm also sure I didn't tell either of you that. I don't know if I've told anybody."

"If that's the book, then we should find it," Titus said confidently.

"No," I said doubting but delighted that he could know that.

"That's the book, right?" Titus confirmed.

"Yeah."

"Then that's the book you need to find."

I stared at him shocked that this could be happening. But leaving Quin, I entered the library and approached the front desk.

"Do you have a copy of the book, 'The Velveteen Rabbit'?"

"I'll check," the dark-skinned girl said from behind the desk. "We do. There's one copy and it should be on a shelf located on the third floor."

The girl grabbed a slip of paper and wrote down the card catalog number. I took and stared at it still not believing this was happening.

Bounding up the stairs, I found where the book was supposed to be.

"It's not here," I said staring at Titus in a panic.

Titus just stared back with his cocky smirk and said, "I thought you were supposed to be good at this game."

That got me. "Oh, it's definitely on."

Heading back to the desk, I told the librarian it wasn't there.

"It's definitely marked as checked in. So it's in the library somewhere," she said confirming on her computer. "If you'd like, I can help you check the re-shelving carts. There's a good chance it's on one of those."

I looked back at Titus who watched me smugly.

"I bet there is. Don't worry, I got it," I told Titus's co-conspirator.

For the next twenty minutes, I checked every cart with books I could find. Luckily, there weren't many. The problem was that it wasn't on any of them. I was about to declare Titus's plan a bust when I glanced out past the fourth-floor balcony and noticed all the students at the study desks below.

I looked back at Titus. He knew I had him. Rushing down, I scanned every book on every desk until I saw another familiar face. This time it was Nero, Titus's ex-roommate and best friend. He was also Quin's soon-to-be brother-in-law. Nero smiled at me as I approached him.

"Nero, in a library reading? Now I know this is supposed to be a clue."

"It's not that weird," Nero said in his rich, small-town Tennessee accent. Titus and Nero had grown up together. But unlike Titus, there was no mistaking where Nero was from.

"What are you doing here? Aren't you supposed to be getting ready for the NFL season?"

"We got a couple of days off so I decided to come in and visit my boyfriend if that's okay with you."

"No, that's beautiful," I said moved by how open he was about his feelings for a guy.

"And if you don't mind, I would like to get back to my reading," Nero said before conspicuously holding up his copy of, 'The Velveteen Rabbit.'

I chuckled.

The night continued like that with clues, tears, and friendly faces until the last clue which simply said, "Now think about all of the things she was to you and you were to her, and let your sadness sail away."

I held up the slip and turned to Titus.

"I could either say that you have no idea how grief works and this is the lamest conclusion ever. Or I could take you to where I go when things get too much and I need a moment. But, I'm absolutely positive that there is no way you know about it. If you do, then I should be worried."

"Then maybe you should be worried," Titus said with a gentle smile.

I smiled back. And taking his hand, I took him to the pond on the far side of campus.

"This is where I go when being me becomes more trouble than it's worth. It centers me. It's the closest I ever feel to home."

"I know," Titus said before directing my attention to the group of people standing by its edge.

As he waved, their faces lit up. It was everyone who had presented me with clues and anyone who meant anything to me. They all had candles and sad smiles.

"Your parents didn't invite you to your grandmother's funeral. So I thought it only appropriate that we have a memorial of our own."

I couldn't stop myself from crying. This time it wasn't out of grief, it was out of happiness. I was the luckiest guy in the world to have had my grandmother in my life. Titus had reminded me of that and had focused me on the positives. The tears that rolled down my cheeks this time were out of gratitude for Grandma Aggie and for having Titus in my life.

Receiving hugs from everyone when I arrived, we placed the tea candles into little ships. With them, we added the clues that had generated such amazing memories and set them free on the pond. We all watched them in silence before everyone else slowly peeled away.

Soon, Titus and I were the only ones left.

"Thank you," I told him still lost in his arms.

"You're welcome. Anything for you," he replied.

Never was I surer that he meant it.

"Titus, could I ask you for a favor? It's kind of weird."

"Of course," he said turning to me as I pulled out of his arms.

I could barely look him in the eyes.

"I'm going to my Grandmother's will reading tomorrow and my parents think I'm engaged. There's a whole story to why they do. But, long story short, do you think you could go with me and pretend to be my fiancé?"

Chapter 4

Titus

"You want me to pretend to be your fiancé?" I asked shaken.

"Yeah. It will just be pretend. I'm asking because my parents saw me get engaged and they already don't think much of me. So if I show up there without a fiancé, it will confirm every negative thing they've ever said."

"I'll do it," I said not needing to hear anymore.

"You will?" he said with the brightest smile he had had all night.

"Of course. You know I'd do anything for you. But, if your parents saw you get engaged, won't they know I'm not Seymour?"

Lou's light dimmed. "You knew."

"I did. I saw."

"I'm so sorry I didn't tell you," he said sliding back into my arms.

"I understand. It's hard to admit a mistake."

He pulled away. "I didn't say I made a mistake."

I laughed. "But, didn't you? If you didn't, I don't think you would be asking me to be your seat-filler."

"He can't go with me because he has a game," he corrected.

"Then why did you hide it from me or ask me to invite him tonight?"

"I didn't know what you were organizing," he admitted. "Putting whether or not I would have invited him aside, there was no way I could have guessed it would be all of this. It was pretty mind-blowing."

Hearing Lou's words sent a warm feeling dancing through me. I liked knowing I had made him happy.

"Now about that other thing. There could be some debate about whether getting engaged was a mistake. No decision is perfect. But it wasn't like I was batting off better offers."

"Maybe if you had waited a second before answering, you would have gotten one," I told him remembering how I watched him say yes with a bouquet of roses in my hand.

"Would I have? From who?" Lou asked staring into my eyes wanting me to say it.

As much as I wanted to and as sure as I was about him, there was no way I wanted the day I declared my love for him to be the day of his grandmother's memorial. Besides, I was exhausted! I had been working non-stop on this from the moment he told me he wanted a game night. I could barely stand up I was so tired.

I wanted what I hoped to be the first day of our lives together to be more than just the aftermath of his grief. And I wanted to be emotionally present for it. I wanted the date to be as special for me as I hoped it would be for him.

"That's what I thought," he said after the silence drew out.

He didn't say it in an angry way, though. It wasn't even sadness. It was more resignation and acceptance. I didn't want Lou to think those things about the way I felt about him.

"You know I'm gonna be the best fake fiancé you'll ever have, right? I'm gonna ruin you for all your future fake fiancés."

Lou laughed, so at least there was that. But as I thought further, something came to mind.

"If your parents have already met Seymour, how are you gonna pass me off as your fiancé? He and I look nothing alike."

"First of all, you do. That was one of the first things I noticed about him."

"That he looked like me?"

Lou tightened his lips and looked as innocent as he could as he looked up into my eyes.

"Wow!" I said never expecting Lou to admit to such a thing. Because, yeah, to be honest, it was hard to miss the resemblance between the two of us.

"But secondly, and more importantly, my parents never looked at him. They looked down the entire time like they were embarrassed to be a part of it. I could bring home Quin and they wouldn't know the difference."

"So, I take it that Quin is busy this weekend?"

"Well, I'm asking you. So, obviously."

I laughed. I didn't know whether he was joking. I never knew if he was joking when he talked about crushing on Quin. But it wasn't like he was a threat.

"Obviously," I agreed. "I would expect nothing less."

"Nothing less," Lou echoed before we both cracked up.

"So you think passing me off as your fiancé will work, huh?"

"After tonight, there's clearly no one who knows me better."

"That is true. So, does that mean we'll be sharing a bed?"

"Don't you get any ideas, mister," he teased. "I'm a good boy," he said pulling his body close to mine.

"I wouldn't dream of it," I told him imagining stripping him naked and pressing his thighs against his chest.

"Oh!" Lou said suddenly pulling away.

"I'm sorry. I don't know why that happened."

Lou stared at me not saying a word. Why wasn't he saying anything? Yeah, I had gotten hard thinking about us sharing a bed, but it wasn't a big deal, right?

"Lou, please don't make this a big deal," I told him hoping I hadn't ruined everything.

I don't know why, but Lou just kept staring at me. When he finally spoke, it felt like an eternity had passed.

"Titus, can you walk me home?"

"Of course."

He then took my hand and said, "Fiancé practice."

I smiled. "Good idea."

Holding hands under the moonlight, I walked him home in silence.

After a lingering hug goodnight, I watched Lou enter his dorm and then took the first deep breath I had had in days. I couldn't believe I had pulled it off. And I couldn't believe that he had asked me to meet his parents as his fiancé.

It would be pretend for now, but would it stay that way? Would I ever have a better opportunity than this one to tell him how I feel about him?

"How'd he like it?" Cali asked me when I entered our room.

"I think he really appreciated it. Thanks for being there. And he invited me to go with him this weekend when he takes care of his grandmother's legal stuff."

When an awkward silence developed I looked up at Cali. That was when I realized he knew more than he was saying. After that, I had a hard time looking him in the eye.

"You like him, don't you?"

"Of course I like him. You've met him. What's not to like?"

"No, I mean you really like him."

I paused, sighed, and then decided I was too tired to continue whatever game I was playing.

"Yeah, I like him. I've always liked him. From the moment I met him, he's been all I can think about."

"You tell him that?"

I thought about it. "I will this weekend."

"Good for you," Cali said with a smile.

Cali was sometimes hard to read, but there was no mistaking how much he meant it. He was happy for me.

"So, you met anyone you like, yet?"

As soon as I asked him, Cali turned beet red. With his eyes locked on the ground, he said, "No, I'm trying to stay focused on football."

"Cali, never play poker," I told him before crawling into bed and quickly falling asleep.

I woke up the next morning relieved and refreshed. Not only had Lou's memorial gone off without a hitch, but I was about to spend the weekend with him.

Between packing and classes, the day flew by and when it was time to pick up Lou, I was in the best mood. Lou was not.

There were many ways people would describe Lou, unpredictable, funny, adorable. But the one thing that nobody could miss was that he was upbeat. He always had a cute little smile on his face. Even when times were tough, he would find the bright side or the humor in it. None of that was there when I picked him up at his dorm.

"Everything okay?" I asked him as we snaked our way to the highway.

"No. Everything is definitely not okay."

"What's going on?"

"Do you not know where you're going? If you don't, that's a problem because you're driving."

"I know where we're going."

"Have you not heard anything I've told you about my family? Wait, what am I thinking? Last night you made clear that you hear everything I tell you. Thank you again for that, by the way."

"Of course," I said feeling good.

"So, I don't have to tell you that we're going to the lion's den. And that pack of hyenas is going to eat me alive."

I reached across the truck and put my hand on his thigh. I loved touching him.

"You don't have to worry. I'll protect you," I told him with a smile.

"Awww," he said moved. "That's sweet." He squeezed my hand. "They're going to eat you alive, too."

I pulled back my hand.

"I don't get it. Didn't you tell me that your Grandmother was going to give you an inheritance? We'll go. You'll get it. And afterward, you'll never have to see your family again. It's only two days. I'll help you through it."

"That's where you're wrong. I didn't just say that she was going to give me an inheritance. I told you that I was going to inherit it all. She said that she was going to give everything to me."

"So? That's even better."

Lou stared at me terrified.

"Titus, you haven't met my family. As soon as they find out that they're getting nothing, they'll kill me and make soup from my bones."

"Lou, you have to be exaggerating."

"Oh, I'm not. After my Grandma Aggie told me that she was giving me everything, she told me to get prepared. She knew."

"And, did you?"

"Did I what?"

"Get prepared?"

Lou looked flabbergasted.

"What does that even mean?"

"I don't know. Get a lawyer, I guess."

Lou completely deflated and turned away in thought.

"Oh. I guess that would've made sense." He turned back to me again overwhelmed. "Where was all of this fancy thinking when my Grandma Aggie was alive?"

"Probably hanging out in my room waiting for you to tell me how your latest date went."

Lou froze. When he replied, he was calmer. "Well, a lot of good that does us now. Anyway, I'm tired of talking about myself. It feels like forever since we've talked about you. How was Nero's new place? Anything new going on in your life? Anyone new?"

I thought and then answered. "Nero's place was nice. And, yeah. There's someone new in my life," I said with a smile.

Lou snapped towards me stunned. He looked like he was trying to be excited for me but was horrified.

"Really? That's great. Are they cute?"

"First of all, I don't know. And second of all, he's my brother."

"I'm sorry, did you say that you have a brother? Since when?"

"Technically, it would be ever since he was born. But my mother dropped that little bit of news on me on Sunday when I went up to see her and caught her and Mike having sex on the couch."

"Okay. Let's start with, ewww. And we will definitely be getting back to that little nugget later. But, you have a younger brother? How?"

"Apparently my father had him before he got deployed to Iraq."

"Do you know who he is?"

"Nope. And my mother's not sharing."

"So, she just dropped that on you and said what, deal with it?"

"Pretty much."

"Wow! So, how are we going to find him? Do you think you two grew up in the same town?" Lou said invested.

"Your guess is as good as mine. I could never lock my mother down on details about my father. But I get the impression that they weren't living together when I was born. I don't even think he was from our town."

"So anyone anywhere could be your brother?"

"Yep."

Lou was lost in thought for a long time after that. At least it took his mind off of his parents. Every so often he would toss out a thought or ask a question, but his adorable thinking face always returned.

He didn't even realize it when we crossed through his grandmother's picturesque town. It wasn't until we approached the gates to his grandmother's estate that he returned to me.

"Oh, we're here," he said perking up.

"We're here."

The stressful look quickly returned to his face. "Are you ready for this? Who am I kidding? Of course you're not ready. How could a lamb be ready for the slaughter?"

He turned to me.

"All you have to remember is that you asked me to marry you on Sunday with four of your teammates singing, 'I Can't Help Falling in Love with You' in the background. It was very romantic. You're very romantic. Everything else about our relationship can be true."

"So, how we met? The memorial for your Grandmother?"

"Yeah. We were best friends who fell in love, a classic romance story."

"I got it. You were in love with me from the moment we met and it took me a while to realize how great you are."

"Please! The story needs to be something they'll believe. If that's the type of storytelling we're in for this weekend, the plan is already lost."

"Wait. Why couldn't that version of the story be true?"

"No times for jokes. We're here," he said crackling as we pulled up to the grand colonial-style home. It looked like a place straight out of the time of slavery.

"How did you say your family got its money again?"

"I didn't."

As soon as I turned off the truck, he took both of my hands and stared into my eyes.

"This has to work. Okay? You can't do anything to screw this up."

"Don't worry. I have you. You'll be fine."

Lou squeaked in reply.

Scrabbling out of the truck, he rushed to the bottom of the stairs and waited for me. When I got there, he took my hand and held onto it for dear life. With a deep breath and a nod, he led me onto the veranda and through the large double doors.

The place looked like the entrance to a grand ballroom. There was a spiral wooden staircase directly in front of us, a dining room that sat twenty to left, a passageway with green marble floors to the right, and two stories of circular balconies visible through the hole in the ceiling above.

As I stared, a woman appeared on the landing on the floor above. I recognized her from the pastry shop. This was Lou's mother and she was dressed like a woman about to go to a fancy horserace.

"Mother," Lou said nervously gripping my hand.

"Louis, one of the handymen has parked their truck out front. Can you kindly inform them to park on the street and that the service entrance is in the back."

"Mother!"

I felt a knot in my stomach hearing her words.

"That's not the handyman's truck. That would be mine," I said with a wave.

She couldn't look further down her nose at me if she tried.

"And who are you?"

I turned to Lou who stared back. After another deep breath, he clamped my hand and turned to his mother.

"Mother, this is Titus. He's my fiancé. Don't you remember? He asked me to marry him with the choir. You were there."

"Ah yes," she said unimpressed.

"Someone parked their service truck out front again," a younger voice said stealing our attention.

This one was attached to someone who couldn't look more like a James Bond villain in training if he tried.

"It's not the handyman's truck," Lou said snapping at him but trying to remain calm.

The guy approached with his eyes set on me.

"And who's this?"

"Chris, this is…"

He cut Lou off when he was immediately in front of us.

"Don't know. Don't care," he said patting Lou on the cheek.

"Woah, watch where you put your hands there," I said immediately not liking him.

He looked at me again. This time like a weirdly clipped poodle.

"Did you bring a bodyguard to your grandmother's will reading?" he asked amused.

"No. I brought my fiancé," he said struggling for courage.

He looked me up and down taking in all of me.

"You never fail to disappoint, do you, brother? At least you're consistent," he said before walking off.

"Wait, you can't just talk to him like that," I said ready to take this guy out.

"Don't," he said putting a second hand on mine. "Don't. That's just how they say hello."

"What?"

I looked up to where his mother was standing. She was gone. So was his brother.

"Any other fine folks I'm gonna meet."

"Just my father. But he lets my mother do his talking for him. It's easier since she's already doing his thinking."

I looked at Lou surprised.

"And yes, they're horrible people. I know they're horrible people. They know they're horrible people. But it's hard when you grow up knowing that the only person who will ever love you is yourself. So…"

"Wow!" I said with sudden realization.

"What?"

"I finally see where you get that from."

"Don't you dare say I'm anything like them."

"I'm not saying…"

"Because you can get back in that truck and drive right back home, Mister."

"Lou," I said trying to bring him back to me. "Lou. Relax. You know I didn't mean anything like that."

"You're right. And I've never once dislodged my jaw and swallowed someone whole. That fact alone makes me nothing like them," he said talking himself down.

I stared at him wondering if he heard it.

"What?!"

"Did I ever tell you how adorable you are?"

My compliment broke through.

"Ahhh." He put his palms on my cheeks. "And that's why I agreed to marry you."

"You mean fake…"

"Shh," he hissed. "There's a massive echo. They can hear every word we say," he whispered.

"So they heard everything you just said about them?" I whispered.

Lou's smile was devious. My baby knew exactly how to fight back against these people. He wasn't as helpless against them as he pretended to be. I couldn't have loved him more.

"Let me give you a tour," he said returning to full volume.

Leading me by the hand, Lou walked me behind the stairs and the dining room. On one side of the room was a grand piano that looked tiny in the large space. On the other side was an elegant wooden floor with a large area rug and a living room set. Taking me back through the dining room, we crossed into the chef's kitchen, prep room, dry storage, and laundry.

The carpeted second floor were all bedrooms. The master bedroom suite was over the side of the house with the grand hall. That was where his grandmother had slept. Next to it was the room that his parents occupied. Next to that was his brother's room.

"Where do you sleep?" I asked after we ran out of doors.

He smiled and pointed to the stairs.

"You get the whole third floor?"

"That's right. Otherwise known as the attic."

Lou led me upstairs and through one of the many doors connected to the balcony. His room was nowhere near as polished as the rest of the house, but it was huge.

"It's also where they store any bit of junk they get from their tacky friends."

I looked at him unsure what I could say.

"Don't worry, they can't hear anything said up here. You're free to speak," he said slumping onto the queen-sized bed.

"I'm starting to understand all of the things you said about them. They might be the absolute worst."

"Might be?" Lou asked with a smirk.

"They don't eat children," I reminded him.

"That we know of. But, come on. Would you put it past Chris?"

I gave him a look and we both burst into laughter. I sat next to him on the bed and wrapped my arms around him.

"Do you regret coming with me yet?" he asked genuinely.

"Not for a second. There's nothing and no one who could ever make me not want to be with you."

Lou pulled away and stared at me with a smile.

"That's so sweet. How do you always know exactly what to say?"

"I guess being with you inspires me," I admitted.

"Awww," he said melting.

"I mean it. I don't think I tell you that enough."

"Well, you definitely don't," he said before wrapping his arms around me and pushing me back onto the bed.

With my back on the mattress, he climbed up and rested his head on my chest. This was the first time he had ever done this. I loved it. The only problem was that in the position I was in, there would be no way of hiding what was definitely going to pop up.

Lou lifted his hand gently gliding his fingertips across my chest. His touches were subtle at first. When I didn't stop him, he rubbed harder.

"Oh my god!" he said causing me to sit up and push him off of me.

"I'm sorry. I don't know why that keeps happening."

"I'm talking about your chest. How are you in that type of shape?"

"What do you mean?"

"I mean…" he waved his hands in front of my torso. "Wait, do you secretly have a six-pack."

I blushed.

Lou's mouth dropped open. "You do! Let me see."

I was beyond embarrassed by what Lou was saying.

"What?"

"We have, like, hours to kill before we have to be back in the snake's den. Show me your six-pack."

"I'm not gonna just take off my shirt like some piece of meat."

Clapping as he bounced on the bed, he chanted, "Show me your meat. Show me your meat."

"Who are you?" I protested. "Is this what you do to all of your dates?"

"No. I save this behavior for my fiancé," he said pretending to flirt. "Come on. Just do it."

"I'm not gonna just take off my shirt."

"Here, I'll be the music," he said before spitting mad beats as if this were an 80's rap battle.

"Seriously?"

"Okay fine," he conceded and then switched up the tune for something a little more country and seductive.

"I'm not gonna get out of doing this, am I?"

"Nope," he said stopping only briefly.

"Fine," I said before getting up and standing in front of him.

"Sway those hips," he said ensuring my humiliation was complete.

Getting it over with, I swayed my hips to the beat and pretended to be a stripper in a club.

"Woohoo!" he cheered.

Feeling a little more into it, I seductively took of my flannel. Grabbing the bottom of my tee-shirt, I slowly eased it up my body. It wasn't so bad. With my eyes closed, I could pretend to be alone in my bedroom.

It wasn't like I had never danced when there was no one looking. This was just like that. And getting into the music playing in my head, I let go and had fun.

I don't know how long it was before I realized Lou had quieted. It might have been a while. But when I opened my eyes again, he was still. It was like the sassy guy I had known for two years was gone. In his place was a stranger staring up at me wide-eyed. His mouth was hanging open.

"What?" I asked not sure what was happening.

When I took a step towards him, he shot up.

"I'll be back," he spit before disappearing through the door.

"What just happened?" I replied when I found myself in the room alone.

I put back on my clothes and sat on the bed for a while. When I realized he wasn't coming right back, I looked around. There wasn't anything that reminded me of Lou in the room. So, twenty minutes after that, I left the room spotting a door on the third floor that hadn't been open when we had entered Lou's room.

I circled the railed balcony to it. Peaking in, I spotted Lou sitting with his back to the door in an old, large desk chair.

I knocked. He swiveled around, offered me a guilty smile, and closed the book he had been reading.

"What happened to you? Where did you go?"

"Sorry. I..." he said trailing off.

I wasn't sure what was up with Lou. But I was sure that being here without his grandmother, was doing something to him.

"What's that?" I asked referring to the book.

He held it up for me to read.

"The Velveteen Rabbit. So that's it, huh?"

"Yeah," he said looking down at it sadly.

I looked around. "Is this your grandmother's library?"

Every wall was filled with old hard-cover books. The only place that wasn't was the window that overlooked the driveway and the woods beyond it.

"Yep. This was where she worked."

"What did your grandmother do for work?"

"She was an author. She was pretty famous."

"Did she write any of these books?"

"A few of them," Lou said looking around but not making a move to show me which ones.

"Are you okay?" I asked approaching the chair and pushing my fingers through his hair. He rested his head on the headrest and closed his eyes enjoying it.

"This is all a lot, you know? I can't believe she's gone. I hadn't called her in weeks. I should have but I couldn't imagine a time when she wouldn't be here."

"I get it. I can't imagine a time when my mother wouldn't be here. Just thinking about being without her…" I stopped when it became harder to breathe. "Have you found out what she passed away from yet?"

"Yeah. My mother says old age, but I wouldn't put it past my family if they killed her."

"Come on. Don't say that. They might not be as warm and cuddly as they should be, but they're not that bad."

Lou looked at me with sadness in his eyes. "You've met them. What about them tells you that they wouldn't be capable of something like that?"

"Because no matter how bad they are, they managed to raise someone like you. And you are pretty great."

Lou stared at me. He didn't smile but the pain in his eyes diminished.

"I miss my grandmother," he said sincerely.

"I'm so sorry for your loss," I told him before he got up and slipped into my arms.

I held him for a while. Afterward, we returned to the bedroom and lay silently on the bed. When it was time for dinner, he looked at what I was wearing.

"You didn't bring anything more formal, did you?"

I looked down at my jeans, flannel, and t-shirt.

"You didn't say that I should."

"Because you didn't have to. You don't have to impress any of them," he told me as if he were telling himself.

"Should I button my shirt and tuck it in?"

"If you want," he said convincing me that I should. "When my family stays here they forget what century we're in. They have outdated views on how we should dress for dinner."

"Are you gonna change?"

Lou looked down at his jeans and what I always thought of as a dress shirt. He looked torn.

"If you wanna dress up, don't let me stop you. You're the one who will have to deal with them if you don't."

"I don't want you to feel uncomfortable," he admitted.

"They already think of me as the service man. How much worse can think of me than that? Lou, wear what makes you feel comfortable."

Lou twisted his mouth, tortured.

"Lou, for me. Do what you need to do," I said taking his hand and finding his eyes.

"Maybe I'll change my pants," he said giving in.

"You do that," I said with an encouraging smile.

Lou opened a wardrobe that separated the bedroom space from the storage area. In it was formal wear. I didn't own a single suit but Lou had everything from dinner jackets to tuxedos.

"So, how formal do they dress?" I asked feeling self-conscious.

"Formal enough to make them feel superior to everyone else."

Lou retrieved a pair of dress pants from the nicest hanger I had ever seen and placed it on the bed. Reaching for the button of his pants, he paused. His eyes blinked up to mine. I was waiting for him to ask me to turn around but he didn't. And since he didn't ask, I kept watching.

When he pulled off his pants, I saw that he was wearing the cutest bikini briefs. He was a smaller guy so I wasn't expecting much. But he had a bulge. It was impressive. No wonder he hadn't asked me to turn around. I would show that off too if I was him.

With his slacks on, he was dressed as fancy as I had ever seen him. God, he was handsome. It took everything in me not to take his cheeks in my hands and pull his lips to mine.

"You ready for this?" he asked nervously.

"You can do this. And no matter what they say, don't forget how incredible you are," I told him meaning it.

"Thanks."

With a hint of fear in his eyes, he looked for my hand and took it. I wasn't sure if this was to convince his family that we were engaged or because he wanted to hold my hand. I chose to believe it was both.

Descending the two flights of spiral stairs, I felt like I was in a different time. I could imagine people dressed in eighteenth-century ball gowns drinking mint juleps. I couldn't believe that Lou grew up in a place like this. Was this who he truly was?

When we entered the dining room, Lou's parents and brother were already seated. The guys were wearing suits while his mother wore a fancy dress. I was severely underdressed.

"I see you invited the help," his brother said referring to me.

"Shut up, Chris," Lou snapped.

"I'm sorry I'm not dressed as formally. I didn't know we would be dressing up for dinner."

"Oh," his mother said fitting more judgment into one word than most people could fit in a speech.

"Yeah, I figured it wouldn't be necessary because we aren't all pretentious assholes who need to dress up to imagine themselves better than everyone else," he said leading me to one of the open place settings. Lou took the one next to his mother leaving me closest to his father and looking across the table at his brother.

"What you refer to as pretentious, others refer to as tradition. And the moment we let go of our traditions, they are lost forever," the uptight blond woman said never looking at her son.

"Have you ever heard of evolution, mother? It's what allows a species to survive as the world changes."

"Your grandmother would disagree," she snipped.

"What would you possibly know about what Grandma Aggie thought? Did you ever talk to her? Seriously, did any of you ever actually talk to her? No. You just showed up here and acted like the royal assholes who owned the place. Did any of you care about her at all?"

His mother turned her cold gaze onto Lou. "For God's sake, Louis, for once can you not be…"

"You," his brother said cutting her off.

I looked at Lou. He was about to explode. I quickly found his hand under the table and squeezed it. It calmed him. I could see all of the thoughts bouncing around in his head, but none of them came out.

"Perhaps we should eat," a voice said from the other end of the table.

It was Lou's father. He was a lean, grey-haired man with a forgettable face. It wasn't that he was unattractive, because it was clear where Lou and his brother got their looks from. It was more that he tried not to be noticed.

Chris looked at Lou. "See what you've done. You've woken the dead."

"Christopher!" his mother scolded.

"I'm kidding. Yes, perhaps we should eat," he said reaching for the bell in front of his mother and ringing it.

As if waiting for their signal, two people exited the kitchen with plates and placed them in front of us. It was like we were at a restaurant. And the food was good.

While we ate, Lou's mother and brother engaged in small talk about his plans after law school. Lou's father spoke up reminding him that there was a job waiting for him at his practice.

"I think I'll be able to do a little better than that," was his smug reply.

While his father seemed hurt, his mother looked proud of him. Lou really did grow up in a world I knew nothing about. I loved him even more knowing what he had to overcome to be as great as he was.

After the two of us were done eating, Lou, who hadn't said a word all dinner, stood up.

"Mother, Father, Chris," he said with a fake smile.

I stood up after him.

"Thank you for dinner. It was incredibly good."

His brother looked at me like he hated me being there, while his mother offered me a fake smile without making eye contact.

"Your family really doesn't like me," I told Lou when I was sure they couldn't hear me.

"My family doesn't like anyone including me," Lou replied with a smile. "But, Sunday morning, they'll read the will and it will be my ass they will have to kiss if they want to keep living this way. Things are going to change," he said confidently.

Returning to his room we sat on the bed. I looked at the clock.

"So, it's 8:30. What do you all do here until it's time to go to sleep?"

Lou shrugged. "I don't know. Read? Sometimes I would play board games with Grandma Aggie. We could pull out her backgammon set."

"Backgammon?"

"It's like an old-timey game where you roll dice and move your pieces from one side of the board to the other."

"Sounds thrilling," I joked.

"Then I must have described it wrong," he said with a smile.

I laughed. "As fun as that sounds, maybe you can give me a tour of the rest of the place."

"I think I've shown you everything."

"Did I see a pool in the backyard?"

"You did."

"We could take a swim."

"You do realize that places like this don't have pools to swim in. It's more like a moat to keep the common people out."

"Well, you did say you'll be making changes when this place becomes yours, right?"

"I did."

"Then why don't we start with the pool."

A light appeared in Lou's eyes for the first time since all this happened. It was nice to see. It wasn't like I needed a reminder, but it reminded me of everything I loved about him.

"I think we should. But we should probably make a stop first."

Again taking my hand, Lou led me downstairs and into the living room across from the piano. His family was there. Each of them held a drink and a book.

"Excuse us," Lou said crossing to the bar and retrieving a bottle and two glasses.

"Excuse us," I repeated trying to sound more sincere than Lou did.

With his bottle in hand, we crossed towards the piano and exited through one of the many glass double doors. Lou was clearly not being subtle about it.

"When you said we needed to make a stop first, I assumed you meant for bathing suits or towels."

"Titus, sometimes it's like you don't know me at all," he said pressing his shoulder against mine and giggling as he jogged forward.

Placing the bottle and glasses on a poolside table, he stripped down to his underwear and dove in.

"Ahh," he squealed when he came up for air.

"How's the water?"

"Not cold at all."

"Really?"

"Strip down and dive in."

I did what I was told and undressed. Lou didn't take his eyes off of me. When there was nothing between us but a pair of boxer briefs, I ran forward and dove in.

"You liar," I shouted when I surfaced.

Lou giggled. "See, this is why we only use it as a moat."

"This thing is freezing."

"Come on. It can't be any worse than swimming in the waterfalls when you were a kid."

"What do you know about me swimming in waterfalls?" I said wading towards him.

"You're not the only one who listens when someone speaks. I remember you talking about how you would catch fireflies and skinny-dip in waterfalls when you were growing up."

"You're making me sound like a character in a bad southern novel or something."

"Did you not catch fireflies in mason jars?" Lou said floating closer.

"We did catch fireflies in mason jars."

"And did you not skinny-dip down at the creek."

"There was a creek and we did sometimes skinny-dip in it."

"Then if the stereotype fits…" he said now inches from me.

Despite the cold water, I could feel his body heat. It encircled me. My heart thumped looking into his eyes.

I wanted to kiss him. My body ached for it. My hard cock throbbed wanting to pull his body onto mine. And finally, when I couldn't take any more, I leaned forward and reached for him. As I did, he leaned back and splashed water into my face.

Not sure what to think of it, I wiped the water out of my eyes and stared at him. He was giggling.

"Oh, you think that's funny, huh?" I said shooting a spray of water back.

Wiping his face, he shot another one at me. I replied with a perfectly aimed shot that caught him between the eyes.

"Are you forgetting that I grew up skinny-dipping at the crick? This is how we fought wars where I'm from," I declared before he sent more water my way.

"Oh, you did it now," I said launching into a full-on offensive.

As much as Lou held his own, in the end, he was no match for the tidal wave I unleashed on him. When he realized it, he tried to swim away. I swam after him. I couldn't tell if his fancy country club swim lessons had let him down or if he had let me, but I caught him. And as he struggled to escape, I turned him until his lips were inches from mine.

He stopped struggling and stared at me. He wasn't going to stop me. He was going to let me collect my prize. But as I leaned in about to do what I had dreamed about for so long, a voice shattered the mood.

"My, my. It's like watching seals on heat. Do seals go on heat? Or is that just something dogs do?" Chris said staring down at us from the edge of the pool.

Seeing him, I let Lou go. Lou swam away as if caught doing something wrong.

"What do you want, Chris?" he asked bitterly.

"Do I need a reason to talk to my brother?"

"When it comes to you, yes. Always. What do you want?"

"You think so little of me. Maybe I just wanted an opportunity to get to know my soon-to-be brother-in-law. You never even introduced us."

I was waiting for Lou to tell him he hadn't introduced us because Chris had been too busy being a prick, but he didn't.

"Chris, this is Titus. Titus, this is my asshole brother, Chris."

"Titus, huh? Is that a biblical name?"

"Roman."

"Oh, like the emperor?"

"I suppose."

"Interesting. And how did the two of you meet?"

Chris sat on a chair near the bottle and poured himself a drink.

"Do you seriously care, Chris?" Lou asked suspiciously.

"If he's going to be a part of the family, shouldn't we at least know a little more about him?"

Lou became weirdly quiet. I couldn't tell if he was worried I would blow our cover or if it was something else. But I had this. People like his brother never got to me.

"We have a friend in common," I told him.

"Quin," Lou added.

"Ah, Quin."

I was waiting for him to say something snide about Quin but he didn't.

"Yeah. Quin was the one who convinced me to go to East Tennessee. So, when I got there, he showed me around. When we arrived back at his place, I met his roommate. It was love at first sight. At least on my part."

"How provincial?" Chris said leaving me confused by what he meant.

"Yeah. Anyway, we started hanging out. And when I realized that there was no one else I wanted to spend the rest of my life with, I asked him to marry me."

"And I said yes," Lou said floating over and wrapping his arms around me.

"Just your typical love story," I said with a smile.

Chris huffed.

"So, what about you?" I asked. "Are you with anybody?"

"I am with a lot of people. Though, I guess you gay guys have a different definition of a lot. Sex is more like a handshake when it comes to you people, isn't it?" he said smugly.

I didn't know how to respond to that. Putting his stupid stereotype aside, as far as I knew, Lou was still a virgin. And the only person I had been with was a girl I thought I was in love with in high school.

"Well, not every gay guy is the same," I said with a smile. "Just like not everyone who looks like the bad guy in an eighties ski movie is a soul-less asshole."

Chris gave me an icy stare, chuckled, and then grabbed the bottle and returned to the house.

I watched him go. When he was out of earshot, I turned to Lou.

"I'm sorry. I probably shouldn't have said that."

"I don't know. I liked it. And he does look like the bad guy from an eighties ski movie, doesn't he."

"He's the guy who's won the ski tournament every year, who the oddball teenagers have to beat to save the lodge."

Lou laughed. "Oh, you're right! I can't believe I've never seen that before."

"It's the hair. Only an eighties villain would be arrogant enough to wear it like that."

Lou laughed louder and stared at me.

"What?" I asked smiling back.

"Nothing."

The two of us continued swimming for a while longer until Lou got out. His underwear clung to his body. Everything about his naked flesh turned me on more than I could have imagined.

I didn't hide my hard cock as I left the pool. Lou saw it and didn't look away until my pants were back on. After, he looked up into my eyes making me think things I shouldn't have.

When we were both dressed, Lou slipped his hand in mine and led me back into the house. With our fingers interlocked, he led me upstairs and into his room.

"We should probably take a shower," Lou suggested shyly.

"Yeah," I said excitedly.

"I mean separately," he said correcting himself with his eyes closed.

"Of course," I replied disappointed. "And, what about the sleeping arrangements? I could sleep on the floor if you want me to."

"No, you don't have to do that."

"Are you sure? Because I don't mind."

"You're only here because you're doing me a favor. I can sleep in the library."

"There's no bed in there."

"I can sleep in the chair. It's pretty comfortable."

"And what happens if someone goes looking for a book because they can't sleep. How would you explain that?"

"Then, what do you suggest we do?"

I looked at the bed again. "Well, the bed's big enough. We could just sleep together. We're both adults, right?"

"Right. And there's plenty of room."

"Right."

"Then, I guess we'll both sleep in the bed," Lou said with his vulnerable eyes locked on me.

Chapter 5

Lou

I stared at Titus barely able to breathe. I couldn't believe I was feeling like this about him. He was my buddy. My best friend. I wasn't supposed to lose my grip whenever he took his shirt off.

On the other hand, there was no way anyone could know that that was what he looked like shirtless. And when he got out of the pool and his hard cock wrapped around his leg? What was I supposed to do?

I mean, my god. He would tear my virgin ass apart with that thing. And what was I doing imagining what it would feel like as he pushed into me?

Now we were agreeing to share the bed? What was I thinking? How was I going to keep my hands off of him? What would happen if he didn't keep his hands off of me?

"I'll shower first," I said needing to get out of there.

"Okay," he said when I was already past the door.

I had to get a grip on things. Titus wasn't one of the guys I dated. He was someone special. There was no way I was going to ruin things with him.

Everyone thought that I dated a lot because I couldn't find anyone good enough. It was something I even told myself. But, deep down I knew that wasn't it.

Everyone treated me like I was fearless. The truth was that I spent every day scared shitless. I knew that if I let anyone truly get to know me, there was no way they would love me.

I mean, how could they? I was a boy who not even a mother could love. So, why would anyone else?

No, Titus was the only person I had shared my mess of a life with, and for some reason, he didn't hate me yet. I couldn't screw things up with him now. If I didn't have him in my life, I wasn't sure what I would do. I needed Titus to breathe. He couldn't also be the guy to take my breath away.

Alone in the bathroom, I got undressed and entered the shower. Looking down I found myself completely hard. I needed this to go away. I couldn't encourage this. Titus was my friend. We could never be anything past that.

Collapsing onto the shower wall, I fought the ache that came from wanting us to be something more.

"No, Lou. You can't do this. He's your best friend," I reminded myself. "Don't screw this up by being you."

It took a while but eventually, I pulled myself together. It helped to remember that nothing Titus was doing was real. He had agreed to pretend to be my fiancé and that was what he was doing. That's all.

He didn't even like guys. I was just his quirky, gay friend who he was doing a favor for. The man was straight. He could never love me like I would want him to. And no matter how his naked chest or hard cock made me feel, that would never change.

"That would never change," I said aloud allowing the words to break my heart. "That will never change," I repeated before wrapping a towel around my waist and heading to my room.

"The shower's free," I said not looking at him.

"And, where is it again?"

"Oh, sorry. I keep forgetting you've never been here before."

"No, I can see why that happens. I clearly fit right in."

That made me look up. When our eyes met, we both laughed.

"That's exactly it," I told him throwing up my hands in mock resignation.

I pointed Titus to the bathroom and then changed into underwear and a pair of shorts. I knew I should probably put on a shirt, but I saw the way Titus looked at me in the pool. He had liked the way I looked. It had felt so go that I couldn't resist hoping for it again, even if I knew I shouldn't want it.

I got into bed and got comfortable. The best-case scenario would be if I was asleep by the time he returned. That didn't happen, but I pretended to be.

With my eyes closed, I followed him around the room. I knew he hadn't taken clothes into the bathroom with him, so he had to only be wearing a towel when he entered. I also knew where he had left his travel bag. It was on the chair on the far side of the room.

When it unzipped, I knew he was facing away from me. That was when I peaked at what was going on. Staring at him in only a towel, I swallowed. But when he dropped it to put on his underwear, I immediately got hard.

How could he have an ass like that? Nothing about him made sense. My straight best friend was secretly hot. How was that fair?

Closing my eyes when his underwear was on, I committed to pretending to be asleep for the rest of the night. There wasn't a moment I wasn't focused on him, though. With his underwear on, I didn't hear him reach back into his bag. Had he already taken out his sleeping clothes? If he had, why wasn't there a rustle as he put them on?

Feeling my heart thump as he climbed into bed, I waited for him to touch or hold me. He didn't. The only thing he did was turn off the light. I kept waiting for him to do more, but nothing happened. It was driving me so insane that my body shook.

It was only then that I felt the bed shift. He could feel me shaking. How would I explain it if he asked? It was a warm night. There was no reason I should have been cold.

Luckily, I didn't have to. While I lay there wishing beyond hope that he would hold me, he wrapped his arms around me. His body was everything I could have dreamed it would be. We were puzzle pieces that fit perfectly together. And with his warm body locked on mine, everything bad that had happened today floated away. I quickly fell asleep.

When I woke up the next morning, it was with me pressed onto the back of Titus like a koala bear. I felt so good bathing in his body heat. The only thing that could make it better would be if I were to wrap my arms around him and pull him to me.

My mind spun lying there. I quickly needed to hold him. Was he was still asleep? If I wrapped my arm around his waist, could I get away with it?

He had held me the night before. But that was just a friend doing what he had to to warm up a friend. It wasn't because he liked touching me.

If I held him this morning, I wouldn't be able to pretend it was for any other reason than me needing to hold him. And I did. I craved being one with him. I had never before realized how great he smelt. I wanted to bite into his back like an apple. I wanted him inside of me.

Unable to resist a moment longer, I lifted my arm like I was going to roll over and then rested my forearm on his waist. My heart clenched at the sensation. Needing more, I adjusted again this time wrapping my arm around him with my forearm on his stomach and my hand on his chest.

Touching him it became hard to breathe. I fought to control my breath needing more air than I was taking in. Even with that, I couldn't resist doing more. Slowly gripping my fingertips, I enclosed one of his strong pecs into my hand. When he didn't move, I explored more of him.

I couldn't stop myself. I wanted to know him. I wanted to have him. But when my hand uncontrollably pushed onto his taught stomach and continued south, Titus stirred.

I shot off of him like I was hit by lightning. Nothing I had done had been subtle. I couldn't explain it away if he asked.

Rolling away from him, I felt him roll over facing me. Crap, I was caught!

"You awake?" he whispered in a groggy morning voice.

He had given me a way out.

I stretched as if his question had woken me. Without answering, I turned laying on my stomach with my eyes closed. I stayed there for a count of five and then turned to him pinching open my eyes.

"Sorry, did I wake you?" he asked cheerfully.

I rolled over facing him again.

"No, no. I was…" I stopped talking as if I were trying to not make him feel bad for waking me.

"Shit, I woke you."

"No, really. I was getting up," I said purposefully muddying the truth.

"How did you sleep?" he asked accepting what I said.

"Good!" I replied with a smile. "I can't remember sleeping better."

"You know that's because I was here, right?" he said cockily.

I wondered if I would let him have this one.

"Maybe," I told him knowing that it was.

I had never slept with a guy before. I had been on a lot of dates. But never once had I slept with them. Not even having a nap in their arms.

I had barely more than kissed Sey before he had asked me to marry him. That was a part of what made his proposal so romantic. I was a Disney princess who found my prince.

But sleeping with Titus had been nothing like I had expected. I had thought that it would make my feelings for my partner more intense if I waited for my wedding night. But that wasn't necessary. I didn't know how I could feel more connected with someone than I did falling asleep in Titus's arms.

Maybe you didn't have to manufacture feelings for someone by waiting if you found the right guy. Was Titus my guy?

"So, what are we gonna do today?" Titus asked still staring at me cheerfully.

I thought about that. I wanted to show him everything. I wanted him to know me in every way possible.

"I'm going to take you on a tour downtown," I told him thinking about all of the great memories I had from going with my grandmother as a kid.

"I love it," he said staring at me like he wanted to kiss me.

Unfortunately, he didn't. He rolled off of the far side of the bed and headed for his bag. I had been right. He had slept in only his boxer briefs. The sight of him made my receding morning wood spring back to life. God was he sexy. Best friend or not, he made me feel like no guy ever had.

With his jeans on, he headed for the door.

"Bathroom," he said as he left.

When he was gone, I rolled over and clutched my throbbing cock. The pressure on it felt so good. I pictured his hand holding it instead of mine. It was almost enough to make me cum.

What the hell was going on with me? It was less than ten hours ago that I had reminded myself why nothing could happen between Titus and me. He was my best friend. I couldn't lose him. At the same time, man did he smell good.

Knowing that my shorts would do nothing to hide my erection and that it wasn't going away any time soon, I scrambled out of bed and changed. When Titus got back, I slipped past him not looking him in the eyes. Doing all of the things to get ready for the day, I returned to find him dressed.

"Are we gonna grab breakfast here or in town? Because I'm kinda hungry. Last night's dinner was incredible, but it wasn't a lot of food."

I laughed. "Right. Sorry about that. I guess everyone in my family is pretty small. We don't eat very much."

"And I can appreciate that. But I would appreciate waffles even more," he joked.

"I can't promise you waffles. But the cook does warm up a few pastries for us if we want them."

"Great! Then point me at them and let's go."

Circling through the kitchen before we headed out, Titus grabbed four croissants and a muffin. The poor guy was probably starving all night.

"Morning," Titus said as we passed my mother on our way to the door.

Her only response was to stare at the food in Titus's hands. I knew what she was implying even if Titus didn't. She thought he was unrefined and not as good as us. But what she didn't know was that Titus was a better person than any of us would ever be. He was too good for my family. I didn't deserve to be with someone as good as him.

Getting into his truck, I directed him into town. Entering, all of my best childhood memories came rushing back.

"We should start at the aquarium," I suggested ushering him forward.

Standing at the ticket window deciding what we should get, Titus turned to me.

"Ah, it looks like fun. But I'm gonna be honest with you, I can't afford this place."

I looked at the prices. It started at $50 per person and went up from there.

"Let me get it for you. Everything today is my treat. Consider it a thank you for putting up with my parents for the weekend."

"You don't have to do that."

"I know I don't. I want to. I really do," I told him sincerely.

Titus wrapped his arms around me for a hug. His touch made me lightheaded. I couldn't deny it. I was falling for Titus and I was falling hard.

Inside the aquarium, we watched the turtles and then took a ride on the glass-bottom boat. We both enjoyed it. After that, we played 18 holes of mini-golf.

"You know I let you win, right?" he said teasingly.

"Whatever you need to tell yourself to sleep at night."

Titus laughed.

From there we teamed up to take down a party of ten-year-olds playing laser tag.

"Crushed them!" I said collecting my high-five from Titus.

And after that, we took a tour of the 'Ripley's Believe it or Not' museum. Titus believed it. I did not.

As the day approached evening, we took a walk through the scenic town. No longer able to resist, I linked our arms. I had an explanation ready if he asked why I had. He never did. It almost made me think he liked holding me as much as I did him. Almost.

"Hey, isn't that one of those DNA testing places?" I asked spotting a new storefront between the candle shop and antique store.

"You mean where they test your DNA to find out where your ancestors came from?"

"Or, find a long-lost brother," I suggested remembering what he had told me on the drive from school.

Titus froze looking at me.

"I mean, if you want to. I just thought that if your mother doesn't want to tell you anything about him, you might be able to find him on your own."

Titus turned towards the business's door and stared at it.

"Do you think that's something you might want? If you don't, we could keep walking. I was just thinking…"

"No. It's a good idea," he said not moving.

"Did you want to go in? It'll be my treat," I suggested unsure what I should do.

"What if I find out something about my dad that I don't like?" he asked breaking his silence.

"What do you mean?"

"I mean, you know how I told you that my father was a pilot who got shot down during the Iraq war?"

"Yeah."

"What if that's not true?"

"What do you mean? Did your father not get shot down over Iraq?"

"That's what my mother has always told me."

"You think she might be lying?"

"What if she just said that to stop me from asking questions about him?"

"You don't believe her?"

Titus turned to me. "Doesn't that sound a little too good to be true? Doesn't every kid who never knew their father wish they were a pilot and war hero?"

"I don't know," I admitted honestly. "So, do you think she also lied about you having a brother?"

"I don't think so. How would telling me my father had a kid with someone else benefit her? That's just inviting more questions. 'Who is it? What does she know about him? Why did she keep this from me my whole life?'"

"Maybe there's a reason why," I suggested. "If you don't want to know it, then maybe you're not ready. She just dropped this on you. Maybe you need more time to process it."

"No," Titus said abruptly.

"No, you don't need more time?"

"No, I think I should take the test."

I squeezed his arm. "You know that you might not get any matches at all, right?"

"I know. But, if there's a chance I could find my brother, how could I not do it?"

"I'm here for you whatever you want to do," I reminded him not wanting to push him any further.

I didn't have to. As soon as I had finished saying it, he was leading me inside.

"I would like to take one of your tests, please," he said looking more nervous than I had ever seen him.

"Right this way," the salesperson said directing him to a display that showed what they offered.

"I think you should get the best one," I told him feeling great that I would be able to do this for him.

"You heard the man," Titus told the salesperson.

Receiving a sealed vile, Titus spit in it and handed it back to the woman.

"Is that it?" he asked.

"That's it. We just need your email address and you should get the results in two to three weeks."

"Wow! That was easy," Titus proclaimed still looking unsure.

I latched my arm around his.

"My fiancé is trying to find a brother he just found out he has," I told the middle-aged freckled woman.

"We get a lot of that," she replied with a smile.

"And how many of them find who they're looking for?" Titus asked.

"I don't get to see that end of things. But if you check the website, there are a lot of people who find family members they didn't know they had."

"Wouldn't it be funny if I do this looking for a brother and it turns out my mother isn't my mother or something?" Titus joked.

"You think that's a possibility?" I asked wondering if I had opened a can of worms.

"As much as I sometimes want that to be the case, there's no chance. I couldn't be more like my mother if I tired. I've accepted it. Don't judge me when you meet her," he said with a playful smirk.

"No promises," I joked back.

Leaving the store, we bought sandwiches, chips, a bottle of wine, and cups and took the ski lift to the top of the mountain. Finding a spot to watch the sun set, we sat and dug in. Again, Titus was starved. I had to remember how much bigger he was than me.

When he was full, we opened the wine and relaxed. Lying on a slope that allowed us to see the horizon, I nestled into his arm pit with my cup in hand.

"I'm cold," I told him as an excuse.

It was sort of true. At the top of the mountain, the temperature dropped fast. I would have survived if I didn't have his warm body to cuddle up to. But I had him. So why not take advantage.

It was either how little I ate or how much smaller I was, but the wine hit me way before it hit him.

"Do you completely regret coming with me this weekend?" I asked needing to know.

"I don't regret a second of it."

"That's good," I said resting my head on his chest.

"You're not falling asleep on me, are you? The sun hasn't even set."

"Uh uh."

"Are you drunk?"

"No!"

"You are, aren't you?"

"I think you would know if I were drunk."

"How's that?"

"I would probably be climbing on top of you and kissing you by now."

Titus didn't reply.

"I might be a little drunk," I realized.

"That's what I thought," he said with a chuckle.

"But, what if I did it?"

"Did what?"

"Climbed on top of you and started kissing you."

Titus laughed. "Yeah, right."

"Don't think I would do it."

"Don't make promises your lips can't keep," he teased.

"You would freak out, wouldn't you?"

"I wouldn't!"

"Oh no, a guy just kissed me. What do I do? Am I gay?"

"You know I wouldn't say that."

"I can't believe my lips touched another man's. I'm going to have to wash my mouth out with soap."

And that was when he took my cheek in his large hand, peeled me off of him, and touched his lips to mine. I didn't see it coming. By the time I knew what was happening, he was starting to pull away. I didn't want it to stop. Did he?

I opened my eyes to see his gorgeous face pulling away from mine. He looked as surprised as I was.

"I'm sorry," he said regretting it immediately.

I could have let him go. I could have done nothing as he backed off. But feeling a rush I had never felt in my life, I sat up, climbed on top of him, and kissed him hard.

It didn't take long for him to react. Pushing his thick fingers into my hair, he gripped and tugged. It wasn't enough to pull me away. It was to let me know he was there. I loved it.

Pressing my lips against his, he opened my mouth. I couldn't believe it was Titus doing this to me, but it was. He took control of me like he knew what he was doing. And when my lips were apart, his tongue entered me. It was everything I thought it would be and more.

Finding my tongue with the tip of his, we danced. Twirling and tugging at each other's, my mind swirled. So when he released me signaling it was coming to an end, my lips left his wanting more.

Pulling away, I stared into his eyes. I wanted to ask him why he had stopped. I wanted to tell him that I could keep doing that with him forever. I didn't. Instead, I returned to his chest, wrapped my arm back around him, and lost myself in the memory.

I desperately wanted to know if he had regretted it. I was terrified to ask him, though. What if he did? What if he never wanted to do it again? What if he could no longer look at me? I avoided looking up afraid that he couldn't.

"I think you wanna see this," Titus said squeezing my shoulder.

Holding my breath, I opened my eyes and looked up at him. He directed my gaze in front of us. The sun was setting behind the mountains in the distance. It was beautiful. I loved lying there staring at it with him. And before I realized it, I had started to cry.

"What's the matter?" Titus asked seeing it.

What could I tell him? I had no idea why I was crying. Was it because I finally knew what love felt like and it was all just pretend? Was it because I never wanted what was going on between us to end? Or, was it because I knew I had just ruined everything and now there was no way to take it back.

"I miss my grandmother," I told him.

After I said it, I wondered if it was true. Before Titus and Quin, she was the only one in my life I could talk to. She was everything to me. Now she was gone. Why hadn't I stayed in better contact with her? How could I have let all of the trivial things in my life get in the way of what was important?

We watched the sun set in silence and when the last of the light was gone, we packed up our stuff and returned to the ski lift. Neither of us had anything to say on the trip back to the estate. I couldn't tell if it was because of the kiss or because he was giving me space to grieve.

Parking the truck in the driveway, I told him, "We don't have to eat dinner with them if you don't want to."

"I'm here for you. Whatever you're up for."

I considered their response if I requested to eat anywhere other than with them. As awful as they were when I was there, they were twice as bad when I attempted to get away from them. It was like the image of us being the perfect family was more important than whether we enjoyed each other's company.

"I'm not sure I'm up for the fight," I told Titus feeling drained.

"Did you want to get dressed up for dinner?" Titus asked me knowing he didn't bring anything formal for him to change into.

He was telling the truth when he told my mother he didn't know dinner would be formal dress. He didn't know because I didn't tell him. What would have been the point of it? I knew everything in his closet. The nicest things he owned, he had brought. What was the point of making him feel self-conscious if I didn't have to?

Maybe that was a mistake. Maybe I should have better prepared him. It didn't matter now because we were here and it was what it was.

"No. I think we're perfect the way we are."

"Whatever you wanna do."

Titus and I left his truck and entered knowing that the others would already be seated for dinner.

"Look who decided to show up," Chris said ringing the bell to be served.

"Sorry we're late. I was showing Titus the town."

"And that somehow excuses you from disrespecting all of our time," his mother barked.

"Mother, did you and father want to have kids?" I asked casually having wondered for a long time.

My mother groaned.

Titus and I sat and Titus immediately reached for his poured glass of wine.

"I'm serious, mother. Did you want to have us or did you do it because kids would look better on the Christmas card?"

Chris burst into laughter.

"Louis, don't be gauche," my father said from the far end of the table.

"That's not an answer," I pointed out.

"Lou isn't wrong," Chris said delightedly.

"We do not use nicknames at the dinner table," my mother corrected.

Chris grabbed his wine glass and took a sip, amused.

"Well, Mother? Did you and Father want to have kids?"

"I think what he's asking is if you had kids for the meme?" Chris joked.

"I said enough, Christopher!" Mother demanded.

My mother's eyes bounced between Chris's and mine, both of which stared at her.

"There are two of you, aren't there?"

"What does that have to do with anything?" I asked.

"Yeah, you could have hit jackpot the first time and taken another roll feeling lucky," Chris replied.

"For God's sake, just be thankful we made the decision we did and consider it enough."

"You didn't actually want kids, did you?" I said realizing they hadn't.

"We were expected to have children if you must know. We come from a time when we did what was expected of us. Do you think I wanted to ruin my body by pushing the two of you out of me? I was once a beautiful woman, no matter what I look like now. Your father was lucky I chose him.

"So I don't want to hear either of you complaining about what we did or didn't do. We had you. Be grateful. My God, when did that stop being enough?" my mother concluded taking a big swig from her glass.

She rang her bell.

"More wine," she shouted before one of the servers exited the kitchen with a bottle.

I didn't know what I was expecting to hear when I asked the question, but it certainly wasn't that.

Considering how quiet Chris was for the rest of the night, I don't think he expected it either.

"Thank you for dinner," Titus said as we got up from the table. "It was, again, very good."

Neither my mother nor father acknowledged him. Normally I would have told them off for it, but I didn't have it in me tonight. My fight was gone.

A lot had happened today. I got my parents to admit they never wanted me, I might have opened Pandora's box by convincing Titus to take a DNA test, and I may have ruined things with my best friend by kissing him. I was ready to bring the day to a close.

The only thing that made me feel better was that tonight, I didn't have to shiver while pretending to be asleep to get Titus to hold me. As soon as we were both in bed, he wrapped his strong arms around me.

"They're reading the will in the morning," I reminded Titus.

"Oh yeah?"

"You won't have to be here much longer."

Titus replied by holding me tighter. I liked his response. It made me think that I hadn't completely ruined things between us. I knew that wasn't true. But, for the night, it was nice to pretend.

Chapter 6

Titus

I could spend the rest of my life with Lou in my arms. If I did, I would die happy. With him there, I felt complete. And lying in bed with him, I couldn't fall asleep in fear that it would end.

This was the day I had kissed Lou for the first time. Not just that, but he had kissed me back. With his body on top of me, his lips had pressed against mine. I never felt more alive in my life.

The last thing I wanted was for this day to end. And I held out as long as I could. But eventually, I fell asleep.

When I woke up, Lou wasn't next to me. He was sitting on the edge of the bed with his head in his hands. There was no question that this weekend had been a lot for him. I could see the pain his family caused him. He pretended like he didn't care what they thought, but he cared deeply.

Watching him sit there with his shirt off, I also couldn't help but think how good he looked. I wanted to grip his small waist in my hands and then slide my fingertips across his smooth chest. With my arm holding him tightly, I would rest my chin on the bend of his neck. As my face brushed against his hair, I would tickle the back of his ear with the tip of my nose.

My cock pulsed thinking about it. I ached to touch him. Being away from him was torture. But I knew this was a big day for him. It wasn't about what I wanted from him. It was about helping him make it to the end.

"You doin' alright there?" I asked touching his hip with my foot.

Lou sniffled and wiped his eyes before looking back. My baby was crying. It broke my heart.

"Yeah. Just being silly," he said forcing a chuckle.

"What time is the will reading?"

"It's at 11."

I looked at the clock. It was already past 10. How had I slept so late?

"Shit! Was there something you wanted to do before then?"

"You mean before my family hated me for life?"

"You don't know how they'll respond. Who knows? Maybe they'll surprise you."

"You think there's a chance they'll find out my grandmother left me everything and they won't declare war against me? Have you met them?"

"I have. But, if you give them a chance, people change. And maybe once they realize that they can't push you around anymore, they'll be nicer to you."

"Yeah, maybe," he said not believing it. "Can you be with me when they read it? They'll probably say some horrible things about you being there, but I want you with me."

"Of course!" I said honored that he would want me there. "And don't worry, I learned a long time ago to not listen to what people say. I hope you don't mind me saying this, but neither should you.

"People who only care about themselves aren't worth winning over because all you'll ever be to them is a means to an end. There's no way you can win with them. So what's the point in playing their game?"

Lou stared at me stunned. "Wow!"

"What?" I asked suddenly feeling self-conscious.

"I've never heard you talk like this. Is it because we slept together? Because if it is, sign me up," he said with a flirtatious smile.

"You're on the top of the list," I said never wanting him more.

"Nice," he said giving me a wink. "But as true as what you said might be, it's not easy to stop caring what they think. I've lived a lifetime with them telling me that what they think should be the only thing that matters. I can't just flip that switch like it's a light."

"I know. I didn't mean it like that. It's just that I wish you could see yourself the way I see you instead of the way they do."

"And how's that," he asked vulnerably.

"As someone who's pretty great. Someone who cares a lot about their friends even if you hide it behind jokes. Also, you're so funny. If I ever want to feel good or have a good laugh, all I need to do is find you. Lou, you're the greatest guy I know," I said showing him my heart.

Lou twisted his mouth not believing it but not wanting to argue.

"You should tell my family that. Because as far as they're concerned, I'm just their embarrassing, too gay son. Ya know, I often wonder if they would love me more if I was a good gay."

"A good gay?"

"You know, like Quin or Nero's boyfriend."

"Oh, you mean boring?"

Lou burst into laughter. "Yes, that's exactly what I mean."

I shrugged. "Who knows? Maybe they would treat you differently. But, you're you. That's not gonna change. And the people who care about you are grateful for that because we all like you exactly the way you are."

As soon as the words came out of my mouth, Lou took a breath and then climbed on top of me wrapping his arm around me. I loved it. The problem was that I still had a massive erection. How could I help it? Lou had been sitting in front of me with his shirt off.

And the last thing I needed ruining this heartfelt moment was my hard cock. How would I explain that? 'I know you're hurting right now, Lou, and I'm saying nice things to you. But really, all I want is to strip you naked and push inside of you as you groan.'

I allowed him to hold me for a second and then pulled away and sat up. I leaned forward trying to bury my aching dick between my legs.

"What's the matter?" he asked responding to my abruptness.

"Nothing. Nothing's the matter. I just thought we should get ready for the reading. It's getting late and this is important to you."

Lou sat up and stared at me.

"You're right. You want to shower first, or should I?"

"You can go first," I told him knowing there was no way I would be able to get up without him noticing my bulge.

"Okay. I'll be back in a bit," he said disappearing into the hallway.

I fell back onto the bed. What the hell was I doing? My whole reason for coming here was so I could tell him how I felt about him. Okay, maybe that wasn't my only reason. I was also here to help him through a hard time in his life. But, me telling him how I felt was high up there.

Why couldn't I just say it? 'Lou, I'm in love with you and I've been in love with you from the moment we met.' Is that so hard to say?

I guess I would also have to say, 'By the way, I'm into guys. I've always been into guys so what I feel for you isn't a passing thing. Also, even though almost no one I know knows I'm into guys, I'll come out for you and treat you like you deserve to be treated.'

Man, that's a lot, I realized before curling into a ball.

Would I be able to be the out gay guy someone as free as Lou deserves? Was I even gay? The only other person I loved was a girl. And how would my mother respond to me coming out?

She didn't say much when I told her about Nero and Kendall, but Nero wasn't her son. She's always cared so much about what people thought about her. Would the way she felt about me change if instead of being her perfect son, she had to admit to her friends that I was dating a guy?

My mind swirled thinking about it all. How was Nero able to do this so easily? He declared his love for Kendall on national television risking his career and future. I couldn't even tell the guy I would die without that I loved him.

I laid in bed repeatedly swearing that I would tell Lou before the trip was done. That lasted until he returned from the bathroom in his towel. I knew I had to get out of there before he got dressed because seeing him in his underwear would prevent me from being able to stand up... again.

Gripping the door handle, I was about to exit into the hallway.

"Um, you probably want to put this on," he said taking off his towel and tossing it to me.

I caught it and stared at him. He was naked. Lou was standing in front of me naked.

"I don't know if my parents would appreciate you walking the halls in your underwear."

I forced myself to breathe and snapped out of my stupor.

"Yeah. Of course. Thanks," I told him before wrapping the towel around my waist and heading to the showers.

If I felt like I was going to explode before, now I felt like I was about to go nuclear. Did he realize he was naked when he threw me his towel? He couldn't have. What would it mean if he did?

I couldn't think of anything else as I took a shower. And still as turned on as all get out, I took my time brushing my teeth and preparing for the day. After thinking about more than a few rounds of baseball, I got my dick down. Once I did, I headed back to our room.

"Don't you look nice," I said finding Lou in a suit. "You sure you want me in there with you. I didn't bring anything near as nice as that to wear."

Lou held up a jacket.

"What's that?"

"I got this from my grandmother's closet. I think it was my granddad's. I knew that nothing Chris or my father had would fit. And I figured you would feel more comfortable at the reading if you had something formal to wear."

I dropped my towel, pulled on a pair of underwear, and then tried on the jacket. It was a little short in the sleeves and tight around the chest but it wasn't bad.

"What do you think?" I asked modeling it for him.

"Umm, yeah," he said stammering and starting to sweat.

"Thanks," I said taking it off and getting dressed.

I had taken a long time in the bathroom. What can I say? I had just seen Lou naked. But because I had, we only had time to grab a muffin and head to the living room next to the piano.

Everyone stared at me when I entered.

"What is he doing here?" Chris asked coldly.

"I asked him to join me," Lou declared.

"And he did, all the way from 1950," he said referring to my jacket.

"Will you be quiet, Christopher. If Louis needs his…," she fought to say the word, "fiancé with him at a time like this, then have some respect," his mother said with shocking kindness.

"Thank you, Mother."

Lou was trying to pretend that her gesture hadn't meant much to him, but I could see that it nearly brought him to tears.

His father, who had been talking to a grey-haired man with more polish than sincerity, turned and addressed the group.

"Now that we're all here, we can begin. For those who don't know, this is Tom, he was the executor of mother's will."

"Doesn't Tom work at your law firm?" Lou asked staring at him strangely.

"Yes, he does. Tom is one of the partners there."

Lou's neck cricked as if processing something that didn't make sense.

"But wasn't the lawyer who managed Grandma Aggie's estate the one responsible for her will?"

"Your Grandmother made a few changes in the last weeks of her life. One of them was to allow my firm to execute her wishes," his father said not making eye contact with his son.

"But, why would she do that after working with the firm for her entire career?"

"For God's sake, Louis. Your Grandmother changed the executor. God knows why. Can you please just accept it and allow the man to do his job?"

Lou stopped talking and stared at everyone with a crinkle rippling his forehead.

"Thank you, Martha," the man said addressing the room. "This will be short and quick," he said holding up an envelope. "As you all know, Aggie made substantial changes to her will in the last weeks of her life."

"She what?" Lou asked confused.

The slimy man pulled a letter out of the envelope and read.

"I, Agatha Armoury, being of sound mind and body hereby leave the entirety of my estate to my son Frank Armoury to distribute as he will to all of my living relatives. I make this decision without prejudice and of my own desire. May the Armoury legacy be in good hands for generations to come," the lawyer said looking up from the letter.

"So, pretty much as expected," Lou's mother said reinforcing what the letter said.

"It looks so," Lou's father said receiving the letter from his friend.

I looked over at Lou who was incredibly confused. Fighting to get the words out, he said,

"That's not right."

"Of course it's right," his mother protested. "You heard it, didn't you? What were you expecting? That she would leave everything to you?" she said with a laugh.

I looked at Lou for his response. He looked stunned. Lou, needing answers, turned to his brother. For once, Chris wasn't an asshole. The look he gave Lou simply said, 'What did you expect from them?'

Lou got up and headed for the back door.

"And where do you think you're going?" his mother chided with an aura of superiority.

Lou took off his jacket and flung it to the ground.

"Louis," his mother called. "Louis!"

"Let him go, Martha," his father said silencing his wife.

I looked around at the joke of a family and hurried out after him. I didn't catch up to him until we were approaching the pool.

"Lou, you okay? Lou?"

"They changed the will. I don't know how, but they did," he finally said as we passed the pool and headed for the back lawn.

"You think so?"

Lou stopped and practically burned a hole in me with his eyes.

"Titus, my whole life my grandmother told me to prepare for when I inherited everything. My whole life!

Now they're saying that in her final weeks she suddenly changed her mind? That doesn't even make sense.

"And what about switching to my father's law firm?"

"Is that weird?" I asked innocently.

"My grandmother was an author! Two years ago she sat me down and explained that her lawyer specialized in managing the intellectual property of authors after they were gone. Her talking about dying brought me to tears. There was no way I would forget that situation. And just like that, she's going to replace him with a firm that specialized in litigation? That's nuts!"

Lou turned away and continued to storm off. I didn't know what to say. Lou was implying that his parents stole his inheritance. How did I respond to that? Certainly, his mother seemed capable of it. But could even the worst mother actually do something like that to their child?

I continued following Lou across the lawn to the woods behind it. About to enter the trees, Lou turned around and stared at the estate. I stood next to him.

"What are you thinking? Should we burn it down?" I asked half-seriously.

"Would you like to know how my family first made their money?"

"How?" I asked having an idea considering we were in the south.

"Cotton. "Just like the great President Andrew Jackson did," my granddad always said. Whenever he was questioned about the morality of slavery, he always brought up "The people's president!"

"But it wasn't just slavery. One of my great, great, great grandfathers saw the civil war coming and convinced his father to invest in iron mines and processing factories. That worked out well for him because once the Civil War broke out, he supplied the south with guns. War is always good for business so he made a fortune.

"Then when the south lost and cotton became less profitable – you know, because plantation owners had to pay their workers – my family transitioned to exploiting miners and putting eight-year-olds to work in their factories.

"Yep, my family has had a long and distinguished history," Lou concluded mockingly.

I listened shocked. I had no idea what to say to all of that. I knew Lou's family was rich and, it being the south, I guessed it was old money. But, I had no idea what that meant.

Lou always seemed so, I don't know, carefree or something. It was hard to believe that this was the tree he fell from… unlike his brother. Because the only thing stopping Chris from sinisterly twirling his mustache was his inability to grow facial hair.

"Wow!" was all I could say.

"Yeah."

"So, what are you gonna do now? Are you gonna get a lawyer and fight the will?"

"Fight my parents? Have you met them? You see what they're willing to do to get what they want, right? There's no winning against people like that."

"Then…?"

"I don't know. Can we just take a walk?"

"Of course," I told him wishing I could help.

I was willing to do anything for Lou. I would fight a bear to be with him. But this problem was in a world I knew less than nothing about. It killed me that I couldn't help him with this.

Turning and entering the woods, Lou led me down a lightly warn path. The mixture of large oak and pine trees reminded me of Snow Tip Falls. We walked for twenty minutes in silence until Lou reached back looking for my hand.

He had never done that before. I took it wanting it and more. Walking beside him, something about him suddenly seemed lighter. I wasn't sure what caused it until after another twenty minutes of silence when we approached a stream. It had crystal clear water and was ten feet wide and three feet at its deepest.

Tightening his grip on my hand, he brought me to a stop at the edge of the water. Facing me as he backed away, he looked into my eyes as he undressed. The smile on his face told me he was about to do something devilish. I thought he was gonna go for a swim, but instead, he walked to the large rocks at the end of the creek. Past him, all I could see was empty sky.

"What are you doing?" I asked amused.

He didn't reply. And when he was finally in nothing but his underwear, he climbed on top of the rock furthest from us, peeled that off, tossed it on top of his clothes, and then fell back.

"Lou!" I shouted watching him fall out of sight.

My heart stopped. What had he just done? I immediately ran towards where he had fallen and before I got there I heard an explosive splash.

Scrambling to the top of the rock, I looked down. Forty feet below was a lake. The water was clear and beautiful. And emerging from the bubbling white water was Lou.

"Woohoo!" he yelled wiping his face.

"Oh my God! You gave me a heart attack!" I said through the pounding in my chest.

"Come down! The water's warm!" he said with a smile.

"Oh, you mean it's warm like the last time?" I asked remembering how he described the freezing pool.

Lou laughed. "Maybe. But you gotta join me. You can't just stay up there."

I looked around at the incredible sight. I was standing on an elevation. The edge of the land above circled around to an area that was on the same elevation as the water. Where the land met the water was a patch of sand.

"Are you really not gonna join me?" Lou asked looking up.

"I'm coming down," I said retreating from the cliff.

Collecting his clothes and shoes, I rounded the edge to the clearing at the bottom. When the entire site came into view, I was in awe. It looked like a flying saucer had crashed into the side of the cliff and then had disappeared leaving a perfect imprint. The cavern it left was 500 feet wide with a smooth stone ceiling and large broken stones that disappeared into the water.

Surrounding it on every side that wasn't shaded were lush green trees. It was breathtaking. The small waterfall from the creek above reminded me of Snow Tip Falls. But this place had something Snow Tip Falls never did, a naked Lou swimming in the water.

"There you are," Lou said with a smile when he spotted me.

"This is amazing!" I said dumbstruck.

"Are you coming in?"

"Yeah. Of course," I told him looking for a place outside of the sand I could put the clothes.

Pulling off the jacket and my shirt, I did my best not to think about what was waiting for me. Unlike this morning, I had just gotten an eye full of Lou's beautiful body. He was a small guy, but his cock was not.

He wasn't completely hard when he had turned to face me on top of the rocks, but he was aroused. How could I not think about that as I undressed? And the longer I did, the harder I got.

I had to do this fast. Doubling my speed, I whipped off my pants and underwear and ran to the water. Approaching, I saw that the bottom dropped off quick enough that I could dive in. I screamed as I did. Honestly, I was just hoping to distract him from the thing growing between my legs.

The chilly water hit me like a hammer. As soon as surfaced I looked for Lou.

"You call this warm? You're insane?"

Lou responded with a devilish laugh and waded toward me. Meeting me where I could stand with just my head above the surface, he latched onto me. Climbing onto my back, he locked his legs around my waist.

That was when I became grateful for the ice bath. If it wasn't for it, he would know how turned on I was. How could I hide my hard cock if it was poking him in the foot?

"Do you like it?"

"Yeah," I said thinking he was talking about him holding me.

"I don't think the rest of my family knows about it."

"Oh, you mean the lake?"

"Yeah," he replied as he got comfortable placing his cheek on the side of my head.

I turned around to get a better view of everything.

"How could they not know about this place? This has got to be the most beautiful site in fifty miles."

"Do you see Martha or Frank walking forty minutes to experience the beauty of nature?"

I chuckled imaging his mother walking here wearing one of her fancy suits.

"I don't know. I could see you and your brother coming here as kids."

Lou huffed. Chris was always the way he is now. I used to think that he was as miserable as I was growing up. But then I realized he wasn't. He was perfectly content to make snide comments and plot his takeover of the world. He just had a resting bitch face.

I chuckled before realizing what he had said.

"So you were miserable growing up?"

"Yeah. This was the place I came when things got too much. I was thinking I would donate this part of the estate to the county when I inherited it. But I guess that's not going to happen now."

"Wait, all of this is your family's land? From the house to here?"

"And beyond."

"Oh my god!"

"It's a lot," he said with sadness.

"I guess none of this matters if you have a sucky situation growing up."

"You can either have love or money. You might get neither or a little bit of both. But you can't have this much of one for this long and expect to also get the other."

"What about Quin?" I asked. "His father is one of the richest people in the world. And from everything he's ever mentioned, he and his parents have a great relationship."

"It's new money. My grandmother told me it takes a special type of person to manage generational wealth. Maybe, in the end, my grandmother realized I was too much of a mess to be trusted."

"You can't think like that?"

"Why not?" he said defeated.

"Because unless you ask your parents what got your grandmother to change her mind, anything you come up with will just be a guess."

"I don't have to guess what my parents think of me."

"You can't let them get to you."

"Why not? It's not like I've ever been able to stop them."

"Lou?" I said peeling him off of me and turning him to look in his eyes. "You can't listen to every awful thing people say about you."

"But these are my parents, Titus. My parents don't love me."

"They're your parents. Of course they love you. They just have a funny way of showing it."

I could see Lou's heartbreak before saying, "You say that because you grew up with someone who loved you. You can't imagine life any other way. But, you don't know what it was like with Martha and Frank. They didn't hide how upset they were when they had to be around us.

"Most of the time they could dump off me and Chris with the nanny and go have fun. But in the times, like when we came to visit Grandma Aggie and they needed us to look like a happy family, they acted like they were in pain."

"I can't imagine that," I said with my heart hurting for him.

"You shouldn't. No one should have to. My parents didn't love me. No one did. I used to think I was unlovable."

"I love you," I said unable to hold it back anymore.

"What?"

"I love you, Lou. I have since the moment we met. And I'm not talking like a brother or a friend. I can't stop thinking about you. I measure time by the next time I'm gonna get to see you, and then when I do, I'm the happiest I could ever be. Lou I…"

That was when he kissed me. Wrapping his arms around my neck, he pulled his body onto mine. Needing more, I cupped his shoulder in one hand and moved my other hand to his naked ass. He didn't pull away when I squeezed.

With him in my grips, I focused on his lips. Pressing them against mine my mind swirled. I wanted to be inside of him, so opening his mouth my tongue went in search of his. When I found it, they danced.

Pulling his body tighter to mine, I could feel the full length of him. His torso was lean and narrow. That made it easier to feel something else.

As we kissed, he got hard. His growing cock fought against my body to stand up. The lack of space between us wouldn't let it. So when I shifted his weight to better carry him to the shore, it sprung free. Stopping where I could kneel, I pulled him back onto me.

His hard cock pulsed against my stomach. He wasn't hiding his arousal. Realizing that caused the tip of my cock to touch his ass. He must have known what it was because feeling it, he groaned and lowered himself in search of more.

Losing myself touching the only man I had ever loved, I gripped his body and found his ass. Still kissing him, I rubbed the head of my cock along the flesh between his cheeks. Getting closer to his hole each time, Lou moaned.

That was when I lost it. His groans, his touch, it was more than I could handle. I needed him. It felt like my heart would explode if I didn't get more of him. So carrying him the final steps to dry sand, I laid him down ending our kiss. His eyes looked desperate for more and he was about to get it.

Clutching his small wrists in either hand, I stretched them above his head and pinned them together. Climbing on top of him, I positioned myself to kiss his palms. I hadn't thought about the rest of my body until a sensation shot through my groin. Instead of lying there passively, he had taken my balls into his mouth. I had never felt anything like it. It was amazing.

Not stopping what I was doing, I leaned down pressing my lips against his soft palms. His fingertips reached up gently touching my face. I could tell he wanted to do more. I wouldn't let him. But that didn't stop him from pushing his tongue up the line of my cock. It felt incredible.

This was Lou who was doing it. He was the love of my life. So when I relented and released one of his hands, he used it to pull my tip into his mouth. I nearly passed out it felt so good. And if I didn't do something to switch things up, this was going to end fast.

Kissing down Lou's narrow wrist and forearm, I rubbed the tip of my nose on his tender flesh. It took my cock out of Lou's mouth just in time. Continuing my kiss past his elbow and bicep and onto his armpit, he giggled.

Crossing his chest to his nipple then stomach, my heart raced.

I knew what would appear next. When I saw it, my heart fluttered.

Lou had the most beautiful cock I could have imagined. Slightly curved, it was rock hard. Needing to touch it, I wrapped my hand around it. It fit perfectly. Lowering my mouth onto it, I felt a connection with Lou greater than I thought possible.

I loved the feeling of Lou in my mouth. Flicking the rim of his head with the tip of my tongue, he became rigid. Then bathing his head like a tangy lollipop, he groaned and then released. Lou's hairless body bounced. As he did, he shot his juices deep inside of me.

Experiencing Lou's pleasure, all I could do was grip my own cock and squeeze. That was more than enough to make me cum as well. I had been on the border of cumming from the moment I pulled out of his mouth. A brush of his leg could have sent me off. So, out of breath from the orgasm and drunk from Lou's exhilarating touch, I collapsed.

I could have lied on his crotch with his cock in my hand forever. That wasn't what he wanted, though. So, when he pulled at my back, I crawled up his body. Rolling on top of me, he placed his head on my chest. I loved it. And wrapping my arms around his warm body, I knew that there was nowhere else in the world I would rather be.

Lou and I laid there until the fall temperature got to us and lying naked with our feet in an ice bath became too much. A few minutes after we both orgasmed, Lou gripped me tighter. Once he started shivering, I spoke.

"Should we get dressed?"

"Can we get dressed without moving? Because I never want this moment to end."

"We can try, but we might have to move a little."

Both of us were quiet until Lou's shivering became intense.

"Okay, we need to get dressed. Get up," I said knowing someone had to.

Lou looked disappointed, but he relented. Crawling up and giving me a quick kiss, he sat up and looked around for his clothes. I pointed him to them and he stood up.

Watching the gorgeous guy walk away from me, I couldn't believe how lucky I was. I had dreamed of being with him for so long and reality was better than I had hoped. I loved him so much that my heart hurt looking at him. And when he bent over showing me his ass, I started to get hard again.

"Wait," I said stopping him from getting dressed.

"What?" he said turning around with his underwear in his hand.

"One second," I said getting up and brushing the sand from his beautifully smooth backside.

Lou stood letting me. His cock got harder with every stroke. It was almost enough to make me pull him into my arms for round two. But he was also still shivering. My baby needed to put on some clothes.

When all of the sand was gone, I let him know and he slipped his tempting manhood into his shorts. That was quickly followed by him putting on his shirt, pants, and shoes.

I grabbed my shorts and Lou quickly did the same for me. I loved feeling his hands on my naked flesh. I was disappointed when he stopped. The only thing that made it better was knowing that this was just the beginning of our new life together. And the more clothing I put on, the more I looked forward to what came next.

"Where do you want to go now?" I asked him as we both stared at each other fully dressed.

"I don't want to leave this spot. Once we do, I don't know what's going to happen."

"What do you wanna happen?" I asked vulnerably.

"I want to spend the rest of my life with you."

I smiled. "That's what I want too. Then why don't we do that?"

"I'm scared."

"Of what?"

"I don't know. What if I can't be happy? What if my family won't let me be happy?"

"I think you're giving them too much credit. If you wanna be happy, just be happy. You gotta choose it. I choose to be with you no matter what happens. I don't care what anyone will say or what it could change. If you wanna be with me, you gotta do the same. That's all."

"You don't know my parents."

"You're giving them too much power." I took Lou's hand. "Lou, do you wanna be with me? Because I wanna be with you."

He looked into my eyes. I could see his heart. "I want to be with you."

A warm wave washed through me making my brain crackle with joy.

"I'm glad. Then, if your family tries something, all you have to do is choose me."

"I will," Lou said making me lightheaded I felt so good.

"Then let's just go back, get our stuff, and head home."

"Yeah. Let's go home," he said with a smile.

Lou took my hand and led me back to his family's estate. Having been with Lou for the first time, the place looked different somehow. Maybe it was because I knew it played such a large role in my baby's childhood. I wish there was something I could do to win it back for him, but I couldn't. All I could offer him was my endless devotion and love. Hopefully, that was going to be enough.

Picking up his jacket from where he had tossed it in frustration, we entered the glass door closest to the stairs. We were about to head upstairs when Chris entered from the other room. He was smiling. It was a creepy sight.

"Louis, Louis, Louis, I didn't know you had it in you," he said approaching his brother.

"Chris, whatever you are referring to, I officially don't care."

"You sure about that? Because it seems that you have finally done something right."

Lou stopped at the bottom of the stairs and stared at him. "What?"

"Oh yeah. Frank and Martha are very impressed."

Seeing Lou being lured back in, I slipped my hand around his upper arm. "Let's just go, Lou. Don't listen to him."

"Louis definitely wants to see this. And again, very impressive," he said sincerely.

"I should just see what he's talking about," Lou said turning to me. "We'll leave right afterward. I promise."

"Lou, you don't want to do this," I told him getting an ache in my heart I couldn't explain.

"Oh, he does," Chris told me. He turned to Lou. "Trust me," he said with a disturbing smile.

"I'm just going to see," Lou said to me. "What is it, Chris?"

"Follow me."

We did and as we entered the living room, we found Lou's parents having drinks with someone I didn't recognize. He was our age, good-looking, and wearing an expensive suit.

"Sey?" Lou asked stunned. "What are you doing here?"

"Wait. This is…?" I stopped myself.

"His fiancé. Yeah," Sey confirmed with a cocky smile. "Lou, I was able to get back in time after all. I decided to drive up and surprise you."

Lou stared at him speechless.

Chris continued. "At first that confused us because you had introduced him as your fiancé," he said gesturing to me. "But then he mentioned that he had met Frank and Martha before and reminded them of his proposal. Turns out he is your real fiancé and this one isn't," he said glaring at me.

Lou looked at everyone flustered. I tried to think of what I could say to explain everything but I couldn't come up with anything either.

"Here's the funny thing," Chris continued. "We like him. Quarterback of the football team, comes from a notable family, and has great taste in cars. Louis, you finally did something right. Well done."

I looked at Sey again. His smug smile couldn't have been bigger. Where had he been until now? Why hadn't he told Lou about his plans? What made him think he could just show up and everything would be fine?

He was clearly the biggest asshole in the universe. There was no way I was going to let him do whatever it was he was trying to do to Lou.

"Listen, Sey…"

Lou's mother cut me off.

"Louis, we like him," she said pointing at the asshole. "We don't like him," she said gesturing toward me. "Send him home and we can talk about your future in this family."

"My future?"

"What are you, in your third year at that school? Your grandmother was funding your tuition and now she's gone. I suspect you're going to want to complete your stay there."

"Are you blackmailing your son?" I asked having had enough. "You're just awful, aren't you? All of you are? You think you can just use your money to bully Lou around? You can't. Not anymore. He's finally free of you."

Lou put his hand on my forearm silencing me. "Titus, can we talk?"

My heart stopped hearing his words. What was happening?

"Come," he said leading me into the other room.

"You see what they're doing, right? When you said they're terrible people, I didn't believe you. Because how could you come from somewhere bad? But you were right. They're all bad."

"But they're my family," Lou said cutting me off. "And, like it or not, I'm stuck with them."

"So, you're just gonna let them bully you around?"

"Titus, Sey is my fiancé."

"But…"

"He is. He asked me to marry him. I said yes. Maybe I shouldn't have…"

"Maybe?"

"…but I did. And, until something changes, he will continue to be the man I agreed to marry."

"You're just saying this because you think if you're with him, your parents will accept you. But nothing you do will change anything. You said it, they are incapable of seeing anything past what they get out of stuff."

"But I have to try," Lou implored. He sighed and looked away. "They're my family and I have to try."

My chest burned.

"So, what does that mean… for us?"

"You should go."

"Lou?"

"We'll talk about this when I get back. I'm sure Sey can give me a ride. It will give me time to straighten things out with him."

"Don't do this, Lou. Remember how you felt just an hour ago. We were meant to be together."

"Are we?" Lou asked confused.

I held his shoulders. "Yes, Lou, we are."

I wanted so badly for him to look me in the eyes. If he did, I knew he would remember what we meant to each other. But he didn't.

"You should go, Titus," he whispered breaking my heart.

"But…"

"You should go," he said pulling away from me.

Standing in front of him desperately wanting to touch him, I felt lost. I was losing the only person I ever truly loved. I had only just won him. I wasn't ready for things to end.

Ready for it or not, I knew what I had to do. I still loved Lou with every part of my being. And if he wanted me to go, I would. So, turning from him, I headed for the stairs. It was a long walk to the third floor, but when I was there, I headed to his room and collected my stuff.

It didn't take long to pack everything into my bag and return downstairs. When I did, I saw that Lou hadn't moved. Looking at him, he still couldn't look at me. I didn't bother to say bye.

Exiting through the front door, I headed to my truck. It was clear why Lou's family liked him so much after I saw what the asshole had driven up in. It was an electric blue, convertible McLaren. I didn't need to know how much it cost to know how rich his family had to be to afford it.

Maybe he was a better match for Lou than I was. What did I have to offer him past my love and endless devotion? He could probably give Lou the world. And wasn't that what Lou deserved?

I got into my ten-year-old truck and pulled out of the driveway. I could only imagine what everyone thought as I drove off. I had just been fooling myself if I thought that someone as great as Lou would want to be with someone like me. I had been such a fool.

I was never going to be made a fool like that again, though. Never. It hurt too much. I wouldn't be able to stand it. Lou had told me to leave moments after telling me he wanted to be with me forever. For over a year I had pretended that life was other than what it is. But I had to accept facts.

Nero had moved on without me. My mother had moved on without me. And now so was Lou. I was alone.

Nothing I thought I had was real. Everyone had just been killing their time with me waiting for something better. I was tired of being everyone's second choice. I needed something real. This pain was too much.

From now on I was going to do what everyone else did. I was going to take what I wanted and only think of myself. I was going to create the life I wanted and not wait for someone to give it to me.

I was never going to let myself feel this way again. Not for Lou. Not for anyone. Never!

Chapter 7

Lou

The last thing I expected to see when I arrived back at the estate that day was Sey. Having not heard from him after I had given him the address, I thought things were over between us. Was I wrong for assuming that?

How could I know that he would show up unannounced? How could I know that he was planning it as a surprise? And what was I supposed to do now that Titus and I had been together?

Sey and I had barely kissed. How could we do more? We had only been on two dates. On the third, he had asked me to marry him. And on the fourth, he was being coddled over by my family.

It was like they no longer cared I was gay. All that mattered was that Sey's family was one of the few Tennessee families that topped our own. Generations ago, they had worked together. And it was in part because of Sey's great grandparents that my great grandparents held onto their plantation after the civil war.

It was ironic that I could be the one to merge our two families. I was gay and despised our family's history. Yet, out of all of the guys I had dated, he was the one who had asked me to marry him. It had to be destiny, right?

Sey and I stayed an extra night at the estate allowing Frank and Martha to gush over him a little more. I definitely didn't like how he had just shown up without a hint that he would, but I did like feeling like a part of my family for the first time in my life.

I didn't know what approval felt like until my mother gave it to me because of Sey. How could I break things off with him now? How could anything feel more right?

At the same time, I couldn't help but think about what I did to Titus. He had to understand why I did it, right? No matter what had happened between the two of us, Sey was my real fiancé.

That didn't mean that what I felt for Titus wasn't also real. It was. That was one of the reasons I had Sey sleep in the guest bedroom instead of my bed. But maybe there was more to being with someone than just loving them.

"Your family really liked me," Sey said as we drove back to campus.

"They did. And they don't like anybody."

"They definitely didn't like what's his name."

"His name is Titus. He's my best friend."

"Oh. And, why did you tell them he was your fiancé, again?"

"Because I didn't know you were coming."

"So, you just told your family you were engaged to someone else."

"How was I supposed to know that you would just show up like that? Why didn't you tell me you were coming?"

"I told you, I wanted it to be a surprise."

"But, you didn't reply to any of my texts. What was I supposed to think?"

"Well, I didn't think you would replace me with the next guy to come along if I got a little busy."

"So, you were busy? That's why you ignored my texts?"

"I didn't ignore your texts. I read them. I just got busy before I could reply. At the risk of sounding like a dick, I do have other things going on right now. I just transferred to a new school. I've been trying to win over my teammates. I'm fighting for my place as starting quarterback. And, unlike you, I have to deal with parents who are having a hard time accepting that their only son is gay. So pardon me if it takes me a minute to reply to you."

"I didn't know any of that."

"Well, now you do. So, maybe instead of beating me up for wanting to surprise you, you can just say thank you for doing something nice for you?"

I considered what he said. Maybe he was right. Maybe I was the one threatening to screw things up between us. He had asked me to marry him. Didn't that mean that he was all in? Didn't that also mean that I had royally screwed up by letting things happen with Titus?

"You're right. I'm sorry," I told him seeing how everything going wrong between us was my fault.

"No. You know what? I'm sorry," he said putting his hand on my thigh. "You're right. I should have texted you. And I should have given you a heads up that I was planning on stopping by. It was stupid of me to just to show up like that. Do you forgive me?"

I stared at Sey realizing that he was actually a good guy. I didn't know what I thinking before. He really did love me.

"I forgive you," I told him forcing a smile.

"We both made mistakes. But, we'll do better, right?" he said joyfully.

"Right," I told him knowing it was what he wanted to hear.

Sey smiled and then leaned across the car for a kiss. I gave him one. It immediately made me think of Titus. How was I going to explain any of this to him?

It turned out that I wouldn't have to explain things to Titus. Because, like after Sey had asked me to marry him, Titus disappeared. But unlike the last time, it wasn't just for a day. Three weeks went by without hearing from him.

"Have you heard from Titus?" I asked Quin when I couldn't take the silence any longer.

"Yeah. Why do you ask?"

"I haven't heard from him."

"Oh," Quin said surprised.

"He hasn't mentioned me?"

"No. But maybe it's because he has a lot going on."

"What does he have going on?"

"He's back on the football team," Quin said surprised I didn't know.

"He's what?"

"Yeah. He decided that he wanted back on, and he made it happen. I think he's a starter. Didn't Sey tell you? You said they met at your grandmother's estate, right?"

"Sey knows who he is. I guess he just forgot to mention it. Or he assumed I already knew?"

"That makes sense," Quin concluded.

"What else has Titus been doing?"

"He started a new business."

"What?" I asked not expecting to hear anything like that.

"Yeah. In Snow Tip Falls. It's with someone he went to high school with. It's a tour guide company. But they're still in the setting-everything-up phase."

"Wow! Anything else?"

"There's some local politics stuff he's also doing. But that's more of a side thing than anything else. He wants to get the town officially put on maps. There's been some resistance to the idea, but Cage has been helping him gain support for it."

"So, what you're saying is he's been doing well… without me?"

"No, Lou. I didn't say that."

"But he is, though. Right? I mean, he's probably never been better."

"He's probably doing as well as you are," Quin said leaving it at that.

How well did Quin think I was doing? Sure, Sey and I had come up with something workable between us. But were either of us happy?

The reason I had fallen for him so quickly was how his flood of attention had made me feel. He used to text me every morning and night. He made me feel loved in a way no one else did.

But then all of that stopped. Nowadays, if he replied to my text on the same day, I had to be grateful. He had a busy life. There was no denying that. But sometimes I wondered where I ranked on his list of priorities.

'I see you have a home game this weekend. I would love to see you play,' I texted Sey.

It took a day, but he texted back. 'I'll leave two tickets at will-call for you.'

'Maybe we could grab something to eat afterward?'

Sey never replied.

Somehow I convinced Quin to join me at the game instead of driving up to Snow Tip Falls to spend the weekend with his boyfriend. I wasn't sure why he would. His boyfriend was smoking hot. But I was glad that he did.

Ever since Titus and I stopped talking, I've felt lonely. Titus was the person I told everything important to. I had really screwed things up with him at the estate. I blame my grief for my bad decisions. I wouldn't have done any of that if my grandmother hadn't died and my parents hadn't stolen my inheritance. I would never have risked our friendship otherwise.

Titus had been my best friend. I loved him. I was happier whenever he was around. And I cared about how he felt. Seriously, I cared about his feelings. Who was I when I was around him?

I might not know who having Titus in my life had turned me into, but I did know who I was without him. I was an incomplete and sad person. I didn't like that Lou. But I had done this to myself. Why had I kissed Titus? How could I ruin our friendship like that?

Taking our seats at the game, I was excited. I wasn't sure why. I had seen Sey play before. It was at the beginning of the year. It was what led to our first date. We had met at the campus bar and after some flirting, he had invited me to watch him play.

I'm not a football fan, so I didn't care that he was the starting quarterback. But there was a moment right before they got into that squat that they all do when he had looked up to where I was sitting and pointed at me. It was like he was saying that this was for me. And then he threw the ball halfway down the field for the game-winning touchdown. How could I not go out with him after that?

That didn't explain why I was excited this time, though. I was getting less impressed by Sey every day we were together. But when the game started and our school's defensive squad took the field, my heart thumped.

"There he is! There's Titus," I said almost giggling.

I had done my research as soon as I found out that Titus was on the team. I found out the number he wore and his position. He was one of the guys whose job it was to stop the other team's quarterback from throwing the ball. He wasn't one of the huge guys that ran into each other at the start of the play. He was the guy who stood at the end of the line and tried to sneak around the guys trying to protect the quarterback.

"Did you know that Titus has had ten sacks for the season?" I told Quin while not taking my eyes off of the field.

"That's good, right?"

"That's like, a lot," I explained. "Doesn't your boyfriend coach football? Shouldn't you know that?"

"Until he figures out what I do working with my dad, I don't need to know what sacks are," he joked.

As soon as Quin said it, the first play of the game began. On cue, Titus faked left throwing his defender off of him, and then spun right. With no one in front of him, he shot toward the quarterback like a freight train. When he hit him, the crunch echoed through the stands.

The crowd was silent before exploding into cheers. Quickly getting off of the guy he had flattened, Titus flexed his muscles and roared. It was amazing. I couldn't be more turned on if I tried.

"That's a sack," I told Quin proudly.

"And, now I know," Quin joked. "Wow! What got into him?"

"I don't know," I said wondering if Titus knew I was here.

That couldn't be it, right? I didn't tell him I was coming. Did Quin? I definitely couldn't ask either of them that. Not after treating Titus like I had.

Whatever it was that was inspiring Titus's play kept inspiring it. The guy had four sacks by halftime. If ten was considered a lot over multiple games, then four in the first half had to be insane.

"Who's Titus showing off for?" I joked as we left for hotdogs at halftime.

"You think he's showing off for someone?" Quin asked.

"I'm just saying he's playing well."

"So is Sey," he said cheerfully.

That's right, I had a fiancé and he was playing too.

"Yeah. Definitely. But... I mean, Titus, right?"

I was sure that I wasn't giving away my feelings for him. Titus was on fire. It was the most impressive thing I've ever seen on a football field. Granted, I'm not a football fan, so I haven't seen a lot. But, damn. Titus was amazing.

The second half of the game mirrored the first. Even though the other team seemed to change their strategy to stop him, Titus got four more sacks by the end of the game. I had no idea he had that in him. It had to be the hottest thing I had ever seen. I couldn't begin to figure out why, but it was.

"Did Sey want to go grab something to eat?" Quin asked me after the game.

Grabbing something to eat after the game was a tradition for our group whenever we came to watch one of our boyfriends' games. Last year I didn't go to any because, you know, it's football. But when Quin would tell me about it afterward, it always sounded like fun.

"I texted him. He didn't say."

"We could meet him at the player's exit."

"You figured out where it is?" I asked remembering the first game we saw together and how we circled the place for an hour after the game trying to find it.

Quin laughed. "I've been to a lot of games since then."

"Okay. Lead the way," I said ushering him ahead of me.

Snaking through a couple of corridors, we exited the back of the stadium in front of the player's parking lot. It took a few minutes but Sey was one of the first to exit. He was with teammates. They looked like they were having a good time after their win. Seeing me, Sey came over.

"Lou, what are you doing here?" he said kissing me in front of his friends. I liked that.

"Quin and I were going to grab something to eat and were wondering if you wanted to join us."

"Didn't I text you back? One of the guys from the team is having something. I would invite you, but it's kind of a team-only thing."

"Oh," I said disappointed.

"I'm sorry, Babe. I'll make it up to you. I swear. Let's get dinner tomorrow," he said cheerfully.

"Yeah. Sure," I told him trying to hide my disappointment.

"Great! And, did you like the win? It was for you," he said cockily.

"Yeah. Thanks."

"Okay. Talk to you later," he said giving me another kiss before catching up with his teammates.

"He has a team thing he has to go to," I explained to Quin.

"Oh. I was going to say that we should ask Titus but if they have a team thing, he probably has to go to it as well."

As soon as Quin mentioned Titus's name, I felt a rush. My face felt hot. I wondered if Quin could tell. If he could, he didn't let on.

"We could ask him," I suggested as my heart thumped.

It was then that Quin looked at me strangely. Was I that red? Quin chuckled and agreed.

I felt so nervous waiting for Titus. Would he even want to see me after what I did to him? I knew I wouldn't want to see me if I were him. I probably shouldn't even be waiting for him. But wasn't it Quin's idea to come down here? It wasn't like I was stalking him or anything.

"Titus!" I said as soon as he stepped into view.

He looked over at me with a blank look. He stared at me for a while before shifting his gaze to Quin and coming over.

"Congratulations on the game! You were incredible out there," I said wanting to play it cool but failing.

Titus gave a faint smile. "Thanks," was all he said.

When the silence drew out, I spoke again.

"Quin and I were going to ask you if you wanted to grab something to eat. I know it used to be a tradition last year."

Quin interjected. "Sey said you guys have a team thing, though. So, if you can't, we understand."

"No!" Titus said startling us. "I mean, I could probably come. A different teammate throws something after every victory. I could just go to the next one," he said turning his sights on me.

I melted under his gaze.

Quin chuckled uncomfortably. "You know what? I just remembered that I told Cage I would do a Facetime with him after the game. I should really go do that."

I turned to Quin wondering if him not being there would make Titus change his mind.

"Are you sure you can't come?" I asked pleading with my eyes knowing Titus couldn't see me.

"No, you two go ahead. He was disappointed I couldn't come up this weekend. I need to make it up to him. And I'm sure the two of you have a lot to talk about."

"How's Cage's team doing?" Titus asked Quin.

"So far they're undefeated," Quin said proudly.

"Tell him I'll have to see a game, next time I'm back home."

"I will. Anyway, you two have fun. And congratulations on the win, Titus. It was an amazing game."

"Thanks," he said as Quin walked off.

With Quin gone, Titus turned his eyes to me.

"So, do you still want to grab something to eat?" I asked vulnerably.

"Do you?"

"Yeah. Definitely. How often can I say that I'm going out with a star football player?" I teased.

"You're engaged to one," Titus said confused.

"I mean, yeah. But you kind of carried the team."

Titus looked away humbly. "It was a team effort."

"Titus, I'm pretty sure you gave their quarterback PTSD. He's gonna wake up screaming because of you. You were insane out there."

Titus huffed proudly.

"Eight sacks in a game? That has to be some kind of record. Like, where did that come from?"

"I just felt like I had a lot to get out today."

"Oh," I said again wondering if his play had anything to do with me.

Walking to a nearby pizza place, I remembered the last time we walked together. We were holding hands. I had liked it. My small hand got lost in his. Everything about that weekend was incredible until Sey had shown up.

"I never got the chance to apologize for everything that happened," I told him breaking the silence as we waited for our order.

"No, I should apologize."

"What did you do?" I asked confused.

"I shouldn't have mentioned how I felt about you."

"Oh," I said remembering it. "Well, you probably wouldn't have if I didn't kiss you… twice."

"You did do that," Titus said lightheartedly blaming me.

"But, to be fair. I was in mourning and I did see you with your shirt off for the first time. So, I can't really be blamed."

"So, it was my fault?" Titus asked amused.

"I didn't want to have to say that. But…"

"Wasn't it you who pressured me to take off my shirt?"

"I don't know what you're talking about."

"You chanted "Take off your shirt" and then beat boxed."

"I don't remember it that way," I said knowing that it was.

"Oh, okay."

"Besides, I was in mourning. You should have known that and resisted my sick beats."

"Resist your sick beats? Lou, I'm only a man," he said before we both laughed.

"But seriously, Titus, I'm sorry."

Titus dropped his smile and lowered his eyes accepting my apology with a nod.

"I've missed my best friend," I told him with a smile. "I'd love to have him back."

"Did you tell Sey what happened between us that weekend?"

It was my turn to look down.

"I didn't see the point of it. It's not like it's going to happen again, right?" I asked hoping that it might.

"Right. Never again," he said firmly.

I could barely hide my disappointment. "Never again. So, can I have my best friend back?"

"I don't know, Lou," he said drifting off into thought.

"Hey, did you get the results back from your DNA test yet?" I asked needing to stop him from saying something that would break my heart.

Titus's eyes brightened with my question.

"I did."

I sat up excitedly.

"And?"

"Nothing."

"At all? Wait, are you not human? Because that would explain your play today."

Titus chuckled.

"I mean, no relatives popped up."

"No one at all?"

"No. It did say that my genetics came from East Tennessee, though. But, I already knew that. Being born there kind of tells you that."

I thought for a moment.

"Does it, though?"

"How could it not?"

"What if your mother and father were born in California and your mother moved here before you were born."

"But she didn't."

"Right. But how did the test know that?"

Titus thought about it without a response.

"Titus, I think you have relatives in East Tennessee."

"I thought we already covered this. I was born here. Of course I have relatives here."

"No, I mean, I think you have relatives who already took the genetic test."

"Then why didn't they show up in my results?"

"I don't know. Maybe they requested not to be shown to others. Maybe they did something where their results were added anonymously."

"Or maybe there's a completely other reason."

"I mean, that could be. But since we don't know which is true, shouldn't we choose the one that offers the most hope."

Titus took a deep breath.

"I might be over having hope for things," he said staring at me.

Ouch!

"Quin told me that you were starting a business in Snow Tip Falls. You have to have hope for that."

Titus shrugged.

"And he mentioned something about getting the town on the map or something?"

"Yeah. It turns out that the only way we can do it is to incorporate the town. It requires a town-wide vote. I've been organizing it while campaigning for it."

"Wow! Looks like I was just holding you back," I said jokingly but afraid it might be true.

Titus looked down instead of responding.

"So, if you could have hope about all of those things, why not have a little hope that you will find your brother?"

"Some things hurt a little more when you're disappointed."

Again, ouch!

"Then, how about if I help you? I could have the hope for both of us," I said with a smile.

"Help me? How?"

"I don't know. But there's got to be someone in your town who knows something, right? Hell, someone there could be your brother without knowing it. I could find them for you."

"Lou…" he said about to brush me off.

"Please, Titus," I said reaching across the table and putting my hand on his forearm. "Let me do this for you. It's the least I can do. Let me help."

Titus thought about it. Waves of pain washed across his face as he did. Had I hurt him that much? It was yet another reason I needed to help him. I couldn't let him be alone. He was too great of a guy. And if finding his brother would cure him of that, it was something I had to do.

"I'll think about it," he told me as our order came.

"You think about it," I told him happy that I might be getting him back into my life.

Chapter 8

Titus

"You didn't come to the after-party?" Cali said when I got back to our room.

"Yeah, sorry about that. Lou and Quin showed up after the game wanting to grab something to eat."

"So, you ditched the party and didn't invite me?" my roommate asked hurt.

"It wasn't intentional. And Quin didn't even end up joining us."

"Oh. So it was just you and Lou?" he asked suddenly giving me his full attention. "How'd that go?"

I considered what I had told him about my feelings for Lou. I hadn't told him that I was in love with Lou, but he had to know I felt something for him. Cali had helped me arrange the memorial for Lou's grandmother. I told him I was spending the weekend at his family's estate pretending to be his fiancé. And he saw how I was when I got back.

I have not been in a great mood. This was the first time I felt anywhere near myself. He had to have made the connection. But, could he have guessed that we had done naked things together?

"It went, okay. We talked. We both apologized for what happened."

"What happened?"

I stared at him wondering what I should say. The only people who knew I was into guys were Quin and Lou. And Lou only knew because I told him I loved him.

Was I straight except for my feelings for Lou? No. I had always found guys hot. So, was I gay? I haven't been able to see anyone past Lou since meeting him. So maybe. But that would mean that everything I felt for girls throughout high school would have been a lie.

"Can I tell you something, Cali?"

Cali froze and then shifted to the edge of his bed. Giving me his full attention he said, "Yeah, man. Anything."

I took a deep breath. What was I doing? This felt like such a mistake. But, didn't Lou deserve to be with someone who wasn't embarrassed about his feelings? Wasn't that the one redeeming quality about Sey?

"When I was at Lou's place, things happened between us," I told him suddenly feeling uncomfortably warm.

"What type of things?"

I took another deep breath.

"That's alright. Take your time," Cali said sweetly. It gave me the confidence to continue.

"We kissed."

"Wow!" Cali said with a lot less surprise than I was expecting.

"Yeah. And I might have told him that I was in love with him and that I have been from the moment we met," I said feeling my face flush.

"Is that true?"

"What?"

"That you were in love with him since the moment you met?"

"Yeah," I admitted for the first time to anyone.

"That's amazing."

"Why do you say that?"

"I don't know. It takes a lot of courage. Thanks for sharing that. It means a lot to me."

Out of all of the ways I could see this conversation going, him saying that it meant a lot that I told him, wasn't one of them. What was I supposed to say to that?

"Thanks for being cool about it."

Cali lowered his head turning red.

"What?" I asked seeing there was something he wasn't saying.

"I had a crush on a guy," he said shyly.

"You did?" I paused and thought about it. "Is it someone I know?"

He shook his head embarrassed.

"Who was it?"

Cali hesitated.

"You don't have to say if you don't want to."

"No, I want to tell you. I just…" he took a deep breath and centered himself. "It was Quin."

"Quin?"

"Yeah. You know that first time when Quin and Mr. Rucker… I mean Cage came to Snow Tip Falls?"

I remembered the time. "Oh yeah."

"Then."

I smiled. "To be honest, I kind of had a crush when I met him, too. But he was with Cage and Cage is great. Also, he introduced me to Lou."

"Oh yeah, Mr. Rucker is great. He got me my scholarship here."

"But, you still kind of have a crush on Quin?"

Cali lowered his head and turned red.

"Listen, I get it. So, does that mean you're… gay?"

He shrugged his shoulders.

"Maybe."

"Maybe, like you don't want to admit it? Or, maybe, like you really don't know?"

"I don't know," he admitted bashfully.

"It's hard to tell, right? You meet someone of the same sex and they're great. So, then you start to think that you could never have feelings for someone of the opposite sex again."

"Right?" Cali said with a big smile.

"I obviously know the feeling."

Cali paused.

"So what are you going to do about Lou? We could still go mess Sey up if you want. We could make him less pretty."

"He is annoyingly pretty, isn't he?" I joked.

"Pretty much," Cali said with a laugh.

"Yeah, but Lou made his choice. If he wanted to be with me, he would have chosen me. He didn't. What else can I do?"

"You could fight for the man you love?"

I thought about that.

"I could. But he knows how I feel about him and what I want. I even think he might feel the same about me. But maybe loving someone isn't enough. He needs to want to be with me. If he doesn't, what am I supposed to do?"

"Fight."

I looked at Cali and smiled.

"You're gonna make some guy a great boyfriend one day. Not Quin, though. He's spoken for," I teased.

Cali blushed.

Thinking about what Cali said as the night went on, I realized that he might be right. The one thing I could do was fight for Lou. But hadn't he kissed me first? Didn't that mean he liked me back? And, didn't that also mean that he chose Sey because the two of them made more sense together?

Sey was an openly gay guy from an old Tennessee family. What's more, Lou's family, who hated me, loved him. And didn't his mother say that they wouldn't pay for Lou's tuition if he didn't choose Sey? If I fought for Lou and won, wouldn't I be ruining his life?

So, what did I do about Lou's offer to help me find my brother? I still loved Lou. It's because I can't be with him that I rejoined the football team.

I needed a way to channel my anger and went to Coach asking for a second chance. There were a few players out with an injury that day so he let me practice with them. When he saw me running through tackle dummies like they were made of straw, he invited me back. I've been leading the country in sacks since.

Football wasn't enough, though. I needed more to take my mind off of Lou, so I told Claude I was in on his business idea. That led to a discussion about marketing. And that led to research that said that the only way to get Snow Tip Falls added to maps was to incorporate the town.

Incorporating a town is a big deal. There is a ton of work involved. I had to get people to sign a petition that I sent to the State. They had to approve it. And now I have to organize an election to decide on the town's charter.

It's a lot of work. And between that, football, and school, it was just enough to keep me from thinking about Lou every minute of the day. But now Lou wanted back into my life.

On one hand, I couldn't be happier. The only thing I want is to kiss him like we did that weekend. A vice grips my chest and squeezes whenever I let myself think about it.

On the other hand, he doesn't want to be with me. The thought of being so close to him and not being able to have him makes me want to get into bed and never get out. I can't take being reminded every day of what I can't have.

That means that I can't accept his help in finding my brother, right? I shouldn't. Then why did I want to?

He was the one who suggested I take the DNA test. It was a good idea. The only thing I could come up with was pressuring my mother to tell me more. But after telling me that first time, she pretended like she didn't know what I was talking about when I brought it up. What other options did I have?

My whole life I wanted a brother. It never felt right that I was an only child. When Nero found his brother Cage, I wished it was me. Could finding my brother transform my life like it did Nero's? When he met Cage, Nero was hosting fight clubs for money. Now he's playing in the NFL.

I don't know if finding my brother would do the same for me. But maybe if I did, I wouldn't feel so god damn alone all the time. And Lou was offering to help me find him. Is the torture I feel being around Lou worth a chance at finding my family?

Not able to decide, I did what I did best. I put it out of my mind and lost myself in everything else I had going on.

Although the team lost almost every game before I joined, we had a perfect record since. I had to keep my intensity up. On top of that, I had to review the budget Claude put together for the business and prepare for the town meeting I arranged. Oh, and classes.

The days flew by in a blur and only slowed down when I got a text from Lou. Every part of me wanted to answer him immediately and then text back and forth for the rest of day like we used to. But I couldn't. I always got back to him, but not until the next day.

'Quin invited me to stay at his place on the weekend of your town meeting. Would you mind if I came? I have an idea that could help you find your brother,' he texted.

Staring at the text, there was so much I wanted to write. What was his idea? Why that weekend? Did he know that I was making a speech? Did that have to do with why he wanted to come? But instead, I texted,

'That's fine.'

His reply didn't come as quickly as it used to. I was torn by how I felt about that.

'Thanks,' he wrote before going silent.

"He's coming up this weekend," I told Cali as we sat waiting for practice to end.

As the kicker, Cali never had much to do during practice. I was sitting out after a brutal hit during the last game that left my shoulder sore.

I had already sacked the other team's quarterback five times. An asshole from their offensive line tried to send me a message. I replied by laying their quarterback out on the next play.

The guy lay sprawled on the ground like an outline at a crime scene. That was me marking the message 'returned to sender'.

That didn't change how much the hit I had taken had hurt, though. It was easy to play through the pain while channeling all of my anger. But, the following morning I felt it. So here I was sitting on the sidelines instead of practicing. And the only one sitting next to me was Cali.

"Who's coming up? Lou?" Cali asked me.

"Yeah."

"How do you feel about that?"

I took a deep breath. I didn't know how I felt. This would be the first time he came to Snow Tip Falls. There were so many things I wanted to show him. I wanted to take him everywhere. I wanted to kiss him under a waterfall. But then I looked across the field and saw Sey.

"What do you think is going on with Sey?" I asked Cali.

"What do you mean?"

"Do you get a weird vibe from him?"

Cali stared at Sey as he went through his drills. He turned back to me.

"I mean, I can hate him if you want me to. Fuck Sey."

"Thank you," I said sincerely. "But seriously, you don't get a weird feeling from him?"

"He seems like he's trying really hard to get people to like him."

"That's what I mean. Doesn't it seem fake to you?"

"Maybe. But he's an openly gay quarterback. I'm sure he feels the pressure of it," Cali said making a good point.

"I guess," I said not sure if that was it.

I had watched what Nero went through after coming out. The team had been nothing but supportive. So was the media. The only ones who weren't were players from the other teams. And that had more to do with Nero kicking their ass on the field.

You try to get in the head of your opponent any way you can. With Nero, it was that he liked guys.

With Sey, it felt like there was something else going on. Sure, we didn't get along. And that was explainable. But the feeling went beyond that.

I had to assume he was treating Lou well. I couldn't imagine Lou putting up with anything less. So maybe it was just in my head. Maybe Sey didn't deserve me picturing his face on every quarterback I played against. But…

"So Lou's coming to Snow Tip Falls this weekend? What are you gonna do with him?"

"What do you mean?" I asked.

"Are you gonna show him around?"

"Should I?"

"You two are trying to be friends, right?"

"Are we?"

"Aren't you?"

Were we? It seemed like Lou was, but what was I doing.

"What about you, Cali? You found someone to replace Quin, yet?"

Cali blushed.

"Have you?" I asked surprised. "Is it someone on the team?"

I watched him react.

"It is!" I confirmed.

I looked around the field again.

"Please tell me it's not Sey."

"Ah, no," he said half-heartedly.

"Jesus, Cali."

"He's the only guy on the team who's into guys!"

"First of all, you don't know that. Second of all… Sey?"

"He's hot."

"Whatever. He's also engaged to Lou."

Cali went quiet before saying, "I'll hate him if you want me to."

Did I want him to? Wasn't Sey making Lou happy?

"Do what you want. I'll see you back in the room," I said getting up.

"Are you mad at me?" he said watching me with vulnerability in his eyes.

I stopped and caught myself. What I said had come out a lot harsher than I had meant it to be. Kneeling in front of him, I put my hand on his shoulder.

"Cali, you're a great guy. Any guy or girl would be happy to be with you. You have a lot to offer someone. So maybe consider someone who isn't already in love with someone else."

He didn't reply. He didn't have to. I could tell he heard it.

I left him and hit the showers. After, I headed to the café, picked up dinner, and then headed to the library to catch up on my reading for the week. It was hard staying focused. My mind kept drifting to Lou and his visit to Snow Tip Falls.

What would it be like to have him there? What would my mom think of him if I introduced them? Should I introduce them?

'I'm thinking about doing games at my place in Snow Tip Falls on Friday,' Quin texted. 'Lou, Nero, and Kendall will be there. Are you and Cali interested?'

I considered it. We had a football game on Friday but it was early. So, we could be there. And it would be good to see Nero. But could I pretend like everything was the way it used to be with Lou?

I knew Cali would want to go. And he wouldn't be comfortable going without me. Cali was a great guy, but he hadn't made any real connections with anyone at university. If nothing else, I felt like I should go to game night for him. He needed it.

"You're coming with me to game night, on Friday," I told Cali when I returned to our room.

"Cool," he said not showing much emotion.

I was counting on him being more excited. If he was, it would be easier to believe that I was doing it for him and not because I really wanted to see Lou. I ached to see him again. And the thought of being around him made me feel all of the things I didn't want to feel for him.

'We'll be there,' I texted Quin.

'Yay!!!' he replied.

I should have been thinking about my upcoming game. I should have been thinking about my speech at the town meeting. But all I could think about was seeing Lou again.

On Friday, I ran through the game like I had somewhere to be. I had seven sacks and each time I pictured Sey's face on the quarterback. No matter how Lou felt about Sey, I wasn't gonna like him. All I wanted was a weekend where he didn't exist.

"Titus!" Nero said when he opened the door.

"Dude! What are you doing in town?" I said greeting him with a hug.

"I had a few days off. I decided to come down to visit Kendall and Mama. Beer?" he said showing me the bottle in his hand.

"Definitely!" I said entering.

"I heard you're running away with the sacks record. I tell ya, us Snow Tip Falls boys know what we're doing," Nero said proudly.

I smiled scanning the house as we walked through.

"Looking for Lou?" Nero asked seeing my eyes dart around.

"No!"

"Right," he said with a chuckle. "He's upstairs with Quin. You tell him how you feel about him yet."

I looked at him feeling the weight of what happened. I wondered how much he knew. The last time I saw him, I was still denying my feelings for Lou. So unless Lou told Quin what happened – which he probably did – and Quin told Nero, he was in the dark.

"I did," I admitted seeing waves of emotions flow through Nero.

"It didn't go well?"

"You know Lou's engaged, right?"

"No shit!" Nero said handing me a beer from the fridge. "Who?"

"The quarterback from the team."

"Bradley?"

"It's a new guy who transferred from Nashville."

"A new guy. How long have they been dating?"

"He proposed on the third date," I told Nero getting a blank stare in return. "Yeah, I thought the same thing."

"So, you don't think it's gonna last either?" Nero said breaking out of his stupor and taking a swig.

"What do you mean?"

"Did he text Lou good morning and good night every day?"

"I think so. Why?"

"Does he like grand gestures?"

I thought about it. Not only did he propose to Lou with a choir singing in the background, he showed up at Lou's place to surprise him.

"He does," I decided.

"Then, all you gotta do is wait him out," Nero said with a confident smile.

"What are you talking about?"

"He's what you call a Love Bomber."

"What's that?"

"He gets off on the rush you feel at the beginning of a relationship. No follow-through."

"How do you know this?"

"I know things," Nero said taking another gulp of beer. "Just wait him out. Lou will realize what he passed up on."

"Did I hear my name?" Lou said entering the kitchen with Quin and Kendall.

Lou had the devilish smile he got before saying something playful. God, did I miss it.

"Nero was just saying that you and I won't have a chance against him and Kendall now that you're engaged and distracted by love," I said testing Nero's theory.

"Ha!" Lou balked. "It's sad watching him grasp for straws, isn't it Titus," Lou said moving beside me. "If you think my mind is anywhere but right here," he said slipping his arm around mine, "then you are in for a rude awakening."

"I stand corrected," Nero said giving me an I-told-you-so look as he took another swig of beer.

We all hung out in the kitchen laughing until Cali arrived. After that, we moved to the living room where Cage joined us. With an uneven number of people, we decided on Wavelength. It was our go-to game and always fun to play.

In our group, Cage and Quin were the super couple. They could practically read each other's minds. Lou and I usually beat out Nero and Kendall, but it was always very close. This time we split the team into brains versus brawn.

"Football players versus nerds," Nero said teasingly.

"So, what you're saying is you want to lose badly," his boyfriend replied.

"That does sound like what you're saying," I added. "They're gonna murder us."

"See. Even your teammate agrees," Kendall said with a smile.

"It's going to be hard to watch," Lou joined in.

"I said football players versus nerds, and that's what we're doing. And, we're gonna win."

I hissed like I had been burned.

"I said, we're gonna win!" Nero insisted.

We lost ten points to two.

Nero sulked for the rest of the night while Kendall gloated for his entire team. Lou wasn't much better, but he at least gave me a hug claiming that he felt sad for us. I took it, enjoying feeling his body on mine.

For the rest of the night, Lou didn't pass up an opportunity to touch me. Every time he did, I was turned on more. Could Nero have been right? Did Sey get off on the rush of new love and grand gestures? Could he and Lou already be drifting apart?

We played games and drank until late into the night. It felt great to pretend like nothing had changed between Lou and me, but I knew things had. And when I could no longer shake the thought of joining him in his bed, I announced I was headed home.

"Are you sure?" Lou asked looking at me like he wanted me to stay.

I stared at him needing to kiss him again.

"I should go before I do something bad," I told the group.

"Like what?" Lou asked me with a flirtatious smile.

What was he doing? He had to know what I was referring to. Whether his fiancé was a love bomber or not, he was still engaged. A good guy respected that.

I laughed and said, "I'm gonna go."

"I'll walk you out," Lou said taking my hand.

I looked around. Everyone was staring. They all knew the situation between us. More importantly, Lou knew it. So when we got to my truck and he placed his chest inches from mine and looked up into my eyes, I needed to know what was going on.

"What are you doing, Lou?"

"Walking you to your car," he said with a smile.

"I'm trying to be good here," I said feeling my resistance slipping away.

"What if I don't want you to be good?"

"Lou, you're engaged."

"Am I?"

"Yes!"

"Then you should tell Sey because it would probably be news to him."

I chuckled uncomfortably. Nero might have been right. If he was, I didn't know what to do about it. What was my responsibility to Lou as someone who cared about him?

"I should go," I said peeling myself off of him. "I think you had a few too many drinks."

As I opened my truck door,

"He and I haven't done what we have," Lou said desperately.

I froze. "What?"

"You know what we did on the beach?"

"Yeah."

"He and I haven't gotten that far," he said looking down.

He was telling me that they hadn't had sex. He had always said he was waiting for the right guy. But after breaking his rule with me, I had assumed that he would go even further with his fiancé.

"Why not?"

"Because he's not you," he said not looking at me.

If he was trying to make me feel uncomfortable, it had worked. How was I supposed to respond to that? I laughed.

"I have to go."

I didn't look at Lou again until my door was closed and I was about to start my truck. He looked devastated. Why? He was the one who had chosen Sey over me.

I had told him how I felt. We had had sex. And then he tossed me out as soon as I got inconvenient. He didn't get to look heartbroken as I respected his choice.

"Good night," Lou said meekly.

"Night," I told him before pulling away.

Driving home I whipped back and forth from wishing I hadn't left, to being pissed as hell. He didn't get to do that to me. I wasn't going to take that from him. He chose Sey. He sent me home. If he was now having regrets, then too bad. You make your bed, you lie in it.

It took everything in me to force the situation out of my mind. So instead of tossing and turning all night thinking about the things I would do to Lou if I got him naked again, I thought about what I would say at the town meeting. It was in a few hours and I didn't feel prepared.

I had wanted it and had arranged it. But what was I going to say? Some people didn't want to incorporate our town. Dr. Tom, the town doctor, was one of them. He was completely against it and would be arguing his point.

He wasn't the only one. My mother was against it. Her boyfriend, Mike, was against it, which made no sense. Mike owned the diner at the beginning of town. More visitors would mean more business for him. Everyone would benefit from incorporating. I didn't understand why they resisted it.

When I had asked my mother about it, she had said that things were good the way they were. But, they weren't. The reason I hadn't explored my feelings for guys growing up was because I didn't feel like there was any room for it. I was supposed to act like everyone else and not rock the boat. If I had had one example of someone my age making another choice, things would have been different.

Meeting Quin and Cage the day they came to town was a revelation for me. They were two guys who loved each other and weren't scared to show it. It changed everything. I'm guessing it did the same for Nero and Cali.

The people of this town needed that type of exposure. We needed examples of other ways of thinking. But, how did I convince everyone else of change when they were happy with the way things were?

My speech had the chance to improve the lives of so many people. What the hell was I gonna say?

Chapter 9

Lou

Watching Titus drive away, I was never surer that I needed him back in my life. I had forgotten how great my life had been with him in it. It was more than just having my best friend back. It was about having a partner in crime.

Sey wasn't a bad guy, but he wasn't a partner. He had his own life. Was that healthy for our relationship? Maybe. I didn't know. But, what I was sure about was that it didn't make me happy.

I didn't feel alone when I was with Titus. I felt supported and loved. I was happy when I was with him. I couldn't deny that.

I wanted to feel his strong arms around me and his lips on mine. I wanted to get lost in his touch as we took on the world together. But, how was I supposed to do that considering everything that had happened?

Maybe the distance between us had become too great. Maybe the two of us weren't meant to be. But retreating to my lonely bed and remembering our nights together, I wished it wasn't.

Sitting next to him, I could smell his scent. He smelled like flowers and musk. It was how he smelled after a game. It made my dick hard. And losing myself in the memory, I pushed my hand into my pants and clutched my throbbing cock.

Laying naked on the beach, he had kissed a path down my body. My muscles had twitched underneath him. When his large hands caressed my balls and took hold of my erection, my chest had lifted. I had inhaled barely able to breathe.

His warm mouth had sent sparks crackling through my body. I was weak to his touch. Anything he wanted, I would have given him.

Remembering as he swallowed me, I pulled down my pants and stroked my cock. I could feel him touching me now. His broad body was all over me. His large hands gripped my chest. The tip of my dick pushed into his throat.

Stroking harder and faster, my breath increased until I could hear myself moan. I couldn't help it. The thought of Titus was overwhelming. And when my toes curled and an itch shot from my inner thigh and tightened my balls, I exploded letting out a yelp as I did.

Out of breath, my mind swirled. I couldn't think of anything but pleasure. Thoughts of Titus floated around me. I ached knowing he wasn't there to hold me.

His absence from my tingling body nearly drove me insane with desire.

Why had I sent Titus away instead of fighting for him? Why had I chosen Sey when I knew that there was only one person I could love?

I needed to make this better somehow. I needed to have him back. What I had planned for his town meeting was a start but it wasn't going to be enough.

It was as I thought about it in my orgasmic afterglow that I eventually fell asleep. And when I woke up the next morning remembering what day it was, I popped open my eyes ready for the rest of my life to begin.

Getting out of bed, I rushed to my travel bag double checking that everything was still there. It was. After heading to the bathroom and getting ready for the day, I left for the kitchen finding Cage.

He and I had never spent much time together. I had always only thought of him as Quin's incredibly hot quarterback boyfriend. That didn't leave us much to talk about now.

"Morning," I said joining him at the stove.

"Morning. How did you sleep?" he asked politely.

"Sleep? What's this sleep thing you speak of?"

Cage chuckled. "You not sleep well? Was the bed not comfortable?"

"Oh, no," I said reassuring him by resting my hand on his shoulder. "Oh!" I said suddenly distracted by how hard his muscles were.

"Are you squeezing my boyfriend's shoulder?" Quin asked from behind me.

I turned around finding Quin looking at me strangely.

"Quin? I… ah… Fine, you caught me. This is exactly what it looks like and now I'm in love with your boyfriend. Sorry, not sorry?"

Quin stared at me tensely for a second and then shrugged and walked to us.

"You'll have to fight every girl and half the guys at the high school he coaches at. But if you win, give me a call," he said brushing past me and kissing his man good morning.

"Well, I'm not gonna go through all of that," I said retreating to a stool at the kitchen island.

"Speaking of fighting for your man," Quin began, "you and Titus looked pretty cozy last night."

I smiled. "Didn't we?"

"So, are you going to be doing anything about it or was it just for show?"

"For show? What do you mean?"

Quin and Cage exchanged looks.

"What?"

They didn't respond.

"What?"

"Cage, do you want to take this one?" Quin asked.

I turned to Cage confused.

"Yeah, Cage, would you like to take this one?" I asked not sure I liked where this was going.

I was half expecting Cage to back down. For some reason, he didn't.

"I think what Quin means is that you can sometimes do and say things for the reaction to it."

I gasped dramatically clutching my imagery pearls.

"Okay, yeah. I saw it that time," I told him admitting he was right. "But, to look at it from my perspective, shut up?"

Quin and Cage both laughed. At that point, I would have been happy to tell them they had been a great audience and to walk off stage, but Quin didn't let me.

"Look, we're not saying it's a bad thing. We're just saying that in your attempt to entertain everyone, you might be missing what's right in front of you."

"You think I was acting like I was with Titus to be funny?"

"Not funny…," Quin said looking at Cage for the word.

"I don't know what the word is. It's more that, we just want the two of you to be happy. And, we know that you're with Sey and your parents like him. But we also know how Titus feels about you. Then you act like the way you acted last night and…"

"We just think that Titus is a great guy and you two work together. But, if you're not serious about being with Titus, maybe you should…" Quin looked at Cage.

"…stop leading him on?" I asked Quin.

"Maybe."

"So, shit or get off the pot?" I confirmed.

"We just think Titus really cares about you and…"

I cut Quin off. "Maybe I care about him too. Maybe I spent all last night trying to figure out how we could be together and that's why I couldn't sleep."

"Did you?" Quin asked.

I stared at them.

"You two don't know how lucky you are."

They both gave an uncomfortable smile and put their arms around each other.

"I'm serious. You don't know how hard it is to find what you two have and then have it. You don't think I see how great Titus and I are together? Don't you think I've always seen it? It's not that simple."

"Isn't it, though?" Quin asked delicately.

"No, it's not. Some of us didn't grow up with parents who loved us and wanted nothing more than for us to be happy. Some of us didn't grow up feeling like we had a choice about how our life could go."

"You're right," Cage said. "Some of us didn't. I was raised by a man who stole me from a hospital and made me feel that the only thing that gave me value was how I performed on a football field."

Remembering Cage's story, I quickly backed down. "I didn't mean you, Cage."

"No. You did. And that's okay. Sometimes we forget that others have gone through hard times too. But, I got through it. And, it wasn't easy. I had to choose to believe that what I wanted was as important as what people wanted for me. And because I did, I now have the privilege of being told that I don't understand how hard other people have it."

"Cage, I didn't mean it like that."

"I'm not blaming you, Lou. I'm not trying to make you feel bad. I'm trying to tell you that there's a way past the obstacles you see now. You just have to make the choice and deal with the consequences. And, the consequences could mean that you lose things and people you care about. But, it also means a chance at true happiness. You just have to make the choice."

"You making breakfast, bro?" Nero said entering the kitchen not wearing a shirt. His eyes bounced between the three of us. "Am I interrupting something?"

"No," I told him. "Cage was just telling me how important it is that I make a choice about breakfast. Pancakes or waffles? Like anyone could ever choose."

"Pancakes."

"Pancakes."

"Waffles," Nero said completing the responses.

I stared silenced.

"Monsters!" I exclaimed before dramatically exiting the kitchen. And, yeah, I saw it that time too.

Cage wasn't wrong. Neither was Quin. What exactly was my plan today? Yes, I wanted to be with Titus. I wanted it more than I had wanted anything. But, if I got him, would I choose him? I hadn't before. And what had changed since then?

Shit or get off of the pot. That was what Cage had said. Why was it so hard? Titus was everything I wanted in a man and a partner. He loved me and showed it. And I never had a better time than when I was with him. So why was this even a question?

"Titus! I choose Titus. I'm sure of it," I told myself finally realizing what I truly wanted. "So, what do I do now?"

What was I supposed to do now? Not only was Titus about to make the most important speech in the history of his town, but I had come to Snow Tip Falls with a plan. I was going to find Titus's brother.

I reentered the kitchen to find everyone sitting around the kitchen island. In front of them were stacks of waffles and pancakes.

"After all of that talk about making a choice, you made both? I feel betrayed," I said getting a laugh from Cage and Quin.

"Are you going to join us or not," Quin asked.

"Fine. If you insist," I said taking the remaining opening seat and reaching for the waffles.

Enjoying breakfast with everyone, it was 10:30 before we left the table and got ready for the town meeting. It was being held at the high school gym and would be going on for most of the day. Someone named Dr. Sonya had suggested that the organizers turn it into a kind of fair. So there would be someone there selling pastries, Titus's new business would have a table introducing itself to the town, and I asked if I could get a spot as well.

I had considered running the idea by Titus but had decided against it. Instead, I told Quin who told Cage. And as a known person in the community, he made all of the arrangements for me.

With my travel bag in hand, we packed into the trucks and headed to the event. As we got closer, I got more nervous. Was I doing the right thing? Would Titus appreciate what I was doing? Would finding his brother help Titus? I was sure it would.

"What's this?" Titus asked when he arrived and saw me sitting behind one of the tables that lined the room.

"Hello, sir," I began. "My name is Louis Armoury and I'm doing a project for school that deals with family trees in small towns. If you would like to participate, I'm giving away free DNA testing for today only. With it, you will be able to find out which part of the world your ancestors are from. You might even find a long-lost relative or two. Would you like to participate? It's free," I told Titus with a smile.

Titus stared at me without saying a word. Getting nervous, I said,

"You said I could help you find your brother. Well, I'm helping. I figured that since your brother could be anywhere, the most reasonable place to start would be close to home. And when I heard about the town hall and was told anyone could get a table at it, I had an idea. What do you think?"

He continued to stare at me blankly.

"Okay, you're starting to make me nervous. I only did it because I thought you might like it. What if your brother was someone in town? You're not mad at me, are you?"

It was only then that his lip twitched. His stone face dissolved into emotion.

"That's the most thoughtful thing anyone has ever done for me. I don't get it. Who's paying for this?"

"At least one good thing had to come out of my parents stealing my inheritance and controlling my life, right? Any samples I get, I'm charging to their credit card," I said with a smirk.

"You're amazing. Thank you for this," Titus said moved. "But…" He paused.

"But what?"

"You haven't been to many small towns, have you?"

"My family's estate is next to a small town," I reminded him.

"No. That's a ski town. It's not Nashville, but it's not Snow Tip Falls, either. As great of a gesture as this is, you might not get as many offers to participate as you think."

"It's free," I reminded him.

"So is a poke in the eye, but no one's gonna line up for it," he said with a sad smile. "But what you did here…" he tightened his lips. "Really. I can't tell you how much I appreciate it even if you don't give away a single test."

"You don't think anyone's gonna get one?"

Titus shook his head trying to erase what he said.

"Who knows? Maybe I'm wrong. Maybe you'll have a line out the door. All I'm saying is that I can't tell you how much it means to me that you've done this. Thank you."

I blushed hearing everything I wanted to hear.

"So, Cage said you have a table here as well. Which one is it?" I asked him.

Titus turned and pointed at the table with the beautiful black guy behind it.

"You're selling hot guys? I'll take one," I joked.

Titus laughed.

"That's Claude, my business partner."

"Oh, that's Claude! Cage mentioned something about him. He's single, isn't he?"

Titus looked at me.

"Not that I am… or that I'm interested," I said trying to back my way out of the corner. "Asking for a friend?"

Titus chuckled.

"Would you like me to introduce you… for your friend?"

"I mean, it would only be polite, right?" I asked continuing the joke.

Titus walked me across the room drawing Claude's soulful eyes to mine.

"Claude, this is Lou. Lou's a good friend of mine. Lou this is my business partner Claude. We played on our high school football team together."

Claude stood and offered me his hand. He was very different than Titus and Nero. Claude was serious and composed. He reminded me of royalty. I didn't feel like joking around in front of him. He looked like he had more important things on his mind.

"Nice to meet you. So, you two are business partners. What's the business?"

I knew bits and pieces of what the two were planning but Claude walked me through all of it in detail. They were going to sell adventure tours focused on the water passageways and falls surrounding the town. It was a seasonal business that would allow Titus to continue attending school. And it sounded like a pretty great idea.

"So, how did you two meet?" Claude asked the both of us.

I told him in detail even mentioning that Titus had met my parents. I could hear myself making Titus sound like my boyfriend. I wasn't sure if Titus wanted his business partner to know he was into guys, but I couldn't help it. I wanted to be with him. I wanted it so badly that my heart ached thinking about it.

"That sounds nice," Claude replied sincerely. "Then maybe we'll be seeing more of each other when the season starts. Has Titus given you the tour yet?"

"The tour?" I asked Titus.

"I had to come up with where I would take people if they signed up."

"When they sign up," Claude corrected.

"Oh, I want to go," I said enthusiastically.

"Really? Because it's a lot of walking through the woods with a canoe," Titus clarified.

"That sounds like fun!"

"Does it? You never struck me as the roughing it type."

"What do you mean? I could be rough. You just have to ask," I said flirtatiously.

Titus's eyes flicked up to Claude who laughed.

"There you go. He likes it rough," Claude joked.

"Yeah, don't tease me," I said looking into Titus's eyes.

I knew I shouldn't have been flirting with Titus in front of his business partner while surrounded by all of his small-town friends, but I couldn't stop myself. It was all I could do to bottle up what I felt for him.

Still, Titus wasn't out. I didn't know if he was attracted to guys who weren't me. I didn't know how he felt about me now. Maybe I was supposed to be his secret. Maybe what I had done had sent him running back to women and he never wanted to think about a man again.

"I'm joking," I added regretting what I said. "I should go back to my table."

"What are you doing over there?"

"I'm offering free DNA tests for a school project. Only you will see the results. You should get one."

"Oh, interesting. Maybe I'll stop by later," he said flashing a brilliant smile.

Claude was Titus's business partner so there was no way I would do it, but the old me would have asked him out. There was something about him that told me he would be open to it.

But that was the old me. The only one the new me wanted was Titus and I might have again screwed things up with him by exposing him like I had.

"I'll walk you back," Titus said joining me as I returned to my table.

"I'm sorry about that," I told him feeling bad.

"About what?"

"Making those jokes."

"Why would you apologize for that?"

"I know I can be a bit of a show."

"A show?"

"Yeah. I just…" I tightened my lips as my swirling thoughts jammed the path to my mouth. "I don't want to embarrass you. This is your home. Everyone knows you a certain way here. I just don't want to ruin anything by mentioning what happened between us."

"Ruining things by mentioning what happened between us?"

"Yeah." I turned to put my hands on his chest and then stopped remembering where we were. "Yeah. I should go back to my table and recruit a few victims… I mean volunteers," I said trying to lighten the mood. "You should work the room, Mr. Politician."

"Lou…"

"You should go," I said wanting to be alone.

Titus listened and left without saying another word. I watched him walk away. I didn't want to ruin his life. I didn't want to lead him on. I didn't want to hurt him. Maybe the best thing I could do for him would be to leave him alone.

I didn't question how much I loved him. I loved him more than I thought it possible to love anyone. But was that enough to be with someone?

I'm a mess. I know that. I've always known that. I've always been more than even a mother could love. If I truly loved Titus, wouldn't walking away be the best thing I could do for him?

That was all I could think about as I sat at my table. Quin stopped by and sat with me for a while. So did Cage. It was good because other than the occasional visitor who kept on moving as soon as they found out what I was offering, they were the only ones I spoke to.

"So, what are you doing here?" A familiar face said snapping me out of my thoughts.

"Cali, right? You're Titus's roommate."

"And you're Lou," he said like we had met more than once.

"Right. I'm offering free DNA tests."

He looked confused. "Why are you doing that?"

I was about to go into my story about it being a school project and then stopped myself.

"How close are you and Titus?"

"We talk," Cali said casually.

"Did he tell you that he has a brother?"

Cali looked at me blankly.

"Maybe."

I couldn't tell if Cali was being coy or hiding the fact that Titus hadn't told him. I was also too in my head right now to figure it out.

"Anyway, he does and I had the idea to offer free DNA tests to figure out who it is."

"Cool," he said casually.

When he didn't immediately run off I felt a glimmer of hope.

"Did you want to take a test? It's free."

"What would I have to do?"

"You just spit in one of these tubes," I said picking up one and showing it to him.

"That's it."

"Yeah. And then you fill out a form. They'll send you the results in a few weeks."

"That's cool."

"So, you want to?"

"Sure."

I walked Cali through everything trying to hide my excitement. I figured that him taking the test wouldn't help me find Titus's brother, but his willingness gave me hope that others might want to as well.

Packing away his sample, I returned to things with a little more enthusiasm. I had a few more participants after him but not many. The only other one who was even close to our age was Claude who came over as promised. Claude was another guy who had no shot at being Titus's brother, but at least today wasn't going to be a complete waste.

Although Titus looked over a few times as he worked the room, he didn't come back to me. I understood. I had told him to go… for the second time. Why would he return?

When the time came for the meeting to begin, the room was full. A fair-skinned, fifty-something woman with a slight Jamaican accent gathered people's attention.

"Hello. Your attention please," she said quieting everyone. "Thank you for coming. As you know, we are here to discuss something important for the future of our town. One of our impressive young community members has proposed that we incorporate and we are here to listen to both sides of the debate. I was thinking that I would have each of them make their argument and then if you have any questions for them, you can find them later as they circle about. Sound good?"

The crowd mumbled and the woman continued.

"Presenting the argument for why we shouldn't incorporate will be Dr. Tom. You all know him. Most of you have removed your pants for him so he needs no introduction. Dr. Tom," she said calling him forward.

Everyone clapped.

As the round-bellied, bearded Latino man talked politics and money, I watched Titus. He wasn't paying attention. He looked like he was going over notes in his head. He looked nervous and all I wanted was to wrap my arms around him letting him know everything would be alright.

When it came time for him to speak, he stepped in front of the crowd and glanced over at me. I wish I had time to give him a thumbs-up, but he looked away too quickly. Mine was just the first eyes he looked into.

As he stood there not saying a word, he scanned the room. It was only when heads began to bend towards each other to whisper that he spoke.

"You have to forgive me, I'm not the speaker that Dr. Tom is. He's been a leader of this community for a long time, and I think we should give him another hand for that."

Titus led the group in applause. Dr. Tom held up his hand in acknowledgment.

"When I originally came up with the idea to incorporate the town, I'll admit that it wasn't exactly for everyone's best interest. You see, I'm starting a new business with a high school classmate. And for marketing purposes, I thought it would help if customers could locate us on a map.

"But, that's not the reason I will be presenting to you today. The reason I'm offering is a lot more personal. Dr. Tom made the argument that Snow Tip Falls has a good thing going here. And we do. It's nice here. Things are… stable.

"But, do you know the day that shaped the rest of my life more than any other? It was the day I met a couple who had come to town in search of family. The couple consisted of two men which shouldn't have been anything new here considering we've all grown up with Dr. Tom and Glenn, his husband. But it was.

"Meeting them changed me. It was because of them that I considered attending university. And I wasn't the only one. It was because of them that I considered something about myself that I had kept hidden. Meeting these strangers from out of town has led to me discovering new passions. It led me to falling in love.

"It was because we opened our hearts and doors to the outside world that I discovered what it is to be in love. I found love because of them. I'm *in love* because of them. And if welcoming two strangers from beyond our community could have such a dramatic effect on my life and the lives of others, what could welcoming the world to our town do for you?

"Please don't just look at incorporation from a political or economic perspective. It's more than that. I fell in love with the greatest guy I could imagine because a couple of strangers showed me what was possible. Consider what you might discover is possible if we opened our doors to others. Consider what you might love. Thank you."

Hanging on his every word, it wasn't until he stopped talking that I felt the tears rolling down my cheeks. There was no doubt that he was talking about me. I wanted to run to him and kiss him. I couldn't, though. Not because I wouldn't let myself, but because the audience had swarmed him in adoration.

I wasn't the only one in tears. He had moved the crowd. I never felt prouder of him in my life. And never was it clearer what I had to do.

Waiting as he addressed everyone's many questions, eventually, he made his way to me. We both stared at each other not sure what to say.

"Any chance you caught my speech?" Titus eventually said with a smile.

"Here and there," I said as my face tingled with warmth.

"You mentioned something about liking it rough. Any interest in taking my tour in the morning?"

My cock got hard as his body heat swallowed me.

"Yeah," I replied barely able to speak.

"I'll pick you up at 8. Be ready," Titus said before leaving me for a group of adoring fans.

When Quin came to collect me, he gave me a knowing look. He also knew who Titus was referring to in his speech. Everyone in our group did.

"Should I ask Titus if he wants to come over tonight?"

"I'm meeting him at 8 AM. He's going to take me on one of his adventure tours," I said feeling my face turn red.

"Okay," Quin said smiling back. "Then I guess it'll be an early night."

Getting the same look from Cage and Nero when we met up with them, I felt so much pressure. Titus had professed his love for me in front of everyone. What more could he have done? I had never felt more special in my life.

After an early dinner and not a lot of conversation, I headed to bed leaving the two couples to have fun without me. I had a date in the morning and I couldn't be more excited. That didn't make falling asleep easy, but it eventually happened.

Awake before my alarm sounded, I was dressed and waiting for Titus at eight. Hearing his truck pull up, I hurried outside. There was a large, yellow, plastic canoe in his bed. Webbed inside of it were paddles and life vests.

"Should I be worried? Am I going to survive this?" I said joking about the life vests.

"There's no way I would ever let anything happen to you," he said confidently.

My heart skipped a beat knowing he wouldn't. I felt like putty in Titus's hands. I was willing to do anything he asked me to. And as the morning went on, he asked me to do a lot.

Parking the truck on the side of the road, we carried the gear for a quarter-mile to a river. Putting on the vest and a helmet, we paddled down the river for half an hour. The crisp morning air was electric and the view was beautiful.

From there we removed the canoe from the water and carried it to the next river. That river had a series of rapids that were as thrilling as they were challenging. With every stroke, I thought we would tip over. We didn't. Titus was not only an excellent guide but the hottest outdoorsman ever.

We dipped in and out of rivers all morning. By afternoon I felt alive but exhausted. I had never done anything like it and I loved it. But carrying the canoe the final few hundred feet, I could barely remain standing.

"Can we rest?" I asked sure I couldn't take another step.

"Do you hear that?"

I listened. The only thing I heard was the sound of crashing water.

"What? The waterfall?"

"The waterfall. It's pretty close. Do you think you can make it there?"

I listened again. It didn't sound that far away.

"Probably, but when we get there, I'm going to need to rest."

"Promise," he said with one of his brilliant smiles.

As the waterfall came into view, I realized why he had suggested that we keep going. Not only was the watery monster amazing, but on the far side of the lake was a blanket. He had set up a picnic complete with a picnic basket. It was the most romantic thing I had ever seen.

"Are you going to do this for all of your tours?" I asked setting the canoe down and walking over.

"No, this one's special," he said with a confident smile. "Champagne?"

"Champagne? What are we celebrating?" I said relaxing my weary muscles on the red and white plaid.

"We're celebrating you," he said retrieving a bottle of champagne from the basket and filling two glasses.

"Me? What are you talking about?"

"I mean that we're celebrating you," he said handing me a glass.

"It's not my birthday or anything."

"It doesn't have to be your birthday. Every day I'm with you is a reason to celebrate. Cheers."

I smiled feeling good. We then both took sips and relaxed.

"I think my body's dead," I told him sinking further onto the blanket.

"Did I work you too hard? You said you liked it rough."

I chuckled.

"I did. And, you did."

"Awww," Titus said with mock sympathy.

I laughed. "Shut up."

Titus sat up.

"Here. Give me that," he said referring to my glass.

I gulped the remainder of the champagne and handed it to him. He looked at me amused and then moved towards me.

"Roll over," he said ordering me onto my stomach.

I complied.

"What are you doing?" I asked open to anything.

"I'm gonna give you a massage."

"Yes, please," I said with a smile.

With my head turned to the side, I watched as Titus climbed on top of me. He sat on my ass and pushed his large hands across my back. His two hands spanned the whole thing at once. I felt small in his grasp. The feeling took my breath away.

"How's that?" he asked.

I couldn't answer.

"Do you want me to stop?"

"No," I chirped terrified he would. "No," I repeated calmer. "It feels good."

Titus's fingertips pushed into my muscles relaxing them. My thoughts swirled bathed in the sensation.

Losing myself, I felt his hands find the bottom of my shirt. His fingers touched my flesh. It was electric. I struggled to breathe.

"Do you want me to stop?"

"No. Don't stop," I begged.

He didn't. Pushing his hand up my back, he lifted my shirt higher and higher.

"Don't stop," I repeated.

When my shirt pressed against my neck, he pulled it off of me. With his hands sliding against the back of my arms, he leaned down and kissed my back.

His was a trail of kisses. Each delicate and seductive.

Finding the canal of muscle down my spine, his lips entered. Spilling onto my lower back, they slowly climbed the gentle slope towards my ass.

"Do you want me to stop?" he asked breathlessly.

"I don't want you to stop," I said offering him the final permission he would need before I lifted my hips and he reached under me unbuttoning my pants.

I was hard, very hard. His hand found it. Caressing it through my pants, his hand returned when my pants were off.

Stroking my cock through my underwear, his teeth pinched the fabric. I wanted him so badly I could burst. Pushing his chin between my cheeks I moaned for him. I wanted more, so much more that when his tongue pushed against the cloth covering my crack, I pushed my ass onto him.

That was enough. With my waist off the ground, he took hold of my underwear and pulled it down. They only got to my knees before he pushed his tongue onto my hole. I had never felt anything like it. My entire body tingled. So, when he danced the tip of his tongue and pushed harder, he pulled me open slipping in.

"Ahhh!" I groaned losing control.

"I want you to fuck me. Please fuck me," I begged.

I couldn't take it anymore. The crashing water, the tongue in my ass. Everything was too much. But when he released me and returned with something wet on his thumb, it was a whole new sensation.

Caressing my opening, he pushed on it. It felt so good. I wanted to feel him inside of me. It was the only thing I could think about. But when his thumb entered me with a pop, I wasn't ready.

"Ah!" I squealed.

The feeling was overwhelming and then it wasn't. Quickly, I loved it. I had never felt this before. Someone was inside of me. Stretching me open, my legs quivered. When he slowly removed his thumb and rested his chest on my back, I was ready to explode.

The first time I felt the head of his cock part my cheeks, it was a revelation. Someone was about to fuck me. But, it wasn't just anyone. It was Titus. It was the only man I could trust. The one who had been there for me even when I didn't deserve it. So when his large head found my hole and pushed onto my prepared opening, I reached back for him.

With my hand on his leg, he measured my pleasure and pushed harder. I could feel every inch of him enter me. It was too much yet not enough. I wanted him to keep going as much as I wanted him to stop. And when the pain gave way to a flood of desire, I sunk my fingertips into his thigh asking to be fucked more.

Titus relented. Placing his legs on either side of mine, he propped himself up using my back. In position, he pulled back his cock. It was only enough to get a running start. When he returned, his crotch slapped my ass.

"Oh!" I moaned.

"Yes?"

"Yes!" I pleaded.

He then withdrew and pounded me again. Faster and harder, he filled me. It was too much and just enough. It felt so good I thought I would cry. I loved everything about it. Titus was inside of me. The two of us were one.

"I'm cumming. I'm cumming," I screamed not having touched myself.

Titus breathed harder. So did I. Sinking my nails into his thigh, I held it back as long as I could. I wanted to hear his groans as he did mine.

He was fucking me so hard I couldn't hold off much longer. My yearning to release was painful. And just when I thought I couldn't take it for another moment, when I thought my body would explode, Titus did. I followed.

"Ahhhh!" I bellowed.

My finger was in a light socket, then it wasn't. Titus held still as his cock flinched. When he moved again, I got another zap. It didn't stop until his large body collapsed on top of me.

"I love you," he whispered into my ear.

I loved him too but I couldn't say it. It wasn't because I didn't feel it. It was because I lost the ability to speak.

Never had I imagined that anything could feel so good. My emotions were all over the place. It was overwhelming. My world tumbled behind my closed eyelids. And when my love wrapped his arms around me and pulled me tight, sinking my body into his grasp was the only thing I could do to not melt into a puddle of goo.

When I could speak, I said, "I want to be with you. I never want to be away from you again."

"How do we do it?" he asked me.

"I don't know," I responded before my thoughts crashed into the real world like the waterfall into the lake beside us.

Titus and I lay naked on the blanket for a while. We both knew the problem. We wanted to be together but I was engaged. More than that, my parents controlled my life. They wanted me with Sey and had threatened to stop paying for school if I didn't do as they said.

I was a junior. I still had another year left. I could never afford to pay for East Tennessee University without their help. I couldn't even afford my dorm room without my family's money.

Yet, I knew who I loved and what I had to do. I was going to have to figure out a way. I couldn't keep doing this to myself or Sey.

Sure, Sey wasn't the greatest boyfriend in the world. He never texted me and we never did anything I wanted to do. But he wasn't a bad person.

"I'm going to break up with Sey. We can't do anything else until then," I told Titus breaking the silence.

"What are you gonna tell your parents?"

I thought about that. I didn't know. Maybe I could not tell them and they wouldn't know. If I ended things positively with Sey, then there was no reason they had to find out.

I could just say that Sey was busy or something if they ever asked about him. But what were the chances of that? No one in my family ever thought about anyone but themselves. I don't even think they remembered they had a second child when I wasn't around.

"I'm not going to tell them anything."

"You're gonna pretend he never existed? Are you sure that's gonna work? They seemed to like him a lot."

"He's the gay son they wished they had. But, that's not saying much. My parents always regretted having kids. So I'll just give them the space to forget I exist. And once my final year of school is paid for, I will walk away from them forever."

"I'm sorry, Lou," Titus said pulling me tighter. "You're just going through this because of me."

I rolled over within his warm embrace and looked him in the eyes.

"That's not true."

"It is. If I didn't tell you how I felt, you would still want to be with Sey and you could still have your family."

"Without you, I would never know how it feels to be loved. Do you know how much that means to me? There have been times I've been so lonely I could barely get out of bed. You rescued me from that.

"It wasn't Sey or even Quin. It was you. You pulled me out of that. Don't be sorry for anything you do. Because without you, where would I be?" I asked with tears streaming down the side of my face.

Titus held me tighter. I wasn't sure he understood how much he meant to me, but if I got my way, I would have a lifetime to explain it to him. For now, I would have to show him by ending things with Sey.

Eventually, the two of us let each other go and got dressed. I watched Titus as he did. This was the first time I could just stare at his nakedness. The man was beautiful. His body was even more godlike than when he danced for me at the estate. It had to be because of football.

Did running up and down the field also explain his incredibly tight ass? What about his incredibly beautiful cock that swung in front of him taunting me?

Nope! We couldn't do anything else until I ended things with Sey. I wanted to drop down in front of him and feed that monster into my mouth. I wanted to feel its ridges and veins with my tongue.

"What are you thinking about?" he asked me when he turned around and saw my rising cock.

"All of the things I'm going to do to you when you're officially mine."

"I'm yours now. I've always been yours," he said with a smile.

It was weird getting rock hard as he watched. As a guy, you spend your life trying to hide erections. As a gay guy living in a straight world, getting caught with a bulge in your pants was even worse. But having Titus see me, all of me as I was, was the greatest feeling I had ever had.

"Do you want some help with that?" Titus asked referring to my brick-hard cock.

"No. That's okay," I told him snapping out of it and getting dressed. I turned to him. "But, ask me again later," I said blushing.

Dressed, Titus packed the blanket into the picnic basket, dropped the basket into the canoe, and called me over. Together we lifted it and everything in it above our heads. As we walked, all I could think of was holding his hand. Maybe that wasn't all I could think about, but it was the one thing I thought I could have.

Completing the loop, we arrived back at the truck. Strapping the equipment into the bed, we got in and pulled away. The drive back to town was silent.

I, for one, didn't know what to say. At one point he lowered his hand close to me on the seat between us. My heart thumped seeing it. Shifting to place my hand near his, I looked out the windshield. There was a lump in my throat knowing his hand was right there.

I moved mine closer needing him. Where was his? All I wanted was a touch. When something tickled my finger, it was electric. Warmth washed through me. I wanted more. I ached for so much more, but when he tried to put his hand on mine, I pulled it away. Not a lot, but enough.

That was when he again found my hand and latched our pinkies. We drove like that until we pulled up to Quin's place.

"Are you coming in?" I asked not letting go of his hand.

"I should probably go."

I didn't know what to say. I wanted him to stay. I never wanted to be apart from him again. But, I couldn't be selfish. He had a lot going on. I would have to wait.

"Okay."

Staring for a moment, I let go of him and got out. It hurt knowing he was leaving. Peeling away, I opened the door. I couldn't do it. Rushing back towards him, I pushed my lips against his. A warm wave washed through me. It would have to be enough. Soon, though. And for the rest of our lives.

"How was the tour?" Nero asked me when I found the group drinking in the living room.

"A+," I told them. "I recommend the ending."

"Titus asked me to invest," Nero told the group. "I'm thinking about it."

Quin looked confused. "Why didn't he ask me?"

"Maybe he didn't want some city slicker coming in and ruining our fair town," Nero joked.

"City slicker?"

"You know, with your New York money," he teased. "He wanted someone who could appreciate the value of the experience."

"It was definitely a valuable experience," I told them.

"That's good to hear! Then he's got my money," Nero declared. "It looks like Snow Tip Falls is moving up in the world. And we're doin' it homegrown style," he said pleased with himself.

Nero looked around at everyone. He was surrounded by Quin, Cage, Kendall, and me. None of us were from here. Frustrated, he got up.

"Mama!" he yelled. "You didn't hear me but I just said that Snow Tip Falls was doing it homegrown style." He left in search of her. "Mama?"

We all looked at each other and laughed. Quin stared at me.

"So, it was good?" he asked knowing there was more.

"It was very good," I confirmed.

He responded with a smile and cozied up to Cage. I couldn't wait to join this group as part of a couple. These people were my family, not the people who raised me. And being with Titus, this town was going to become my home. A tear rolled down my cheek from joy.

As anxious as I was for my new life with Titus to begin, it took me a day to text Sey asking to meet. It took him two more days to agree to it. If I had had any doubts about breaking up with him, that exchange removed them. The two of us weren't meant to be together.

Yeah, we were both gay, from an old Tennessee family, and hot. But we only worked on paper. We were very different people who moved and communicated differently.

We wanted different things. At least I think we did. Who knew what he wanted? It wasn't like he shared anything deeply personal with me.

We had to bring this to an end. Maybe then we could both get what we wanted.

Arriving at the restaurant first, I was seated. It took him twenty minutes longer than the time we arranged for him to get there, but I was willing to forgive him considering what I was about to do.

"Sorry I'm late," he said leaning across the table to kiss me. I shifted my head to offer him my cheek.

His gesture reminded me of what I had liked about him. No matter where we were, he was never ashamed to show his affection. It was something Titus was still working on. Him declaring that he was in love with a man in front of the whole town was a great first step. But there's something undeniable about Sey's unashamed confidence. I hope the next guy he's with appreciates it.

"That's fine. But I was thinking, since the restaurant will be closing soon and you probably have something you have to run off to, maybe we should just order drinks."

Sey sat and stared at me suspiciously.

"No, you have me for the night. And, this place will be letting people in for another thirty minutes."

"I was just thinking that…"

He cut me off. "Lou, what's going on?"

I was going to have to say it. I took a deep breath, centered myself, and spoke.

"Sey, you're a great guy. But I think we need to break up," I said sensitively.

Sey's mouth dropped open. He looked stunned, but only for a moment. Regaining his composure, he looked around for a waiter. Making eye contact, he signaled for them to bring him whatever I was drinking. He then turned to me and casually said,

"No."

I stared at him confused. Was he in shock? Had he not heard what I said?

"What do you mean, no?"

"No," he said as if it were obvious.

"I don't think it works like that," I said unsure what was going on.

"Can I tell you a story?"

Before I could reply, the waiter put his drink in front of him.

"Thank you," he said with all of the charm in the world. He then turned back to me not waiting for my answer.

"Do you know how my parents found out I was gay?"

"How?" I asked still confused.

"I was 14, still not sure what I was, and there was a boy in my class I had feelings for. Brock. I didn't know if I was straight or gay, but I knew how I felt about him. I couldn't stop thinking about him. I decided I needed to be friends with him. The funny part was that he wanted to be friends with me too.

"So, what happens when you put two horny boys in the same room together and they like each other? Stuff happens. And stuff happened one day when I had invited him to my place.

"God damn, the tension between us was insane. It was like being near him made me lose my mind. Losing my mind was the only way I could describe it too, because in my bedroom, without locking my door, the two of us got naked and… let's just say stuff happened.

"At least, things began to happen. Maybe my mother was walking by and heard Brock groan. Maybe they suspected something and were keeping a watch. But, when my mother opened the door to find me naked with my cock working its way into Brock's ass, I didn't have to come out to them," Sey said with a chuckle.

"And I guess I should have been grateful because after my mother told my father, neither of them tried to pretend it was anything but what it was. Their son was gay and they accepted it. Although, "accept" might be too strong of a word. They tolerated it. But I could see how they truly felt about it every time they looked at me.

"They didn't despise me. They were just disappointed. It was like their dream died the day they discovered what I was.

"It wasn't like I could blame them. You know what it's like to be a part of a family like ours. You are a part of society. There are parties and responsibilities. And now that they had a gay son. I wouldn't be able to play the role I was born to play. After two hundred years, the power our family wielded would come to an end.

"I, of course, didn't care anything about that. At the time, all I cared about was finishing what my mother interrupted. Once I did that, and a lot more, I started to care about other things. Things like the shift I felt from my parents.

"It was like, because I was gay, they didn't have a use for me anymore. I was dead to them. I wanted to get their love back. It felt gone forever.

"And that was when I started hearing about a boy from a prominent Tennessee family who was also gay. I looked him up online and he was cute. It gave me an idea. What if I could still have everything I deserved? What if I could have my birthright as if I were straight?

"That was when I decided to transfer to East Tennessee and find you. I thought convincing you to go out with me was going to be the hard part. But, you asked me out. Gotta say, that was unexpected!" he said raising his glass to me with a smile.

"And meeting you, I knew exactly who you were. I knew what you wanted.

"You wanted to feel loved. We had that in common. I knew how you would respond to grand gestures, so I gave you one. And it only took two dates for you to agree to marry me. Amazing! We were meant to be together, Lou," he said with a confident smile and a lift of his glass.

I stared at him stunned. If given a thousand years, I would never have guessed any of that. It was disturbing.

"As creepy as all that sounds, Sey, I don't love you," I told him delicately.

"Is it the texting?" he asked casually. "It's the texting. I just get wrapped up in stuff. But, I get it. I'll do better," he said taking a relaxed sip of his wine.

I looked at Sey confused.

"I'm not sure you understand what's going on. I'm breaking up with you. I'm not going to marry you."

"Yes, you are."

"I'm pretty sure I'm not."

"But you will."

The ridiculousness of this situation finally hit me and I laughed. Sey laughed with me.

"Would you like me to tell you why you will?"

"That would be entertaining," I told him.

"It's because, like me, you desperately need your parent's approval."

Heat burned across my face.

"No need to be ashamed of it. I'm right there with you. And, like me, there's only one path you can take to get it. I'm that path and you know it. Being with me will give you the only thing you've truly wanted your whole life. That's why you're going to choose me," he said with a smug smile.

I thought about it. His words were scalpels peeling my skin from my body. I was exposed.

"I can't deny what you said," I admitted. "My family's approval was the only thing I've ever wanted. It *was*. You know what the greatest thing is about finally being loved, it makes up for all of the love you didn't get when you needed it most," I said realizing that I was finally free.

The smile on Sey's face disappeared. When I saw that, I smiled.

"Titus?"

"Titus," I told him.

Sey leaned back in his chair and released a slow deep breath.

"This would have been so much easier if you just saw it the way I did."

"Well, we can't always get what we want," I said feeling good.

"I'm glad you said that because you're right. But here's the thing, I always do."

As I watched, something sinister entered Sey's eyes. It sent a chill down my spine.

"I didn't want this. But it seems you've given me no choice."

"What, Sey?"

"Did you know that Titus is paying for school mostly with a state grant? It's to help less privileged kids pay for college. I didn't know anything about it, but it was explained to me by a family friend who's in charge of the program."

Terror washed through me.

"No, Sey."

"Wouldn't it be a shame if he lost the grant that allowed him to attend East Tennessee? It would certainly be a bummer for our football season."

"You wouldn't."

"I would, and more. In fact, did you know that the town he's from is applying to become incorporated? They want to self-govern. Isn't that adorable. They're growing up. And, do you know whose name is on the petition? Titus's! A different family friend told me that."

"You wouldn't," I said horrified.

"Didn't you hear what the stakes are for me? Of course I would ensure his petition isn't approved. It would be so easy. What you really should be worried about is the hard thing. Do you know what 'eminent domain' is?"

"Oh Sey," I said feeling my heartbreak.

"Eminent domain is the right a state has to acquire land from its owners in the name of progress."

"No Sey."

"You see, for decades, the state of Tennessee has been wanting to build a freeway. But where? That's a decision being made by another family friend.

"Funny thing, I ran into him recently. When I did, I suggested a route. It missed every populated area but one. And the place it cut through didn't even appear on a map, Snow Tip Falls. Ever heard of it?

"Luckily, eminent domain would allow the state to acquire the land and build the freeway. How does that sound? To me, it sounds like progress."

Tears rolled down my cheeks.

"Why are you doing this, Sey?"

"Why am I doing this? You're really asking why I'm doing this? You agreed to marry a guy after three dates to prove something to your parents and you're asking me why I would do this? For love, Lou. I'm doing this for love," he said with heartbreaking anguish in his eyes.

That's when I was sure that he had never loved me. He couldn't love anybody. All he wanted was the approval I was willing to do anything for just days ago.

The drive for that approval was powerful. It blinded you to everything else. His weren't idol threats. He would destroy Titus's life and Snow Tip Falls if I didn't agree to marry him. He… had me.

Catching himself, he sat up and looked around. He was back to looking like the guy I had fallen for. Every moment I had spent with him had been a lie.

"But, I digress. Let's not focus on the negative."

"And, what's the positive?"

He smiled. "The positive is that I've already discussed it with your parents. We will be having a December wedding and your parents have graciously agreed to pay for it. You're going to be the second best-looking groom in Tennessee." He looked at me enthusiastically.

"You have to know that we are going to have an incredible life together, right? Merging our two families, in no time we're going to be running this state. Maybe even the country.

"And where ever we go, you are going to be the perfect husband. Poised, charming. You're going to have to work on that, of course, but I'll help you with it. By the time we're ready to make our mark on this world, you'll know exactly how to act. It's going to be amazing.

"Oh, and you can never see Titus again. But that went without saying, right? We can't have a repeat of whatever happened last weekend," he said with a laugh. "Now, how about we order dinner. I'm starved."

I couldn't respond. I couldn't breathe. In that moment everything went dark. I passed out.

Chapter 10

Titus

Driving away from Lou after we had had sex for the first time was the hardest thing I have had to do. I was uncontrollably, head over heels in love with him. Lying by the waterfall with Lou naked in my arms, I could see the rest of my life in front of me. Lou was my future and he agreed. That was why it was weird when I stopped hearing from him.

He had said that we couldn't do anything together until he spoke to Sey. But that didn't include texting each other. Between when I left him at Quin's place and his meeting Sey, we had to have texted 100 times. Most were just a few words letting the other know we were thinking about them. But after he said Sey had arrived at the restaurant, it all stopped.

'How'd it go?' I texted him.

'You still with him?' I texted later in the night when I didn't get a response.

'Seriously, let me know how it went,' I wrote hours later.

'You're freakin' me out a little,' I sent before starting with the calls.

A day went by and then two. What had happened? Did he lose his phone? Was he alright?

'Have you seen Lou? It's an emergency,' I texted Quin.

'Yeah. What's going on?' He responded quickly.

'He okay? I haven't heard from him.'

Quin's response wasn't as quick.

'He says he's fine.'

That didn't make any sense. If he's fine, then why hadn't I heard from him?

'You sure about that?'

Quin sent me a shrug emoji.

'I'll keep asking to see if I can get any more out of him.'

'Let me know if you do.'

"Something up?" A voice asked pulling my attention away from my phone.

I looked up and fire ripped through me.

"I'm fine," I told Sey who was standing above me half-dressed after a shower.

I shoved my phone into my bag and started taking off my football gear.

"It just looks like you lost something. Lose something there, Titus?" he asked smugly.

That's when it hit me. "You did something to him. If you hurt him…"

I got up, shot across the room, and grabbed him. He was ready for me, but that didn't mean much. I was bigger and strong than him.

What surprised me was how much he fought back when we both knew he didn't have a chance. By the time teammates pulled me off of him, I had pounded him pretty good. That still hadn't stopped him. He was a man possessed. That was fine with me, though, because I wasn't done.

"I'll kill you. You hear me? Hurt with him and I'll kill you."

A crowd had gathered.

"Hurt him? The man I love?" Sey said not backing down.

"You don't know what love is! He doesn't love you."

"And yet, he's agreed to spend the rest of his life with me. What, you thought you could sneak in and take him from me? I LOVE him! You hear me? You think you can sneak in and take him away from me, his fiancé? You will never have him."

"Is that true?" One of my teammates asked. He was one of the guys who sang when Sey had proposed.

"Not cool," another guy said.

I looked at them both.

"You all don't get it. I love him, and he loves me." I pointed at Sey. "He was meeting to breakup with him and this one did something to him."

"You can't snake a teammate's girl, even if it's a guy," another teammate said.

"You should get out of here, Titus. Take a walk," the first guy said.

I looked at everyone surrounding me.

"You don't understand. We love each other. I've loved him from the moment I met him."

"Take a walk, Titus!" The guy demanded.

I was willing to fight the whole team for him if I had to. But I knew that wasn't going to help me figure out what was going on with Lou. Instead, I ripped off my shoulder pads, threw them into my locker, and grabbed my bag.

Knowing where I needed to go, I headed across campus to Lou's dorm. I had to see him. Something was going on and I needed to talk to him. I had to know he was alright.

Slipping into the building as someone exited, I bounded the stairs two at a time. In front of his door, I banged on it.

"Lou, this is Titus. Are you alright? I need to know if you're alright. Lou!" I shouted before the door opened.

"Quin? Lou here? I need to see him," I said desperately.

"He's here," he said blocking the door.

"Quin, what's going on?"

Quin looked away.

"He's here but he doesn't want to see you."

"What? What are you talking about? I need to see him. Something's not right," I explained desperately.

Quin looked heartbroken as he squeezed out and closed the door behind him.

"What are you doing?"

Taking my arm, he pulled me back towards the stairs to talk in private.

"Titus, he doesn't want to see you."

"What? Why?"

"Because he said it's over between you two," Quin said sadly.

"Over? What are you talking about? He went to the restaurant to break up with Sey. He was doing it so that we could be together."

"I don't know what to tell you, Titus. He told me it's over between you and him and he's not changing his mind."

"No. I won't accept it. If he wants to end things after everything we've done, what we've been through together, then he's gonna have to tell me himself," I said trying to push past Quin.

"Titus, stop. Stop!" Quin insisted. "You can't force yourself on him," he yelled getting my attention.

"I wasn't trying to force myself on him. I was trying to talk to him."

"But he doesn't want to talk to you!" Quin caught himself. Pain appeared in his eyes. "He doesn't want to talk to you," he said sympathetically.

"Why not?" I said realizing what was happening.

"I don't know."

"This isn't fair. So, now what? Am I not invited to game nights anymore? Am I not supposed to talk to you or Cage?"

"He's moving out," Quin said heartbroken.

"What?" I said shocked. "Why?"

"I don't know."

"Where's he moving to?"

"I don't know."

I looked around lost before finding Quin again.

"But, I love him. And he loves me. I know he does."

"Sometimes it takes more than love," Quin said with tears in his eyes. "I'm sorry," he said before we both fell into each other's arms.

Why? Why had he disappeared on me? The possibilities tortured me. As the weeks followed, I could barely think of anything else. It affected every part of my life. I lost my edge on the football field. I rarely attended classes. I felt like a zombie walking through life.

Luckily, the speech I gave at the town meeting was enough to give incorporation a life of its own. Others began volunteering their time to it. I didn't have to be the one doing everything anymore. And when we won the vote and submitted our proposal to the state, the state's response was very encouraging.

The letter said that our petition would be evaluated at the beginning of the new year. That was a lot sooner than any of us would have guessed. Considering we had followed the state's requirements to the letter, there was no reason why Snow Tip Falls wasn't going to be made official.

I only wish I could have felt our victory. Whether it involved Snow Tip Falls or our team's wins, I felt nothing. The only thing I could think of was Lou. Where was he? Why didn't he want to talk to me? Didn't he love me?

"You leaving bed today?" Cali asked as he got ready for his first class.

"Probably not," I told him rolling over.

"Okay, this is ridiculous. I've had it," he said with a fire I'd never seen before.

"What? Are you gonna leave me too?"

I could feel Cali staring at me. I had my eyes closed. But if I had to guess, I would say he was looking at me with his mouth hanging open offended.

Did I care? I didn't care about anything. What was the point in caring? It would just break your heart in the end. If I let myself care again, I…

"Hey," I yelled when I felt his hands wrap around my ankles and pull. "Hey!" I shouted as he pulled me off of the bed and I hit the ground with a thud. I opened my eyes and stared at him. He stood with my ankles in his hands staring back.

"What are you doing?"

He didn't respond but I figured it out when he began dragging me across our bedroom floor to the door.

"Quit it! What do you think you're doing?"

He didn't say, but it was clear. He decided that I would be leaving our room today. I fought it, but the guy had gotten pretty strong. I would have been impressed if he wasn't pulling me into the hallway.

"Stop it!" I said before finding the strength to kick him off of me.

It was too late. He had won. I was lying outside my door in my underwear. I looked up at him like he was insane.

I had never seen this side of him. The guy wasn't backing down. He had to know that I could still take him if it came to that. It never would, but he had to know that, right?

I stared up at him waiting for some type of explanation. It never came. Once he broke eye contact, he went back into our room and returned with his book bag. Looking down at me again, he paused as if he was going to say something and then walked off.

I watched him go. Without looking back, he traversed the hallway to the stairwell and disappeared behind the door. It only took a moment before I heard,

"Are you okay, man?"

I looked back and saw a guy who lived down the hall. He wasn't the only person staring at me. Our scuffle must have been louder than I thought. Everyone was staring out their doors like there had been a fight.

I lowered my head thinking about his question. Was I okay? I was lying in the hallway in my underwear and I didn't give a shit. I was definitely not okay.

"Do you want me to help you back to your room?" The concerned guy asked.

Did I want to go back to my room? What was I gonna do there? Lie in bed and think about Lou for another twelve hours?

"Fuck it," I said having had enough.

I got up, brushed the dirt from the carpet off of me, and reentered my room. It was just for a second. When I returned to the hall, I was in a towel.

I was going to take a shower. If I was being honest, that was probably why Cali dragged me out. I kind of stunk. No more, though. I was done with whatever bullshit I was going through.

The water droplets pelting my naked body felt good. It made me feel alive again. So did dressing in clothes that smelt like detergent instead of me. Everything I did felt better than what I had been doing. And bundling up before entering the crisp winter air, I headed for the cafeteria to get something to eat.

The longer I was out of bed, the more life returned to me. What had I been thinking over the past few weeks? Yeah, Lou refused to talk to me and it hurt. It hurt a lot. I had thought I meant more to him. But wasn't there more going on than just that.

Lou had also moved out of the place he had lived for two and a half years. He had been living with one of his best friends. Why would someone do that? And where did he go? Did he move in with Sey? That wouldn't make sense. Why would he do that?

That was it. Instead of wallowing in self-pity, I needed to ask myself why he would do that.

I thought about it as I shoveled a fork-full of pancakes into my mouth.

"Why *would* he do that?" I said aloud.

He and I had had sex. It was his first time and not from a lack of opportunities. He had chosen to share that moment with me. We had talked about starting our life together. He had texted me at the restaurant saying that Sey had arrived and then had ghosted me. What happened between him and Sey that had changed everything?

"Lou's in trouble!" I said as it hit me like a lightning bolt. "Lou's in trouble," I repeated as it slowly set in.

Flinging my chair aside, I shot up and ran like my life depended on it. It did, didn't it? Lou was my life and he needed me. I know he did. I had lost myself in my own bullshit, but I saw it now. How had I not seen it before?

Sprinting across campus, I went to the last place I knew he was. Buzzing the intercom to be let into the dorm, I couldn't be sure Quin was home. Cage always used a code to tell Quin it was him at the door. I pressed the button in the same way.

"Hello?" Quin asked confused.

"Quin, it's Titus. I need to talk to you."

"Titus? I ahh…"

"Quin, Lou needs our help. You need to let me in."

There was a pause, but eventually, the door buzzed open. Bounding the stairs two at a time, I exited the stairwell on the second floor and ran to Quin's door.

"Titus?" he said again when he looked me in the eyes.

It was almost like he wasn't going to let me in, but I pushed past him and entered. Pacing the living room, I took a second and looked up. Quin was standing in front of me in a pair of boxers.

"You coming back to bed?" Cage asked exiting Quin's bedroom in a towel. He must not have heard me because the bulge stretching across the front of it told me I had caught them in the middle of something.

"Titus?" he said spotting me. "What are you…?"

"I'm sorry. I can see I'm interrupting something, but this is important. Lou needs our help."

Cage and Quin gave each other a knowing look.

"What?" I asked feeling the tension.

"You should tell him," Cage said to Quin. "I'll get dressed."

"Tell me what?" I said with a knife ripping down my chest.

"We, um, got this in the mail yesterday," Quin said retrieving an envelope from the dining table.

He handed it to me. It was square-shaped. With the flap already open, I reached in and pulled out a card.

"Seymour Charleston and Louis Armoury cordially invite you to share the special day of their wedding…"

I stopped reading aloud when I realized what it was. I looked at the date.

"It's in less than two weeks," I said shocked.

"I'm so sorry," Quin said.

"No. No, this isn't right. Something's wrong."

Quin opened his mouth to speak but didn't.

"Quin, you can't tell me you think everything's fine. When was the last time you spoke to him?"

Pain washed across his face.

"The day he moved out."

I was shocked.

"And that didn't tip you off that something was wrong?"

Quin shrugged defeated.

"Do you even know if he's been to class?"

"I don't know. He hasn't been texting me back."

I looked at him convinced.

"And does that seem like everything is right with Lou? I mean, even a little," I emphasized.

"Hey! Tone it down," Cage barked when he return dressed. "We're as concerned about him as you are."

"Are you? Because it doesn't seem like you've done anything about it."

"Titus, we got this yesterday," Cage said holding up the invitation. "Why do you think I'm here? I came down to help Quin figure this out. We understand you're concerned about him. But you're not the only one. We're on the same side."

"And which side is that?" I asked angrily.

"Yours," Quin snapped. "Titus, we think you two should be together. We always have. You two love each other." He approached me reaching out to touch my shoulder like I was a wild animal. "We can figure out what's going on with Lou together."

Realizing I wasn't alone almost brought me to tears. Seeing my head droop, Quin wrapped his arms around me. It felt good. Cage was next.

We were going to figure this out. Together, I knew we could do it. But the first thing we needed to know was where he was.

Between Quin and me, we figured out his class schedule. With that, we could figure out the name of his professors. The classes at East Tennessee University were often pretty big. But with a little luck, at least one of them would have seen him or noticed him missing.

With Cage and Quin taking two professors, I took the other two.

"Neither of them could tell me anything," I told Cage and Quin when we met for lunch to share our results.

"The same here," Cage said. "I would have thought Lou would be hard to miss," he joked.

"And what about tests?" I asked. "Shouldn't they notice if someone was missing from that? Or, at least their grade?"

"He's in a lot of large classes," Quin volunteered.

"Okay. So, what do we do now?" I asked.

"If they're getting married, Sey probably knows where he is," Quin suggested.

"You're right," I agreed. "But, he's not gonna tell me that. And neither of you know him so, he's not gonna tell you."

"There's gotta be someone who knows where he is," Cage insisted.

I thought for a second.

"There is."

"Who?" Quin asked.

"Did you see where they're having the wedding?"

"I didn't recognize it."

"I did. It's at his family's estate. I stayed there with him the weekend they read his grandmother's will."

"Do you think they know?"

"Lou's probably involved with the wedding planning, right? That doesn't seem like something Sey would do," I said. "Someone there has to be in contact with him."

"Can you call them?" Quin asked.

"There are two problems with that. One, I don't have their number. And two, they love Sey and really hate me. I wouldn't be surprised if they were behind their shotgun wedding just to keep us apart."

"So, you agree that Lou might be pregnant?" Quin asked.

I stared at him confused for a second and then laughed. We all did.

"He's probably not pregnant," I assured them. "Unless your family has invented something I don't know about," I told Quin.

"No, that's still impossible as far as I know," Quin conceded.

"So, how are we gonna ask Lou's family where he is?" Cage asked.

"And if we can talk to him," Quin added.

"I'll go there," I told them after some thought.

"You said they hated you," Cage reminded me.

"They do. But what other choice do we have? I could suggest trying to beat it out of Sey, but something tells me that he would die before giving Lou up."

"He loves him?" Quin asked.

"Didn't you tell me that sometimes it isn't about love?"

"What could it be about?" Cage asked.

None of us had an answer.

Deciding I would drive to the estate in the morning, I left them and attempted to continue my day. I had a class that I attended and as evening approached, the team had practice.

After my fight with Sey, there weren't many people who were still talking to me. I couldn't blame them. From the outside, it looked like I was the bad guy. I would have thought the same thing if I was them.

As far as they knew, Lou was Sey's fiancé. A few of them were there the day he proposed. I was the asshole who cheated with Lou. I was the homewrecker as far as they were concerned. And now I wasn't even making up for it with my play on the field.

There was one person who knew the truth, though. I kept my eye on him from the moment he arrived. If he gave the slightly indication that he was hurting Lou, no one would be able to stop what I would do to him.

He never dropped his charm. Not a hair was out of place. He almost made me believe that I was the crazy one. After all, how could someone as perfect as Sey be doing anything wrong?

Sey was the proud out gay man who had proposed to the guy he loved while playing a sport that didn't accept him. Who was I but the closet case sneaking behind people's backs? Sey was the hero while I was the villain.

I was sure that Lou's family would see me the same way. His mother had told Quin to make me go away. I was nothing to them. They probably saw me as less than nothing. Hell, they had stolen their own son's inheritance. If they were willing to do that to him, what would they do to the country bumpkin showing up at their door trying to stop their wedding?

I couldn't think about that. Someone in that family had to know where he was. I was going to get it out of them. I didn't know how, but I would.

Although I had seen him at practice, it wasn't until I returned to our room that Cali and I spoke.

"Hey," he said unable to meet my eyes.

"Hey."

"Sorry," he said saying it all.

"No. Thank you," I told him.

He looked up at me and smiled.

Retreating to our beds, he popped in his earbud and we both lost ourselves in thought.

The next morning it was me who woke Cali up.

"Where are you going?"

"To find Lou," I told him determined.

"Do you need me to go with you?"

"I'm good. Thanks, though."

Cali nodded and rolled over.

If I had asked him, I was sure he would have gone with me. Maybe I should have asked him. If there were two of us, at least I wouldn't have to worry about his mother making me disappear. I wondered if she would be capable of that. She was clearly someone who got what she wanted. What would she do if she decided she never wanted to see me again?

A lot of things flashed through my mind as I drove the two hours to the place where Lou and my romance had begun. As badly as the weekend had ended, it held some great memories. I couldn't help but smile remembering him chanting for me to strip. It was very Lou-like.

What wasn't was when he kissed me. Having his lips on mine was the most incredible experience of my life, that is until I saw him naked. Damn, was he beautiful. I had never seen anything like him. And when I kissed a trail down his body and took him into my mouth…

Adjusting my hardening cock within the folds of my jeans, I shifted my thoughts to what I would say to his family when I got there. Who was most likely to answer the door? It probably wouldn't be Chris though I had the best shot at getting him to help me. There was a moment that weekend when it seemed that he didn't hate me. It ended quickly, but wasn't it the most I could hope for?

Driving the narrow, tree-lined road to the estate, I slowed down. I knew what I wanted but I still didn't know what I was going to say. I couldn't tell them the truth, which was that I was in love with their son and needed to rescue him from people like them. They might not like that.

I was going to have to lie. I needed to come up with something they would care about. Maybe I had to find Lou because there were puppies that needed to be turned into a fur coat? They would connect with that, wouldn't they?

Pulling into the large, circular brick driveway, I parked my truck to the side. Taking a deep breath, I steadied myself and got out. Seeing cars parked out front, I guessed that everyone was home. This was going to be a disaster. But what choice did I have? Lou needed me. I had to try everything.

Approaching the door my heart thumped. My knees were weak as I reached up to the doorbell. I rang it.

What would I do when they tried to throw me out? Would I insist on staying? Would I demand that they tell me where he is? What was I going to do to find the man I loved? What would I do to rescue…

"Lou!" I said seeing the gorgeous face I hadn't seen in far too long. "Oh my god, Lou!"

Surprise, excitement, and panic washed across his face. He threw his arms around me. I gripped him pulling him tight. Before I could get enough, he pushed me away.

"You need to get out of here," he insisted.

"I'm not going anywhere without you."

Knowing I wouldn't, he looked behind him and came outside closing the door.

"You don't understand. You have to go."

"Then you're coming with me."

Frustrated and rushed, he gripped my bicep and led me back to my truck.

"I told you, I'm not leaving without you."

"I'm coming with you. Let's just get out of here."

Hearing he was going with me took my breath away. I had done it. I found Lou and was bringing him back.

Hurrying into my truck, he hid below the dashboard.

"Go. Quick. Before they see you."

Starting the truck, I did what I was told. Quickly pulling back onto the feeder road to the estate, I looked down at my guy. I had missed him so much. I couldn't believe that I had him back.

"There's a road to your left coming up. Turn there and park on the side of the road."

"Shouldn't we just get out of here?"

"I'm not going with you. I'm only here to talk."

My heart sank. I prayed it wasn't true. He was right there. He couldn't blame me if I was rescuing him from a horrible fate. I could just keep driving. I could have, but I didn't.

Making the left and pulling as far off the road as I could, I shut off the truck. Lou slowly left the floor and sat close to the door. He couldn't look at me. My heart ached realizing that he wasn't coming home.

It took a while for either of us to speak.

"What happened, Lou? Why'd you leave?"

"I left because I had to."

"What does that mean? You didn't have to do anything. You went there to break up with him. We had said we would figure everything else out, didn't we?"

"There are some things we can't figure our way out of."

"Like what? What could make you leave school and your friends? You left me and you didn't even say goodbye."

"I couldn't."

"Why not?"

"Because if I saw you, I wouldn't be able to go," he said with tears pooling in his eyes.

"Then you should have stayed."

"I couldn't!"

"Tell me why. Tell me how you could do that to us. Explain to me how you could so easily break my heart. I love you!"

"And I love you!" Lou said in an explosion that sent tears streaming down his face. "I did it because I love you."

"You love me?" I asked having heard it for the first time.

"I do. I love you with all of my heart. From when I wake up to the second I fall asleep, all I think about is you. You're the one who's always been there and who I know will never give up on me. You're the man I want to spend the rest of my life with, Titus. You!"

I stared at him achingly confused.

"Then why?"

Lou looked down shaking his head refusing to say.

My heart broke for him. There was something painful going on. In a life that battered him around and had made him feel worthless, there was yet another thing that tore him apart.

I eased across the bench seat and slowly pulled him into my arms. He came without resistance. He wanted to be there. It gave me a glimmer of hope.

"Lou, whatever it is, you can tell me. I think, maybe, you're trying to protect me. Thank you for that. But, if there's one thing I know, it's that the two of us work better when we're together. Whatever it is, we can figure it out together."

Lou listened and sniffled. I pushed my fingers into his hair and scratched his scalp. He chuckled.

"Now you're just not playing fair," he said with a smile.

"I play to win," I joked. "You can tell me, Lou. I promise we'll figure it out together."

Lou wiped his face on my shirt. I don't know why, but I liked it. It felt intimate.

"He threatened to hurt you," he said with his cheek on my chest.

"Who? Your brother?"

"No. Sey."

"He… What? How?"

"His family has a lot of friends in the Tennessee state office. He said you have a state grant for your tuition. He said he could take it away."

"Sey did?" I asked confused.

"Yeah," he said pulling away and looking into my eyes. "And he could. He said it would be easy for him."

My mind swirled. Yeah, Sey was right. My entire tuition was being paid for by a grant from the state. If I lost that, it would hurt.

"If he took that away, then I would apply for a federal grant. Or maybe I'd get a loan. That's how most people pay for college, right? I could do that. It's not a big deal."

"That's not all he said," Lou admitted disappointed.

Despite what I said, losing my grant would be a big deal. It would throw my life into a mess that it would take me all summer to work my way out of. The thought that there could be more sent a chill down my spine.

"Oh? What else did he say?"

"He said he would reject your petition to get your town incorporated."

"He can't do that."

"He can. I didn't even have to tell him about the petition. He knew. He said he saw your name on it."

"He can't do that," I said seeing my future slip away from me.

"That's not all."

Hot prickles washed across my face.

"What else did he say?" I asked hesitantly.

"He said that he could get the government to build a highway through Snow Tip Falls. He could destroy your town. That's why I left. I couldn't let him do that to you, not because of me. I wouldn't let you risk it."

I couldn't believe it. I knew Sey. We weren't friends but we were teammates. How could he consider doing such a thing?

"Does he love you that much?" I asked grasping for answers.

"No. I don't know if he cares about me at all. He wants to merge our families and to have me on his arm. He doesn't love me."

"I don't understand this."

"I tried to tell you. This is what people like my parents and Sey do to keep power. They take what they want. They don't care about who they have to hurt to get it."

The thought of bulldozers destroying my home flashed through my mind. It was a nightmare. I saw kids and families becoming homeless. I pictured them being scattered like ashes. I couldn't let that happen to them. But, I couldn't let Sey destroy Lou's life, either.

"What if we fought back?" I said capturing Lou's attention.

"How? We have nothing. No money. No connections. He has us."

I thought for a second.

"When your grandmother told you that you were going to inherit everything, didn't she also tell you to get prepared?"

"She did, but I didn't listen," he admitted regrettably.

"Was your grandmother the type to take her own advice?"

"What do you mean?"

"Would your grandmother tell you to get prepared and not prepare herself?"

Lou thought about it.

"I mean, I think she did prepare. At least she tried. She had that law firm that was supposed to handle her will."

"The one that specialized in the estate of authors?"

"Yeah."

"The one that your father's law firm got her away from?"

"Yeah."

"Do you think she knew what was going on in her final days? I mean, did she have dementia or anything?"

"She died in her sleep. Before that, she seemed like she would live forever. That's why I wasn't in contact with her as much as I should have been," he said looking down.

"Then, if she was of sound mind, and told you to prepare, she probably knew that there was going to be a fight. Mightn't she have taken steps to win that fight? Steps that could give her side the advantage. Secret steps."

"You're saying that she might have left something behind that might help me get my inheritance?"

"Does that sound like something she might do?"

Lou thought about it. His eyes darted from side to side. As he did, excitement covered his face. I recognized this person. It was the man I fell in love with.

"It does. Did I tell you that she wrote mysteries? Clues were everything to her."

I smiled.

"Lou, you did not tell me that."

"I think you're right. She might have left clues. But what?"

"If she did, it would be somewhere back at the house, right?"

"Maybe," Lou said. "I can't imagine where else she would have left it."

"Then we need to get back there."

"We?"

"You think I'm gonna let you go through this alone? Besides, it's a three-story house. You can't search that place on your own. Not in the time you have left."

"The wedding's in a week and a half," he said starting to panic. "Titus, I really don't want to marry Sey."

"You won't have to. I promise. Even if it means fighting him with everything I've got, I won't let him do that to you."

That was when Lou took my face in his hands and kissed me. It took my breath away. I had missed his lips so much. And when I cradled the back of his head in my hand and touched his tongue with mine, I knew I had found my way home.

Over the next hour, we came up with a plan. I needed to get back into the house. The place was big enough that I could be there without anyone realizing it. That was our advantage. I could search without them suspecting anything. Together we could cover more ground.

Secure on what we had to do, Lou walked back to the estate while I drove to the nearest diner and killed the rest of my day. I wanted to start searching right away, but Lou thought it better that I wait to sneak in when it was dark.

When the time came I returned to the side street and parked my truck. I pulled as far into the trees as I could get. Although anyone who went looking for it would see it, people driving by wouldn't.

After that, I jogged to the grounds I remembered so well. It helped that the place was lit up like a Christmas tree. Seeing where I was going made it easy to navigate. But having to run from shadow to shadow definitely exposed me more than what was safe.

What would Lou's father do if he saw a stranger running across their lawn? He seemed like a, shot-first, ask questions later, type of guy. And if he wasn't, Lou's brother was.

With my heart beating in my throat, I readied myself and ran from one pool of shadows to the other. Lou had said that this would be the time they were eating dinner. He said he would make sure that all of them were there.

That made me feel better, but that didn't mean I wouldn't be spotted by someone who worked for them. If they thought I was a burglar crazy enough to break in while everyone was home, they would probably try to stop me.

Sweat dripped from me as I got closer to the side door Lou had unlocked. And when I got there without hearing an alarm or gunshot, I knew my real challenge would begin.

Opening the door, I entered the guest bedroom and made my way to the hall. I had to stay low. On the opposite side of the house was the dining room. The only thing between us was a short divider and the spiral staircase that was aligned with the front door.

Depending on where I stood, the person seated at the head of the table could see me. Yet, I had to get from the guest bedroom to the stairs and up it with nothing but railing pedestals to hide me. It seemed impossible.

"My father will sit there," Lou had told me. "His eyesight isn't very good and he refuses to wear his glasses. So as long as he's not staring at Martha, he probably won't notice you over her shoulder."

Lou also promised to create a distraction. The bad part was that he couldn't say what the distraction would be. I just had to make sure I was in place when I should be and wait for it.

"I'm tired of you guys!" Lou shouted from the dining room.

"Sit down, Louis," his mother yelled.

"It's my wedding!" he screamed. "You hear me. It's my wedding. I may as well go upstairs right now considering how much of it you're letting me plan. I may as well go upstairs right now!"

I smiled hearing Lou's cue. With my head down, I peeked into the other room. Exiting the hallway, I could see Lou throwing a fit at the dinner table. All eyes were on him. That was my guy. And knowing I would have all the time I needed, I ran up the stairs circling them until I reached the third floor.

Finding the door to his room, I locked myself in. I had done it. My heart was beating a mile a minute. It was such a rush. If I had Lou in front of me, I would toss him onto the bed and make love to him.

Getting here was more exhilarating than a football game. The only thing I could do to come down from it was to throw myself onto his bed. The sheets smelt like Lou. It didn't help how much I wanted to fuck him.

By the time I heard a knock on the door, I had come down from my high. I hurried out of bed and approached the door. A step away, the floor creaked. I couldn't breathe.

"It's me, Titus. Let me in."

Recognizing Lou's delicate whisper, I unlocked the door and stepped back. He slipped in carrying a plate of food. When he was past the door, he locked it behind him.

"I brought you some food. I told them I was going to eat my dinner in my room," Lou said with a laugh.

"I heard you in there. You really care about planning your wedding," I joked.

Lou smiled.

"What got them was that yesterday I yelled at them about how much I didn't care what they planned. They have to think I'm losing my mind."

"Well, they're forcing you to get married. I think you're allowed," I said with a chuckle.

He didn't think it was as funny as I did. I could see the pain of it wash through him.

"Titus, what do I do? I really don't want to go through with it. I can't marry him. I can't be someone's armpiece for the rest of my life."

I held his shoulders looking into his eyes.

"I won't let that happen, Lou. If we have to, we'll run away together. I'm not going to let anyone hurt you."

"And I can't let anyone hurt you," Lou said sincerely.

"Then I guess we're gonna have to find this clue to protect each other."

"I guess we will," Lou said finding comfort in my eyes.

After giving me a few minutes to eat, we got started.

"If she left me a clue, wouldn't it make sense for her to leave it in my bedroom?" Lou suggested gesturing to the endless supply of boxes that filled the other half of the attic.

"That would make sense," I agreed overwhelmed by the task. "I guess we should get started."

"It would help to know what we're looking for," Lou admitted.

"You knew her. What type of clues would she plan in her books?"

"Jade amulets. Portraits that have been painted on top of the pictures of murderers."

I slowed hearing that.

"Do you think… Do you think your parents killed your grandmother?" I asked unsure how else to say it.

Lou looked at me defeated.

"I keep asking myself that. Nothing about the way she died made sense. And any time I ask them about it, they say that she's dead and I should move on."

"Parents of the year," I said.

Lou gave a sad chuckle.

"That's them."

"So, what do you think doesn't make sense about her death?"

Lou grabbed a box, put it on the floor in front of the door, and went through it. I did the same.

"I know my parents are heartless. But why didn't they invite me to the funeral? Even if they don't care about me, they care about what people think. They should have wanted me there. The only thing they care about is us looking like the perfect family. In perfect families, grandsons don't miss their grandmother's funeral."

"Maybe they were trying to hide something they knew you would catch?"

"Maybe. But, what? And, I know my parents are monsters, but I have a hard time picturing them killing anyone. My father wouldn't have the balls for it. And my mother wouldn't dirty her hands with something like that."

"Maybe they got your brother to do it. He looks like the type who would enjoy plucking the wings off of things."

"But killing her would put him even further under my parent's thumb. He would want that as much as I would."

"Then maybe no one killed her. What other reasons would they have for not telling you that your grandmother died until after the funeral?"

"Maybe that's when they changed the will," Lou said sitting up in thought.

"So, they didn't tell you she died because they needed time to arrange things?"

"Yeah."

"How long do you think it takes to change a will?"

Lou considered it. "Well, it's not just changing the will. They would have had to switch law firms. How long would that take?"

"When my grandmother died, she was buried within a few days. What's the longest people usually wait to hold a funeral?"

"I don't know. A week?" Lou guessed.

"What if the reason they didn't tell you about the funeral was because she had been dead longer than a week?"

"How much longer?"

"How much longer would they need? When was the last time you spoke to her before she died?"

"I don't know. Two months before?"

"What if she was dead for two months?"

"Wouldn't that be illegal?"

"If they didn't report her death it might be," I guessed. "And what if they didn't invite you to the funeral because they thought you might ask too many questions."

"Like, how long ago did she die?"

"Or, why did it take so long to tell people?"

"Would that mean there's a record of it somewhere? Like, where did they keep the body after they found her dead? Don't they need a funeral home?"

"Or maybe they kept her here. Like, on ice or something."

"We need to find out. That would give us more answers than looking for a needle in a haystack," Lou said slamming down a stack of papers.

I looked at the seemingly endless number of boxes in front of us.

"Maybe, but I don't think we should stop. Both of our lives depend on it."

Conceding, Lou and I continued through boxes for the rest of the night. We didn't stop until neither of us could see straight. Besides an endless collection of travel magazines, there were publishing contracts and story notes for her books. There were even a few boxes of Christmas decorations.

If his grandmother had left a clue in any of them, she hadn't made it easy to find. That didn't make sense to me. If she had left something for him, she would have put it somewhere he would find it.

Too exhausted to open another box, the two of us retreated to the bed. He climbed into my arms. I had missed this so much. I never wanted to let him go.

He fell asleep a lot sooner than I did. But, once I did, I was out until the sun shone in through the window.

"Morning," I said when I found Lou awake and staring at me.

"I don't want to lose you," he told me with a sad look in his eyes.

"You're not gonna lose me. I told you, we're gonna figure this out. Once we do, we're gonna be together forever," I said with a smile.

My words did nothing to raise his spirits.

"I'm gonna need to help my mother with wedding planning today. It was what I fought for last night. If I changed my mind now, they might suspect something's up."

"I understand. I'll, um… I'll keep looking up here," I agreed fighting the urge to poke my eyes out at the thought of the monotony.

"Okay. I'll bring you something to eat," he said getting out of bed. "Oh, and if you use the bathroom, don't flush the toilet. The pipes are old in this place. If they hear the rattling and I'm not here, they might come looking for you."

"Then I'll try not to do anything that might need flushing," I joked.

"You do that. So, how does a breakfast burrito sound? All the fixin's?"

I looked at him wondering if he was joking.

"Kidding. I'll bring you something light. No fiber."

"Right," I said having another reason to dread my day without him.

Lou was gone for a while and returned with a plate of fried eggs, hash browns, and a croissant. It was filling enough. And when I was done eating, I returned to the endless supply of boxes.

Nothing had changed from the night before. Each box contained a small piece from Lou's grandmother's interesting life. She clearly loved two things, traveling and her books. The two seemed to overlap. But none of it revealed the clue Lou and I hoped she had left.

After a lot of hours and getting halfway through the boxes, I began to consider that she hadn't left a clue for Lou to find. Maybe this was all a wild goose chase. Even if she had left something in one of the boxes, how was I supposed to recognize it? In that case, how was Lou supposed to?

I paused considering that. If his grandmother had left a clue for him, how would he recognize it? If she intended for him to find something, she wouldn't have buried it, would she? She wouldn't have.

At the same time, she wouldn't want anyone else to stumble upon it. If a clue was out there, it had to be hidden somewhere personal. Maybe there was somewhere the two of them went together. Didn't Lou say that some of his best childhood memories involved heading into town? Could she have left it there?

No. That would be too hard. And anyone could have stumbled upon it there. If there was a clue, it had to be in this house. Or, at least on this estate. It had to be somewhere that Lou might think to look.

Where would a mystery author leave a clue for her favorite grandson? In a book. She would leave a clue in a book. It wasn't in this mountain of boxes, it was in her library.

Scrambling to my feet, I worked my way through the stacks to the bedroom door. Pressing my ear onto it, I listened for footsteps. It was quiet. Lou had said that his family never came up here. I had to rely on that. So, unlocking the door and slowly pushing it open, I eased my head out.

No one. At least not standing outside the door. Opening the door further, I checked the halls. Nothing. Slipping out and closing the door behind me, I looked over the railing. The second-floor balcony and the space around the first floor's stairs were empty.

Moving as quietly as I could, I circled the balcony on my floor keeping an eye on everything below me as I did. The door to the library was closed. Opening it as slowly as I had the last one, I peeked through the crack. The room was empty. Slipping in and closing the door behind me, I scanned the room. There were thousands of books.

Heading to the nearest shelf, I began reading titles. There were a lot that sounded like mysteries. Some of them listed Agatha Armoury as the author. I pulled out one and flipped through it.

"When one describes a cold and stormy night, it must pale in comparison to the one Emma Miller suffered the night of her birth," I said reading the first line aloud.

I put it back and pulled another. Returning that, I pulled another. There was nothing special about any of them. She might have left Lou a message written within a book's text. But, which one? And how would she have gotten him to open it?

It was as I thought about it that I saw a book that Lou had told me about, 'The Velveteen Rabbit'. It was the book she had read to him when he was a child. If he were feeling nostalgic, wouldn't that be something he might pick up? Hadn't he already picked it up thinking about her?

I made a move to cross the room when a creak sent terror cutting through me. The sound was coming from the hallway's aging wooden floor. There was someone outside the door heading this way.

Abandoning my path, I spun around looking for a way to get out. Finding none, I looked for a place to hide.

There were bookshelves and a desk. That was it. I could hide under the shallow desk or I could…

There was a gap. It was between two of the standing bookshelves. It was where two perpendicular walls met each other. There wasn't much of a space between them, but I could get in. It offered me a shadow to hide in. But if someone looked in that direction, they would see me.

It wasn't great, but I had no choice. If I didn't try, I was going to be discovered. I needed to at least try.

Compressing my chest against the bookshelves' rounded edges, my body filled the gap. The shelves rocked back into place. I didn't have time to consider if all of me was in. It had to be. The door was opening, and all I had left to do was pray.

As I watched, a distracted man with grey hair entered and retrieved a book from a shelf. It was a mindless gesture. He had to have done it a dozen times. When he had it, he pulled out the desk's chair and took a seat.

For two hours, Lou's father sat lost in whatever book he was reading. Throughout every second of it, I stood watching him. On the other side of him, I could see the book I had reached for. Now that it was on my mind, the children's book was all I could see.

During every moment that passed, I expected Lou's father to see it too. How could he not retrieve that one next? I was sure the secret to everything was in it. And as I thought about it, my stomach growled.

'Shit!' I thought bracing myself for the man's reaction. He didn't budge. Could he hear it? How loud had it been?

Sure, it had been a long time since breakfast, but it couldn't have been that long. Of all times, why now? When would my stomach growl again?

I didn't have to wait long. With a tightening of my gut, my intestines rumbled echoing the sound of my doom. He heard that one. Snapped from his reading, he looked up. If he turned, he would see me. Trapped, there would be nothing I could do.

About to turn my way, he quickly spun back to the window. I heard it too. It was a car pulling into the driveway. That prompted him to get up and return the book. Without a word, he walked to the door and left.

I fell onto the wall of my tomb and closed my eyes. My heart beat louder than my growling stomach could ever be. I had made it. I was free.

Pulling out from between the shelves, I crossed the room and retrieved the book that had haunted me. Exhausted by standing as long as I did, I fell into the desk chair. It was warm. I didn't care.

Opening the book, I found an inscription. As I read it, the door flung open behind me.

"Titus, what are you doing in here? Anyone could come in and see you," Lou said entering and locking the door behind him.

"How long has this been here?"

"How long has what been here?" he said coming over.

"This," I said showing him.

He took the book and examined the inside front cover.

"To the new park preserve, dig deep in the bramble. Always be prepared. Agatha Armoury."

Lou continued staring at the text.

"Is that your grandmother's handwriting?"

"I think so," he said unsure.

"What do you think that means?"

"I don't know."

"If she were trying to leave you a message, wouldn't this be the book she would leave it in?"

Lou flipped it over and looked at the cover.

"Would she?"

"It's something you would pick up to remember her, but it wouldn't hold meaning for anyone else."

"Maybe."

"So, do you remember there being an inscription when you were a kid?"

"It's been ten years," he said reading the note again.

"Be prepared. Isn't that what she told you? That you should be prepared?"

"It is."

"Then what would 'To the new park preserve' mean? It's gotta mean something."

"The lake," Lou squeaked.

"What about the lake?"

"I once told her that it was so beautiful that I thought everyone should get to enjoy it."

"You said you wanted to make it a state park," I said remembering.

"And that's what I said to my grandmother. But she said that it was on private property so it couldn't be a park…"

"It had to be a preserve," I said finishing his thought.

"Right," he said turning to me.

"This is it. And it says, 'To the new park preserve'. She's telling you to go to the lake. This is your clue!" I said excitedly. "What else does it say?"

Lou read, "Dig deep in the bramble." He looked at me. "Bramble is a bush. She's telling us to dig deep under the bush. This is real," Lou said stunned. "She left me a clue!"

Getting emotional, Lou bit his lip. He tried to stop himself from crying but he couldn't. My heart broke for him. Wrapping my arms around him, he leaned into my embrace.

"She didn't forget about me. She loved me," he said with a painful release.

I hadn't realized how much what his parents had done had affected him until now. They had stolen more than just his inheritance from him. For Lou, they had stolen his connection to the only person who truly cared for him. She was the only person Lou thought he could count on growing up, and the one thing she had promised him, they had erased.

If he couldn't trust her, who could he? What about his life could he hold onto as truth?

"We have to find what she left you?" I told him needing to do this for him.

"It's in the bramble," he repeated.

"We can go there now."

"No," he said pulling away and looking up into my eyes. "We need to wait until it's dark. If we crossed the lawn now, anyone looking at the backyard would see us. We can go after dinner. Maybe after everyone has gone to bed," he said planning.

He withdrew from his thoughts when my stomach growled again. He looked at me.

"You must be starved."

"I think my stomach just likes living on the edge," I joked.

"What do you mean?" he asked confused.

"Nothing. Yeah, I could use something to eat."

"I'll get you a snack. But maybe you should return to my room. It's the one place that no one in this house will visit."

"I'll go back."

Leaving and returning with the thickest sandwich I've ever seen in my life, I ate it without question and then washed it down with soda.

"Well, that's a start," I joked.

"How much do you eat?"

"A little more than you," I said again having the strength to smile.

Lou kept the food coming until I couldn't eat another bite. When he left for dinner, all I could do was stretch out in the bed. When he returned, it was with a slice of pie.

"You do know how to feed a man," I said amused by it.

"You don't want it?"

"You're gonna lose your fingers if you try and take it from me," I joked. "Wait. Where's the topping."

"You want topping?" he said sitting next to me on the bed.

"Got any?"

He cut a piece of pie off and fed it to me. When the fork was free, he kissed me on the lips.

"That's the best topping I ever had."

"There's more where that came from," he said kissing my cheek and ear as I continued to chew.

When the pie was gone, I pulled him onto the bed and rolled him onto his back. Kissing his face everywhere but on his lips, I slid my hand up his shirt.

My god, did I love touching his naked flesh. I could have held him all night. Sliding my hands across his chest, I almost did. It wasn't until I moved my hand to the bulge in his pants that he reminded me of our plan.

"We can probably leave now."

"I can think of a few other things I would prefer to be doing," I said gripping his hard cock.

With a nervous laugh, he moved my hand away.

"What's wrong?" I asked wanting to put my hand back.

"It's just that…"

"What?"

"I'm engaged," he said hesitantly.

I stopped and looked at him confused.

"You're only engaged because he's blackmailing you."

"I know."

"So, what's the problem? You don't owe him anything."

"I know," he said racked in guilt.

I rolled off of him.

"I don't want you to stop, though."

"Well, I don't want to do anything that makes you feel uncomfortable."

"I don't know why I'm like this," he said disappointed.

"It's because you're a special guy. That's why I love you."

"I love you, too," he said with a smile.

Staring into my eyes, he sat up and kissed me.

"I love you," he said.

"And I will always love you. We'll stop him. I promise."

Lou curled into my arms.

"And when we do, I'm yours, forever."

Kissing him one more time, he climbed out of my arms. When I got up, his eyes dipped. There was no way to hide how hard I was. He blushed. It just made me want him more.

Pushing my uncontrollable lust for him aside, we made our way to the door and into the hall. Taking a quick detour to get grandma's emergency flashlight, we descended the stairs and snuck out the back sliding glass doors.

"The lights are on motion sensors after 10 PM. As long as we don't get too close to them, we should be fine."

Some of the lights were easy to avoid. Some were not. I held his hand as we walked. Even in the dark, I wondered if someone looking out their window could see us. The full moon made it a bright night. But making it to the end of the property, we entered the trees.

"Ya know, this has to be the most romantic caper ever," I suggested.

"Caper?"

"What would you call it? What we're doing isn't a crime. There's nothing illegal. But it definitely feels dangerous."

"I'd call it, righting a wrong," Lou said determined.

"So it's more of a superhero thing? You're so right. I can see that now."

Lou laughed. I liked hearing him laugh.

Following the path we had months ago, we heard the water falling onto the pool before we saw it. Standing above it on the spot Lou had once jumped from, he shined the flashlight on the plants below.

"Dig deep in the bramble," he repeated.

"Brambles are bushes with thorns, right?"

"Yeah, like…" Lou turned to me in realization.

"Like what?"

"Look for a raspberry bush. When I was a kid, my grandmother and I used to pick wild berries. She used to joke that raspberries were the brambliest bramble of them all. We made a joke about it."

"Did you ever pick berries around here?"

"No," Lou said confused.

Heading down, the two of us spread out searching the brush on either side of the beach that stuck out of the pool like a tongue.

"Ouch," I said when something scratched my arm. "You said they have thorns, right?"

"Did you find one?"

I shined my phone's light at the sea of green leaves in front of me.

"It's a raspberry bush!" Lou declared.

"The brambliest bramble of them all. She said to dig deep. Did you two have a joke about that?"

"No. I think she just wants us to dig deep. There were never any raspberry bushes when I came here as a kid. This isn't even the type of place bushes like this grow. I think she might have planted it here."

"You think she buried something under it?"

"Maybe. How do we dig it up?"

I reached down getting a hand full of thorns. Moving the branches around with my shoe, I found where the stem disappeared into the dirt. Stepping on it, I bent it all back. When that didn't release the roots, I took off my shirt. Wrapping it around my hand, I took hold of the stem and pulled.

The beam from Lou's flashlight left the ground and shined on me. The roots were deep. I was going to have to give it my all if I was going to pull it up. So, repositioning myself over it, I squatted and pulled at it like a medicine ball at the gym. Every muscle in my body tensed.

"Wow!" Lou said under his breath.

Right after he said it, the bush let go of its grip on the earth and I fell on my ass.

"Ahhh!" I yelped when I landed on the thorns.

Lou burst out laughing.

"Are you all right."

"I feel like Wild E. Coyote."

"Beep beep."

I looked up at him. He was smirking amused. Reaching out his hand, I took it. Standing up, I turned around.

"Is there anything attached to me?"

Lou slowly placed his hand on my ass and caressed it. The pain I had felt quickly turned to pleasure. He explored every inch of it squeezing a little as he did.

"Everything looks good here."

When he eventually removed his hand, I turned around. Staring at him, all I wanted to do was strip him down and make love to him on the sand like we once had. I knew I couldn't. We were on a mission.

"So, what do you see down there?" I said pointing.

He took his longing eyes off of me and shined the flashlight at the hole I had made.

"I think it's your turn," I told him.

He looked back and handed me the light. Getting on his knees he dug with his hands. With the soil loosened from the uprooting, he got deep fast.

"Wait, there's something down here."

"What is it?"

"I don't know. It's hard and big."

I kneeled next to him and helped. With anticipation rattling through us both, we found the edges of whatever it was. Pushing our hands down the side of it and finding the bottom, I counted to three. With a yank, the box was free and we lifted it to the surface. It was lighter than either of us expected.

"Do you recognize this?" I asked once it sat between us.

"No. How does it open?"

I pushed my hand over it. It was the size of a small microwave oven.

"I think it's rubber."

"Rubber?"

"Yeah. Like one of those containers you store leftovers in."

Lou reached down exploring it with me.

"You're right. So it's probably vacuum sealed. Doesn't that mean we just have to pull the top open?"

"Try it."

I gave Lou space. As he searched the lid, he found a tab and pulled it. It didn't release on his first attempt. But digging all of his fingers into it, he popped it open. It was his turn to land on his ass.

I shined the light into the box. Neither of us expected what we found.

"It's a video camera."

"I know this camera," Lou said. "This was my grandmother's. She got it as a Christmas gift about a decade ago. For a while, she was recording everything. She couldn't believe how small it was," Lou said with a nostalgic smile.

Lou took it from the box.

"What's in that?" I said seeing a sandwich-sized rubber container.

Lou took it out and handed it to me. I gave him the flashlight to free my hands. Opening it with a pop, I found a small videotape.

"I think it's for that," I said handing it to Lou.

Fidgeting with it, Lou pressed the power button. After a series of flashes and some buzzing, it turned on.

"There's still juice in it."

He opened the flip-out screen.

"It's still half charged. She couldn't have buried it that long ago."

With our hearts thumping, Lou loaded the tape and moved so both of us could see. An old, spritely looking woman appeared on the screen.

"Grandma Aggie," Lou said with heartbreak.

She steadied herself in front of the camera and spoke.

"I, Agatha Armoury, being of completely sound mind and body, hereby leave the entirety of my estate including my properties, books, and all of my holdings to my grandson, Louis Armoury. This is not a decision I'm taking lightly. Nor is it one where my mind will change. If a will appears saying anything otherwise, know that it is fraudulent.

"There is only one person I trust with the future of this family and it is my grandson. He has the kindness and compassion to steer this family in the direction it needs to go. And although I'm hoping that he won't need to look for this, if he does, well, I want to tell him, I love him. And wherever I end up, I will miss him. He might be the only thing that this family ever got right."

The old woman then leaned toward the camera. The image turned to static.

I looked over at Lou. He was drowning in tears. When he looked up at me, he didn't have to say what he was thinking. I could see the love and adoration all over his face. I pulled him to me wrapping my arms around him.

"I miss her."

"She misses you, too."

Turning to wrap his arms around me, I pulled him into my arms. I knew I just needed to be there for him right now and I was. But eventually, when his wave of sorrow passed, he pulled away preparing for what happened next.

"This is legally binding, isn't it?" he asked.

"I would guess it is. And did you see the date on the screen? It was recorded a few months before she died. Do you think something your parents did inspired her to make this?"

"Probably. But, what do we do with it? Do we show it to them?"

"I think the first thing we do is make a duplicate. Do you know how to do that?"

"No, but I'm sure we can find somewhere in town that can."

"We'll go there tomorrow. Also, we need to know what we're dealing with. Was she alive when her will was changed? If she was, we're dealing with a whole different situation. If she was alive, she was coerced. I have to think something like that is hard to prove. But if she had already passed…"

"My parents committed fraud. They could go to jail."

I looked at Lou wondering how he felt about that. I couldn't tell. He had looked away lost in thought.

Lou remained quiet as we collected everything and replanted the uprooted bush.

"You're gonna have to guide us back," I told him.

"Of course," he said taking the flashlight while I carried everything in the box.

Lou's stunned state didn't change during our 40-minute walk back. Re-entering the estate's lawn, he seemed less concerned about getting caught.

"We don't have enough proof yet," I reminded him.

That got him to be a little more careful, but clearly, something in him had changed. He seemed less scared. I liked the way confidence looked on him. And when we made it back to his room with the door locked behind us, he watched me set the box aside and then stared at me with lust.

"What?" I asked unsure what he wanted.

I didn't have to wonder long because, as if unbottled, the man I loved rushed towards me finding my lips. Slipping his hand behind my neck, he took control. Parting my lips, he inserted his tongue. Finding mine, he sucked it while pressing our bodies together. Wrapping a leg around me, I grabbed his ass and lifted him.

Never in my life had I imagined Lou being this aggressive. He had been released. I loved it. With his limbs locked around me, I stumbled back. Finding the edge of the bed, I sat.

As he gripped and pulled my hair, he pushed me onto the bed. I complied loving every moment of it. And when I was sprawled under him helpless to his will, he straddled my hips and found my hard cock. Rubbing it with his clothed balls, he didn't have to tell me what he wanted next.

Staring up at him as he moved with his eyes closed, I reached between the two of us and unbuttoned his pants. As soon as I did, he reached down and pulled off his shirt. He didn't stop there. My shirt was next. Then when I had unbuttoned and unzipped his pants, he rolled off of me to take them off and to allow me to do the same.

Both of us were naked when he climbed back on top of me. We were rock hard. Staring down at me, he placed his hand on my chest and rocked his hips. He stroked my dick with the space between his balls and his thigh. It was driving me wild. And just as I grabbed his hips to control the speed, he climbed off of me reaching something under his bed.

Sitting back up, he slid down my legs and took my cock in his mouth. He could barely pull it back I was hard. And when his tongue rode the rim of my head, I had to grip the sheets to handle the sensations.

Mercifully, the teasing didn't last long. Again sitting up, he revealed what he had retrieved. It was a bottle of lube. Popping the top, he poured some of it into his palm. He slathered a part of it on my cock. The other part he applied to his hole.

Were we doing this? I couldn't be sure. He had said he wanted to wait. But that was before everything in his life had changed. With that change came a new Lou. And that Lou climbed on me, gripped my cock, and guided it between his cheeks.

Lifting his chin, he leaned forward opening himself up. The friction created on my lubed head felt amazing. When he stopped focusing on his folded skin, I held my breath. When he leaned back onto me, my chest reached for the ceiling. His tight hole squeezed the life out of me as he pushed me in. I felt him on every part of my cock and his groans made my thoughts spiral.

Placing his second hand onto my chest, he started fucking me before either of us was ready. The painful pleasure that stole my breath had to be tearing him apart. But he was in control. This was what he wanted.

Slapping my crotch with the meat of his ass, the sound echoed. It was like he no longer cared who heard it. Lou was free. Lifting his arms, he pushed his fingers through his hair. I grabbed his hips and guided us both to pleasure.

It didn't take long. Without touching his cock, Lou groaned and exploded all over me. Seeing him cum made me fuck him harder. With the pressure building, I came like a fire hose. Lost in the release, my mind swirled as I filled him.

Slowing my thrusts, I looked up. Lou was moving in slow motion. I could practically hear his thoughts. He had never imagined anything like this was possible. He looked high. I pushed my hand up his stomach. He recoiled. Lou's skin was electric. His entire body was an open socket.

It took a while for the Lou I knew to reawaken. I was still inside of him when he did. Bracing himself as he pulled himself off of me, I felt every inch of him as he did.

"I'll be back," is what he said as he exited his room naked. When he came back with a warm washcloth, he cleaned me off.

I wasn't going to say anything about it, but he was definitely different. Sure, it was late and the chance of anyone still being up and walking the halls was slim. But they weren't zero. So him walking around naked didn't match with the guy who, up until hours ago, had been so desperate for his family's approval.

When we were both clean and relaxed, Lou climbed back into my arms.

"I love you," he said making me feel as good as I had ever felt.

"I love you, too," I reminded him before we both fell asleep.

Though he had been incredibly bold the night before, he wasn't quite that the next morning.

"We need to sneak you out somehow."

"If we were thinking, I could have slept in my truck last night."

"But then we wouldn't have been able to do what we did," Lou said with a smile. "And that was pretty great."

A warm wave washed through me remembering it.

"Yeah, it was. So, what do we do now?"

"I mean, we could just walk out. What can they do to us now?"

"We don't know what we have yet," I reminded him. "If your grandmother was alive when she changed her will, we don't have anything."

"You heard her, though. She said that she wasn't going to change her mind and that if her will says differently, it's fraud."

"Sure but your parents don't seem like people willing to give up without a fight. We need proof that they faked her will. Until we have it, we can't tip them off."

Lou conceded.

"Well, my mother had planned to do more wedding stuff today. I'm going to have to do something about that. Maybe I could throw another fit?"

"Bridezillas are a thing for a reason, right?" I said with a smirk.

"Then I guess I'm about to have a problem with the flower arrangement."

"Will I know when I should come down?"

"I think you'll know," he said with a smile.

He wasn't wrong. It took 5 minutes before he entered the backyard with both of his parents in tow. He carried dishes that he broke one by one. His mother was irate. His father was mostly trying to calm his wife down.

Making sure I had the camera and tape, I exited the room and descended the stairs. When I got to the second floor, I looked around and jumped at what I saw. Lou's brother was leaning against his bedroom's doorframe with his arms crossed. It was like he was waiting for me.

When we made eye contact, he laughed and retreated into his room. Shit! That had not gone as planned.

Continuing down and out the front door a little less cockily, I jogged across the driveway and onto the feeder street. Winding my way to the truck, I got in and waited for Lou.

"Chris saw me," I told Lou when he got in.

"Shit!"

"Yeah."

"Did he say anything?"

"No. And I got the impression that he wasn't planning on telling anyone."

"He likes having something to hold over people. He probably thinks I'm cheating on Sey with you. If he knew what we were about to do, things might be a little different."

"Then I'm glad he doesn't," I said starting the truck and pulling away.

Our first stop in town was at a store that sold cameras and video equipment.

"We're looking to make a copy of what's on this," I told the attendant holding the tape in my hand.

"What is that, mini DV?" he asked examining it.

"I guess. We brought the camera in case you need it."

I held it up and he took it.

"How long is the footage?"

"Two minutes?" I suggested looking at Lou.

He shrugged.

"To what format?"

"Something we can email," I said confirming with Lou.

"Give me twenty minutes?" he said taking the tape and camera into the back.

Lou and I looked at each other barely able to believe what was happening. We were doing it. If we got it onto the cloud, his family could never take it away from us. Lou was almost free.

Paying for it minutes later, a copy of the file arrived in Lou's inbox. Opening it and watching it again brought tears to Lou's eyes.

"Now what?" he asked me.

"Now we figure out when she died."

"How do we do that?"

I thought about it and then turned to the attendant.

"You guys have a library in town, right?"

"We do," the guy said brushing back his unruly hair and adjusting his glasses.

"Do they have things like local newspapers or town announcements?"

"They should," he asked confused.

"Thanks," I said with a smile.

Leaving the camera store and arriving at the library, I asked the woman behind the desk where I would find the local obituaries. She walked us to a rack with the most recent newspaper.

"How would we find information on the funeral for Agatha Armoury?"

The old woman lifted her glasses and straightened her back.

"You could ask me."

"Were you there?" Lou asked awestruck.

"I was. She was a local author. She meant a lot to the community. It's a tragedy she's gone."

"How was the ceremony?" he asked vulnerably.

"To be honest, surprisingly small. She had millions of fans around the world, yet her whole family wasn't even there."

Lou jerked back like she had ripped out his heart.

"If someone wasn't there, I'm sure there was a good reason," I quickly replied.

"One would hope," she said not backing down.

"Anyway, we were hoping to find out what funeral home took care of her body."

The woman's posture broke in surprise.

"Well, that's a morbid thing to want to know."

"Please, it's important. If you happen to know, we'd be grateful if you can tell us."

Gathering herself, she removed her glasses. Hanging from a chain, she rested them on her chest.

"The funeral home that assisted at the funeral was the same for all funerals in this area, Thompson's Funeral Home. I hope you're not asking that to make a Youtubes or a TikkyTokky or something," she said sternly.

"No, Ma'am. It's nothing like that," I reassured her. "And thank you for your help."

Getting the address to the funeral home, we drove there next. Sitting out front, we came up with a plan. Walking in, a solemn man dressed in black came over. Nothing about him was out of place and he moved with a deliberateness that was sure not to startle anyone.

"Can I help you?" he asked in hushed tones.

"We're hoping you can," I told him. "This is Louis Armoury. He is the grandson of Agatha Armoury. I think you conducted the funeral for her a few weeks back."

"Of course. I'm sorry for your loss," he told Lou.

"Thank you," I said, allowing Lou to remain silent. "We're not sure how to tell you this, but you might have been unknowingly tricked into committing a crime."

The man froze. "I'm sorry, and who are you?" he asked me.

"Right now, who I am isn't important. What is important is that you might have, unknowingly, committed a crime that could shut down your business and put you in prison for the rest of your life."

"I'm really going to have to ask you who you are," he asked me nervously.

"You prepared the body of Agatha Armoury, a world-famous author, and knowingly put the wrong time of death on the death certificate. I don't need to remind you that a death certificate is a federal document."

"I am aware of what a death certificate is."

"So, you will also know putting the wrong time of death on the certificate to aid a crime makes you an accessory. Depending on the crime committed, you could be looking at a long time in prison."

The man stared at me as if fighting to remain calm.

"Do you commit crimes often at this funeral home? Is forging documents something you usually do here?"

"I did not forge a document," he said trying not to snap.

"What would you call it, creative criminality? Call it what you will, but Agatha Armoury's family was wronged and your business is about to become world-famous for committing fraud and embezzlement."

"Embezzlement? What are you talking about?" He turned to Lou. "Your family asked me to put that date to save them the embarrassment of having discovered her weeks after she died. They said that they didn't want anyone to think that someone so famous was the subject of neglect.

"I was sympathetic to their situation and instead put the date they found her. That's all. I did it as a favor for a respected Tennessee family."

The guy was sweating watching his world crumble around him. I wasn't sure if he felt better or worse when Lou pulled out his phone and showed him that we had recorded what he said. But after, he looked calmer.

"What's going on?" he asked, his eyes bouncing between the both of us.

"What's going on is that you are going to tell us exactly what you did for his family. You are going to include all of the gritty details or we're going to make you one of the most famous criminals in America," I told him knowing we had him.

Along with a lot of claims that he didn't know what was going on, he walked us through what happened. Not everyone in a town as small as this required an autopsy. That was the case with Lou's grandmother. She was in her eighties and could be listed as having died from old age.

Having examined the body, he said that that was what she died of. We had no reason not to believe him. That was especially after he admitted to, not only putting the wrong date on the death certificate, but ignoring the damage to the corpse's skin which was most likely caused by it being in direct contact with the floor of a walk-in freezer.

"We got 'em," I told Lou when we returned to the truck. "We have your grandmother's will. We have a recording where someone admits to putting the wrong date on the death certificate. All we need is the date your grandmother's power of attorney was switched to your father's law firm. If it was after your grandmother's death, it's done."

I stared at Lou. I expected him to be a little more excited than he was.

"What's the matter, Lou? You've won. Why aren't you happier?"

"I've gotten back my inheritance, but how does that change things with Sey?"

"What do you mean? Weren't your parents pressuring you to marry him? They don't have anything they can hold over you anymore."

"But Sey does. He still could take away your scholarship. He could still destroy Snow Tip Falls. Me winning back my family's estate doesn't affect that."

It slowly dawned on me that he was right. We had done what felt like mission impossible, but we hadn't changed anything that affected Lou's fate. He was still trapped into marrying the guy blackmailing him, and we still couldn't be together.

"What do we do, Titus?"

I wasn't sure what we could do. But I knew what I had to do. I had to drop Lou back at his estate. We had been gone a long time. Unless we were planning on confronting his family tonight, he had to keep playing along.

"What do you mean you're not coming back with me?" Lou asked when we approached the estate's driveway.

"We found what we were looking for. We've done all we can here. But, as the official representative of Snow Tip Falls, there might be something I can do."

"I can come with you," he said taking my hand.

"You can't give your parents a reason to suspect anything's up. Who knows what they'll do if they think their life is on the line."

"I don't want to be away from you," he said with tears in his eyes. "I don't want to lose you again."

"You'll never lose me. I'm yours and you're mine," I said before giving him a kiss.

Lou wanted to leave the truck as little as I wanted him to go. But, he did. And when he disappeared past the gates and into his driveway, I turned my truck around and headed back to campus.

"Where have you been?" Cali asked me when I was back in our dorm room. "You've missed practice."

"There's something more important I've been taking care of."

"You should talk to Coach. He's really upset. He was talking about kicking you off the team."

I considered what Cali said. But as much as I knew I should have cared about my place on the team, I didn't. The only thing I cared about was Lou. He needed me. So did my town. Nothing else mattered.

Having arrived late, I went to bed soon after. When I woke up, I got back into my truck and drove to the state's capital. I needed to know if there was anything to Sey's threat to prevent Snow Tip Falls from incorporating.

Arriving at the office where I had sent all of our correspondents, I entered and found the receptionist. She sat behind glass in a sterile room by herself. When she spoke, I recognized her voice from my many calls to her office.

"Hi, I came to check on the status of a petition I filed. I think we've spoken before," I said with a friendly smile.

The sturdily built older woman looked me up and down.

"What petition is this regarding?"

"It's to incorporate Snow Tip Falls."

She stared at me with a scowl.

"If you need the petition number, I can give it to you."

She looked away and returned to the paperwork in front of her.

"All status update requests must be in writing and mailed in," she said dismissively.

"I know. And I'm more than happy to fill out any form or go through any procedure you require. But, I was told that there was some chance that the petition won't go through. If that's the case, I figured that since I'm here, I can address it. Might save you some work. Who needs more work, right?" I said with a smile.

"All requests need to be made in writing and mailed in. No exceptions," she said pointing to a sign on the wall beside me.

"Yep, there it is. It says it right there," I said losing faith.

Unsure what else I could do or say, I was about to leave when I stopped.

"Listen, I know it's your job to be a gatekeeper for your boss and I respect that. And from what I can tell, you're very good at it. I can't imagine that anything happens here without you knowing about it…"

"What's your point?" She said cutting me off.

I stopped startled. Realizing that she wasn't going to listen to anything I said, I took a deep breath and steadied myself. "The point is that there's this boy and I love him. He loves me too. But there's a chance he might have to marry someone else because of you."

"Because of me?" she asked replacing her stone face with confusion.

"You control what happens in this office, don't you? You decide what and who your boss sees?"

"What does this office have to do with who anyone marries? We handle governmental petitions."

"Well, today you handle love."

"I really don't see…"

"Snow Tip Falls. And I know you recognized the name. It was all over your face when I said it."

"And if I do?"

"Then you know the petition has been filed with all of its parts satisfied yet there's a chance it might not go through."

"All petitions are pending the approval of…"

"Your boss. I know. But, I've been told that your boss is willing to refuse the petition if the man I love doesn't marry his blackmailer. And my love is willing to spend the rest of his life with a man who treats him like property because he loves me. If I love him, how can I let that happen?"

"I didn't…" she faded to silence.

"You didn't know. How could you? We're just pons on other people's chess board. There are those, like your boss, like the man the love of my life is being forced to marry, and they take what they want not caring what happens to the rest of us. Maybe they rob us of opportunities. Maybe they send us off to die in wars that only benefit them.

"We're nothing to them. What's the term? Cannon fodder? But we have goals and ambitions just like them. We love and feel lose like they do. We feel the harsh sting of loneliness on long, dark nights and ache to have the touch of a loved one. And when we don't have it, our heart breaks like theirs."

I stopped and thought about what I was saying. It was hopeless. There always were and will always be those who make people like me their puppets. No one cared. And they especially didn't care about two guys in love.

"You know what? I'm sorry I bothered you," I said realizing I had failed Lou. "I'll go."

Stepping towards the door, I heard, "You said, Snow Tip Falls?"

I turned.

"Yes?"

"We received your petition."

I returned to the window.

"And?"

"There has been some question about its legitimacy."

"I don't understand. I submitted everything exactly as it was asked for."

"It's the signatures on the petition. There's been a suggestion that they aren't real."

"They're all real. Who's suggesting otherwise."

"I don't know. Maybe it's one of the folks you talked about, the ones who play games with the lives of good people."

"Then, what do I do?"

"There's not much you can do?"

"So, you're telling me to just wait and see what happens?"

"Unless you're willing to prove that every signature on the petition and every vote cast in your town is real, there might not be anything you can do about it."

"I have to prove they're real?"

"If you can do it in a way that no one can dispute, they'll have no choice but to grant your town incorporation."

"And all of the protections that go along with it like preventing it from being torn down to make room for a highway?"

"I guess."

An idea flashed through me like the current to a lightbulb.

"Okay, thank you," I said rushing out.

Pulling my phone from my pocket, I called Lou.

"What is it? What did you find?" he asked me in a hushed tone.

"The answer. I know how you can fix this."

"How's that?" he asked with building excitement.
"You have to get married."

Chapter 11

Lou

I stared down the aisle looking at the people seated on either side. They were all looking back at me. I waited for the music cue before I moved. When I heard it, it was time to begin.

I looked ahead at Sey. He stood at an altar set up feet away from the pool. Behind him were the priest, enough flowers to choke a bee, and a video screen.

I stepped forward. There was a rhythm to the walk. I had practiced it. Falling into step with what Sey and my parents had wanted, I followed the white silk cloth laid on the grass and approached my fiancé.

This was it. I was getting married. Looking down at the tuxedo I had spent way too long in fittings for, I took a deep breath.

"Dearly beloved, we are gathered here today to celebrate the joining of Seymour Charleston and Louis Armoury in holy marriage," the priest began.

I listened to him not making eye contact with anyone. How could I? I was too busy waiting for exactly the right time. How would I know it was the right time?

"Lou!" I heard Titus shout from across the lawn. "I love you, babe. It's all you."

That was when I looked up. The audience murmured. I could hear people asking what was going on. Why would someone rudely interrupt a wedding ceremony? It was because I needed to know when I could begin. It was time.

I turned to Sey and smiled. I felt good. It had been a long time since I had.

"Ladies and gentlemen, I have to stop the priest, who was giving a lovely sermon by the way, because there's someone who isn't here today who should be a part of this. My grandmother Agatha Armoury, who many of you might know as a world-famous mystery author, and I simply knew as Grandma Aggie. She would have loved what's going on today and for that, I would like to make her a part of the ceremony.

"Recently I found… I say "I" but, in truth, it's we," I gestured to Titus who now stood at the end of the aisle staring at me with a smile. "We found some lost footage of my grandmother that I would like to share."

I looked for the man who had duplicated the video. He wasn't hard to find. He was the one recording the wedding. Finding him, I signaled. That was when he lowered his camera, took a remote control out of his pocket, and pressed a button.

There were awes when Grandma Aggie's image appeared on the screen behind me. My mother couldn't understand why I had insisted that a giant projection screen be placed behind us at the altar. I had told her that the videographer needed it. And instead of fighting, she let me have it. I looked over at her sitting in the front row. She was starting to understand.

"I, Agatha Armoury, being of completely sound mind and body, hereby leave the entirety of my estate including my properties, books, and all of my holdings to my grandson Louis Armoury," the recording began.

As my mother watched, the vein on her forehead looked like it would explode. When it was done, my mother, father, and brother were staring at me with their mouths open. My parents were horrified. Chris looked impressed.

"As I said, I truly wish she could be here with us. But as her one and only heir, I have to be the one to thank you for being here today."

Right on cue, my mother stood up. Her face bounced between horror and an uncomfortable smile. She was frantic and I was ready for her.

She laughed and turned to everyone gathered. "What Louis means to say is that as a part of the family that has inherited Agatha Armoury's estate, we all welcome you."

"No, I said it right the first time," I said casually.

My mother whipped around to face me.

"I don't know where you got this video from, but you heard the will," she snapped. "This was clearly made before she changed her mind and altered it…"

"I'm going to stop you right there, Mother!" I said loud enough to shut her up. "Before you say anything else, I would like to thank a few people for being a part of this very special day. Everyone, I would like you to meet Butler Thompson from Thompson's Funeral Home. Mr. Thompson was the person who prepared my grandmother's body for the funeral.

"It's so rare that we thank the people who do thankless jobs. So, can we give Mr. Thompson a round of applause for the job he did preparing my grandmother. Mr. Thompson, please stand up."

I started the applause. Titus joined in and quickly everyone was clapping. When it died down, I looked back at my mother who had a look of terror on her face. It made me smile.

"I met Mr. Thompson about a week ago when I visited him asking about my grandmother's funeral. I wasn't able to attend. And, what was that thing you mentioned to me about the death certificate?" I asked gesturing to him.

"I said that," he began under his breath.

"Can you please speak up so everyone can hear?"

He straightened his back and gathered his courage. "I said that I had written the day your grandmother was found dead on the death certificate instead of her actual death date."

"I'm not going to ask you why you did it. I'm sure mistakes happen in all professions. But how different were the two dates?"

"There was a three-week difference between the two."

"Three weeks? That's a long time."

"It is," he admitted.

"And that means that if paperwork was filed with my grandmother's signature on it during those three weeks, it would be considered fraud. Right, Mr. Thompson?"

"I'm sorry. I'm not a legal expert. I would know nothing about that," he replied sheepishly.

"I guess you're right. You wouldn't. Luckily, another person I would like to thank for being here is, Anthony Dean. He is the lawyer at the firm my grandmother hired to execute her will and manage her estate after her passing. Can you stand Mr. Dean?"

A round, mid-fifties man stood up. His balding head shined in the sun.

"Mr. Dean, as a lawyer, is it your expert opinion that any documents filed with my grandmother's signature on them after she died would be considered fraud?"

"Indeed. Whether it was signed before their passing or not, she must be alive to file that paperwork. It's a law that prevents bad-faith actors from claiming they stumbled upon documents that were created by illegal means."

"Illegal means?" I asked.

"Yes. To file manufactured documents after a person's death would be illegal."

"And I imagine it would come with quite a bit of jail time."

"That, I do not know," Mr. Dean said confidently.

"I guess you wouldn't. Luckily, the last person I would like to thank for coming is Sheriff Bradley McGee and his lovely wife. Can everyone kindly give Sheriff McGee a round of applause for keeping our town safe and being here today?"

I gestured for him to stand as the guests applauded. When they stopped, I spoke.

"So, Sheriff McGee, can you answer that question? How much jail time does a person get for illegally filing paperwork after someone's died? And since I know it's a broad question, we'll narrow it down and say that the paperwork was filed to steal a rather large inheritance."

The sheriff stuck his thumbs behind his belt buckle and dipped his head as he considered the question.

"It would, of course, be up to the judge. And I'm not an expert on white-collar crimes. We don't get a lot of that around here," he said with a practiced smile.

"I'm sure. But if you were willing to oblige a groom on his wedding day, how long would you guess?"

"Ten years? Maybe seven with good behavior," he nodded agreeing with himself.

"That's a lot of time in jail," I acknowledged.

"It is. But, as I said, we tend not to have a lot of crimes like that in this town. Most of the time they are misunderstandings that can be cleared up and easily corrected."

"That's good to know. Thank you for that, Sheriff McGee. And, again, thank you for coming."

I turned back to my mother and father. Both were ghostly white. Chris was doing his best not to laugh his head off.

"So, Mother, was there something you were going to say. Wasn't it something about Grandma Aggie?"

She looked at me in terror. "No. There was nothing," she said backing down and returning to her seat.

I had won and she knew it.

"Impressive," Sey whispered grabbing my attention. "I guess I won't be marrying into a wealthy family, I'll be marrying one of the richest guys in Tennessee," he said with a slimy smirk.

I was about to reply when I turned back to the audience.

"I'm so sorry. I almost forgot. There are a couple of others I wanted to thank."

I turned back to Sey with a smile. His smile quickly faded.

"Everyone, I would like you to meet Heston Parker. He's a friend of the Charleston family. I invited him to be here today. Thank you for coming.

"Interestingly enough, it's Mr. Parker's job to approve towns that have applied for incorporation. You see, recently Titus, a very good friend of mine, applied for his town to be incorporated. But Mr. Parker had to put the petition on hold."

I turned to Heston Parker. Having seen what I had just done to my parents, his face turned 50 shades of red.

"It seems he had some question as to whether the signatures on the petition were real. I imagine signatures are faked a lot. But luckily, to help clear things up, I invited the entire town of Snow Tip Falls to the wedding. Titus can you show them all in," I said turning to my love.

Titus beamed watching me. When our eyes met, he put his fingers to his lips and blew. That was when an endless stream of people crossed from the other side of the house into the backyard.

"I also invited a notary public to verify that each and everyone one of these 1500 people is from Snow Tip Falls and is indeed a real person. So, you see Mr. Parker, you no longer have a reason to doubt the legitimacy of Snow Tip Falls's petition. And the only reason you would have to deny their petition now might be considered fraud. I'm sure there's no need to remind you what happens with that."

A hand gripped my bicep. It was tight. Wincing, I turned around finding Sey's bubbling anger.

"If you think this somehow gets you out of marrying me, you are sadly mistaken. Do you hear me? Nothing's going to stop this from happening. Nothing!"

"Get your hands off my man!" Titus shouted from the end of the aisle.

Titus was furious. I had never seen him so mad. Startled, Sey let me go. That wasn't enough to stop Titus, though. Like a defensive back finding the pocket, he charged down the aisle with his sights set.

Sey couldn't get out of the way fast enough. Nor could he react. In a flash, Titus's shoulder connected with Sey's stomach. Folding over Titus's back, Titus picked him up. Carrying him through the flowers and the projection screen, he found the pool and flung him in.

"And never, ever, touch my man again," Titus yelled as Sey floundered trying to catch his breath.

It was done. I was free. With the never-ending stream of Snow Tip Falls residents confirming their identity, the state would have no choice but to incorporate the town. So any threat Sey made about getting a highway planned through it, would be void.

The only thing we wouldn't be able to stop would be if Sey took Titus's grant from him. But, what did that matter? I had my inheritance and Titus had helped me get it. The least I could do would be to pay for his tuition. The most I could do was to love this incredible, gorgeous man for the rest of my life.

Realizing where I was, I turned back to the gathering crowd.

"Oh, and if you didn't already realize it, I'm calling off the wedding. There's a man I love so much more. Let me introduce you to him."

I gestured for Titus to join me at the altar. He came. When he did, I hung my arms around his neck.

"I would like to introduce everyone to Titus, my lover, my best friend, and the man I hope to marry someday."

The crowd applauded. Losing myself in his eyes, I spoke just to him.

"So, what do you think? You think you can stand spending the rest of your life with someone like me?"

Titus smiled, pulled me tight, and said, "Lou, I love you. I want to spend the rest of my life with you. And when we do, I know that we will live it happily ever after."

He then pulled me to his lips. We kissed.

Titus's Brother Revealed

Titus

Returning to campus after everything that had happened on Lou's wedding day, I felt incredible. Free from Sey and his parent's grasps, Lou was mine. He was my best friend and I loved him. More than that, he loved me.

Quin, who had come to lend moral support at the wedding, allowed Lou to move back in with him. I was happy about that because now that our relationship had become physical, we were going to need somewhere on campus we could be together.

It was great spending an extra few days after the wedding at his estate to make sure all of the deeds were transferred, but we had to return to school. I had to see if I was still on the football team after missing more than a few practices. And Lou needed to catch up after missing weeks of classes.

Stopping at my dorm to pick up a change of clothes, he and I were anxious to get to his place. Our celebratory sex had been non-stop since his parents had left the estate with their tails between their legs. But I couldn't wait to celebrate his return to campus. I was planning on doing it like a birth day, naked and in someone.

Exhausted but still exhilarated by everything that had happened, we entered my room finding Cali. He was lying on his bed when I unlocked the door. But as soon as I stepped inside, he charged towards me stopping an arm's length away.

"Hey," I said stepping around him and inviting Lou in.

"Hey," he said looking at me wild-eyed. "How was the drive?"

I looked at him confused. Cali wasn't known for initiating small talk. He was more likely to snare at you and then ignore you than ask about the weather.

"It was fine. What's going on?"

"What makes you think something's going on?"

I stared at him as I collected my clothes.

"Okay, now you're freaking me out," I said ignoring him.

Lou, on the other hand, squinted as he looked at him.

"You have news?" Lou asked starting to read Cali better than I did.

Cali blushed and looked away bashfully.

"You do," Lou confirmed.

"Oh seriously? You break a new record during the last game?" I asked getting excited.

"Nah. And Coach is pretty pissed at you, by the way."

"You think he'll understand why I've been gone if I come clean with him?"

"Sey's already on Coach's shit-list for suggesting he might transfer out of here. I think everyone will be on your side once you explain what Sey was up to and why he transferred to East Tennessee to begin with."

"Good to know. I'll talk to Coach tomorrow."

With my stuff packed I headed towards the door. Cali continued to stare at me with a big smile.

"So, are you gonna tell us the big news or are we gonna have to guess?"

"I figured you would know already," he said shyly.

"Sorry, man. I don't. You wanna clue me in?"

Cali looked down turning bright red.

"Remember when I took Lou's genetic test at the town meeting?"

I froze. "Yeah."

He gave me a knowing look.

"No?"

He smiled confirming it.

"Wait, you? We're brothers?" I asked shocked.

"Half-brothers," he said with a smile.

I couldn't speak. He and I had gotten close since becoming roommates and I had often wondered if this was what having a brother was like. Turns out it was.

Without saying a word, I threw my arms around him. He didn't resist. Feeling him grip me and knowing who he was, I was brought to tears.

Pulling away, I looked at him as if for the first time. The similarities were there. My hair was longer so it curled more. And he had his mother's fair skin and full checks, but the eyes, the dimples, they were just like mine.

"I can't believe it. Lou, do you hear that? You found my brother," I said looking back at the man I loved. He was already wet with tears.

I grabbed Lou and pulled him into a group hug with Cali. These were now my two favorite people in the world. Cali could contain his smile as little as I could.

"There's something else," Cali said slowly pulling away.

"Yeah? What's that?"

"The app says it found another connection. Turns out that you're not my only brother."

I stopped smiling.

"Seriously? Your mother had another kid."

"No," he said saying enough.

"Then, I have two brothers?"

He shook his head. "I think so."

Backing up, I found the edge of the bed and sat.

"This is a good thing, isn't it?" Lou asked.

"Ah, yeah. Of course," I said stunned. "Does the app say who the brother is?"

Cali nodded his head. I braced myself.

"Who is it?"

"Claude."

"My business partner, Claude?"

Cali nodded.

"How?" I asked knowing that we had to find out.

Thinking about rereading this book? Consider reading it as a male/female story in, the sexy sports romance 'My Best Friend', a steamy wolf shifter romance in 'My Mate's Curse', or a wholesome romance in 'I Don't Date My Best Friend'.

*****

Sneak Peek:
Enjoy this Sneak Peek of 'My Tutor':

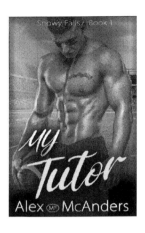

My Tutor
(Sports Romance)
By
Alex (MF) McAnders

Copyright 2021 McAnders Publishing
All Rights Reserved

CAGE'S PROBLEM: He needs to pass his class or he won't be able to play football, get drafted, or become the NFL star he was meant to be.

HARLEQUIN'S PROBLEM: People

Luckily, Cage is great with people. Everyone loves him as soon as they meet him, including Harlequin. And Quin is the smartest girl in the class.

So, what's the problem? Cage, the drop-dead gorgeous quarterback, has a girlfriend. And Quin, who can figure out everything in the world, can't figure out guys, much less relationships, or, you know… people.

But when the two of them agree to tutor the other in what they're good at, more than a few sparks fly. Where those sparks take them is 'Snowy Falls', a small town that causes the two even more problems in this steamy sports romance.

Swoon-worthy guys; twisting story; crackling sexual tension.

Note: This book is a part of the author's 'Love is Love Collection', meaning that it is available as a spicy romance in 'My Tutor', a wholesome romance in 'Going Long', a steamy wolf shifter romance in 'Son of a Beast', and a Male/Male romance in 'Serious Trouble'.

*****

My Tutor

With the deafening silence enveloping us, I couldn't take it anymore. Cage was so close that it was torture not to touch him. I had to at least see the beautiful body whose heat consumed me. So, moving like it was the most natural thing in the world, I rolled over settling on my side.

Buried in the shadows, I opened my eyes. He was facing me. His eyes were closed. Maybe he was asleep. If he was, it meant that I could look at him unhindered. I could examine every contour of his angular, masculine face.

Cage was the most gorgeous man I had ever seen. His wavy hair that lay gently across his forehead, his broad shoulders that sat uncovered, his lightly hairy chest, I desperately wanted to touch him. To feel the heat of his skin next to mine would be enough to live the rest of my life on.

Needing to be closer to him, I moved my hand onto the bed between us. I was less than a foot away from his sleeping body and didn't dare to get any closer. I wanted to. God did I want to, but I knew I couldn't... until, as if sensing me there, Cage moved his hand between us an inch away from mine.

I could feel the heat of him on me. I could barely breathe. Parting my lips as my heart thumped, I couldn't stand it. I needed to be closer. Being apart from him hurt too much.

Moving my fingers slowly, I stretched them out. They weren't long enough. He was right there. I could practically feel them. I would need to move my entire hand if I wanted his touch. Could I do that, though? Should I do it?

My debate didn't matter because as if he needed it too, his strong hand crossed to mine and moved on top of it. It was him who had done it. It could have been the reflex actions of someone asleep, but I didn't think it was. He wanted to hold my hand and I wanted to hold his.

So, shifting my fingers delicately, I allowed his fingers to fall between mine. When they did, I moved mine so that they touched his. It was everything I had hoped it would be. I tried to breathe without making a sound but it was the most sensual moment of my life. His touch was a swirling wind that encircled my warm, naked body. What was I supposed to do now?

Read more now

Sneak Peek:
Enjoy this Sneak Peek of 'Furious Chase':

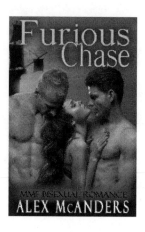

Furious Chase
(MMF Bisexual Romance)
By
Alex McAnders

Copyright 2021 McAnders Publishing
All Rights Reserved

A secret royal, his bad boy best friend, and the curvy woman they both want, fall into an epic MMF bisexual romance. Sharing a room, and a fake relationship lead to, a first time gay relationship, sizzling encounters, and longtime best friends giving in to their heart-aching passion.

KAT
Katherine couldn't have worse taste in men. After thinking she had found the love of her life, she finds herself stranded on an island in the South Pacific without money or a way of getting home. If she hadn't met Angel, a tall, sizzling hot stranger who offers to rescue

her, she might have been there forever. And the only thing he asks in return is for her to pretend to be his fiancé first.

Why would he need someone to do something like that? She didn't know. And when they end up sharing a room together at a nudist resort, and the sparks between them turn into a blazing inferno, what could possibly go wrong?

ANGEL
Angel lives in a world where nothing is ever what it seems... and he loves it. His life would be perfect if not for the occasional complication... the biggest of which is Chase, the one person he can't escape and who forces him to confront his dark secrets.

So when Angel meets Kat and sees a way to escape Chase, he takes it. But could he have a perfect life without Chase? Or, is his childhood best friend the only one who can rescue him from another of his complications, an unbearably lonely heart?

CHASE
Chase found his purpose early in life. It was to clean up his best friend's messes. He couldn't stop himself. He was hopelessly in love with him. But, how did his old friend feel about him?

Everything Angel did told Chase that he wasn't interested. So, why was Chase still following him around the world protecting Angel from himself? And, when Angel introduces him to his beautiful, new fiancé, what does it mean for the two of them?

Will Kat bring Chase and Angel together, or tear them apart? And, if Angel creates a mess like he always does, will Chase clean it up, or make an unexpected decision that leads to the three of them finding the love they all desperately desire?

'Furious Chase' is a steamy bisexual romance with twists, turns and heat. Loaded with crackling MM, MFM, and MMF scenes that will make your toes curl, it will make you laugh as much as cry before leaving you satisfied with its tear-jerking HEA ending.

Author Promise: Swoon-worthy guys; twisting story; crackling sexual tension

*****

Furious Chase

Seeing this, Kat knew she had to do more. With a hand on either of their thighs, she pushed their knees together. Leaning onto them, she slid out of her chair and between their legs. Easing forward, she sat on their knees.

With her legs spread, their meaty thighs pressed against her flesh between her legs. She hadn't realized it until now, but she was aroused. She wanted to rock her hips back and forth to enjoy it. But this wasn't a night for her pleasure. It was a night for theirs.

Balancing on their knees, Kat moved her hand onto Chase's muscular chest. She couldn't help but explore it as her fingers crawled up. Caressing his neck, she took a light hold of his chin. He had a bit of scruff. She liked that. And leaning towards him, she pulled his face to hers.

With the heat pulsating between them, they kissed. Falling into it, Chase quickly lifted his hand and held her back. He parted his lips and found her tongue. The sensation overtook Kat swirling her mind like melted caramel.

It took everything for Kat to break away. She did, though. And when the pleasure crested and subsided, she opened her eyes and turned to Angel.

"Now you," she said barely above a whisper.

Angel did not hesitate. Leaning forward, he kissed her like his life depended on it. His passion was intense. A chill descended Kat's spine feeling his strong lips on hers. She had remembered this feeling. It was like watching a rainstorm from under her covers. It was hard to let go of, but as she had with Chase, Kat pulled away.

Catching her breath, Kat placed a hand on both of their chests. This was it. This was all she knew how to do. If this didn't work, the two might never be together.

With that thought in mind, she looked up, peered into each of their eyes, and said, "Now, you two."
Read more now

*****

Follow me on TikTok @AlexAndersBooks where I create funny, fun book related videos:

Printed by Amazon Italia Logistica S.r.l.
Torrazza Piemonte (TO), Italy